COLD QUERY

COLD QUERY

A BLUE WATER MYSTERY

Ivanka Fear

First published by Level Best Books 2025

Copyright © 2025 by Ivanka Fear

This novel is entirely a work of fiction. The names, characters and incidents portrayed in it are the work of the author's imagination. Any resemblance to actual persons, living or dead, events or localities is entirely coincidental.

Ivanka Fear asserts the moral right to be identified as the author of this work.

Author Photo Credit: Amanda Belec

thirteen13designsnphotography

First edition

ISBN: 978-1-68512-892-0

Cover art by Level Best Designs

This book was professionally typeset on Reedsy.
Find out more at reedsy.com

For my husband, Brian, my best friend
and partner in this crime writing adventure.
And to our family
With all my love.

Praise for Cold Query

"The concept is as brilliant as it is chilling, and Fear presents it in a tense and suspenseful manner that keeps you turning the pages anxiously to the very end."—Kelly Young, author of the Travel Writer Cozy Mystery series and the Haunted & Harassed Paranormal Mystery series

"A chilling twisty thriller that I couldn't put down. Ivanka Fear keeps you guessing to the end!"—Erik S. Meyers, author of the Sally Witherspoon mystery series

"When a member of the Blue Water Murder Club is found dead, aspiring mystery writer and teacher Ivy Rose is devastated. When another member dies, she begins to realize they may all have targets on their backs. As if that weren't enough, the detective investigating the murders is someone from Ivy's past, and she's not quite sure how she feels about that. Ivanka Fear's *Cold Query* will keep you guessing until the very end. For fans of Charlaine Harris' Aurora Teagarden mysteries and Richard Osman's Thursday Murder Club."—K. B. Jackson, author of the Chattertowne Secrets Mystery series and the Cruising Sisters Mystery series

"In her latest book *Cold Query*, author Ivanka Fear again takes readers on a compelling journey, full of twists and turns that will keep them hooked—and guessing—until the final page. This story is perfect for those who enjoy puzzles, intrigue, and unexpected surprises—even in a seemingly charming Canadian town on a beautifully expansive lake. I couldn't put the story down and can't wait for future tales in the Blue Water series."—Daphne Silver, Agatha Award winning author of the Rare Books Cozy Mystery series

"True crime imitates fiction in this page-turner of a mystery. *Cold Query* captured my attention from the beginning and kept me guessing until the final pages."—Anna St. John, author of the Josie Posey Mystery series

"*Cold Query* is a wonderful read for all mystery lovers, both readers and authors of the genre. The latter may even, after reading what can happen to a group of crime writers, choose to work in a different genre! Imaginative and possibly precedent-setting, *Cold Query* will surprise you in every chapter."—J. Ivanel Johnson, award-winning author of the JUST (*e*)STATE mysteries

"*Cold Query* pulled me in from the first page and refused to let me go! The perfect book to curl up on the couch with a cup of tea. Whether you're a seasoned mystery fan or brand new to the genre it will leave you wanting more!"—Hannah Grieve, author of *The Secret of Markie Beach*

A Note from the Author

Cold Query takes place fourteen years after the previous book in this series. But not to worry. The past is ever present.

Prologue

**Mystery writer searching for a critique partner from Blue Water
County to share each other's work. Must love murder, lol. Must be
local. DM me if you're interested in being partners in crime.**

A 'laughing my ass off' emoji followed.

When she read the post on the online Blue Water Writes page, her first
thought was: redundant and repetitive.

Her second thought was that she'd found a kindred spirit.

After several messages back and forth, they made a date to meet in person.
As she sat in a corner booth at the back of the cafe that May afternoon, she
wondered what he would be like. Although they had shared photos of each
other along with some basic personal information, she knew that people
weren't always who they presented themselves to be.

He entered through the glass doors and scanned the tables and booths.
When he spotted her, she waved, and he strode up to her with a warm smile.
The man was every bit as attractive as his photo. She herself had gone to a
lot of trouble to do her makeup and hair and choose an appropriate outfit.

"Hi, nice to meet you in person," she said as he extended his hand, then
lowered himself into the seat across from her.

It wasn't, of course, her first glimpse of him. She had seen him around. It
was a small community, after all. Whether he remembered *her* or not, he

didn't let on.

It was the start of a mutual partnership in more ways than one. They had a lot in common, not the least of which was an affinity for murder. Their conversation revolved around crime fiction and writers who kill for a living.

"I've read all her work," he exclaimed when she told him about her favorite author. "Where do you think she gets her ideas?"

"Probably where most writers get ideas—from real life. Personal experiences, dreams, news reports…" She asked where he got his.

"I have a vivid imagination. I create stories for people." He paused to sip his latte. "For instance, that lady with the short blond hair and purple hoodie, focused on picking out doughnuts? I bet she's a serial killer, stalking her next victim right here in the local cafe. No one would ever suspect what she's capable of doing. Look at her. Mild-mannered doughnut eater by day, cold-blooded killer by night."

She shook her head. "You couldn't be more off the mark. I know her. She's the nicest person, an English teacher with two kids, wouldn't hurt a fly."

"No, she's definitely capable of murder."

She laughed so hard she nearly gagged on her iced mocha.

"You never really know anyone." He joined in the laughter. "Some of your best friends could be psychopaths. They're experts at masking who they really are."

"I highly doubt I know any psychopaths. How about you? Are your best friends psychos?" She bit into her croissant.

"Not that I'm aware."

After breaking the ice, they spent the next hour in an easy conversation about their personal lives, then exchanged manuscripts and agreed to read them by the next week.

* * *

They met again for a picnic, spreading the blanket under a maple tree, away from others who were enjoying the warm spring day at the lakeside park.

"So, what did you think? Did you like my story?" His eyes lit up as he talked about his book, not the first he'd written, but the one he was most excited about.

"Well, it's definitely an interesting premise." She wasn't quite sure what to say. The whole idea was preposterous. But then again, she'd often read news stories that were equally bizarre.

"But did you enjoy reading it? Do you think it will sell?" He was like a little boy with a new toy or a teenager with his first car.

"I think it has potential. It's your main character I'm not sure about. She seems a bit unemotional. Detached. Hollow."

"Exactly. That's the way she's supposed to come across. She *is* a cold-blooded killer." He lay on his stomach, elbows digging into the grass, resting his chin on his hands. "There's only one thing she cares about."

"And that's selling her books?"

"Yes."

"So, she's killing off *other* mystery writers because…?"

"Because she wants to get rid of the competition. Because she's bitter. Angry others are getting the recognition she's not."

"And because she's a psycho?" She couldn't help using that word again. She laughed as she said it, but this time, he didn't join her. "The whole idea is just so absolutely crazy."

"No. No, she's not a psycho," he said, his expression stone cold sober as he explained his main character's motivation.

She lay down next to him. "It seems a bit contrived."

"Aren't all murder plots?"

"And now that I think about it, it's been done. I read a book with a similar plot last year."

"Great minds think alike, I guess," he laughed. "Although they do say there are no original ideas, they've all been thought of already."

"I suppose so. Maybe you just need the right twist to set your story apart."

"You didn't like it, did you?" His face fell as though she had squashed his pet bug.

"I did. Like I said, I see lots of potential in it. Let me help you with a few revisions, and it'll be perfect." She attempted to salvage their relationship, having found someone who would understand her frustrations as a writer.

He rolled over onto his back. "Anyway, I loved *your* book. Wasn't sure what to critique. Great voice, loved your main character. No plot holes. And the way you described the setting, it's like that mansion was another character in the book. You shouldn't have any problem getting an agent and finding a publisher."

"Thanks, but I'd have to be crazy to think it's that easy."

Chapter One

"The first day is the toughest," I called to the newbie across the hall, who flitted around her room, dropping papers and books across the shiny linoleum. "But you'll get through it." I smiled before turning left into my own little haven housed in the large two-story institution. The plaque on the door always surprised me: Ivy Rose, Head of English.

The first day *was* the toughest, even though it was my twelfth first day of teaching high school literature. As usual, there was the excitement and anticipation of a fresh start with all its possibilities. As always, there was the underlying anxiety that everything would blow up in my face. Imposter syndrome was an apropos word for the feeling—but in more ways than one. My claim to imposterhood went way beyond my professional life.

I glanced around my classroom one last time, satisfied I'd done everything possible to make it inviting. The bulletin boards were eye-catching, the desks arranged in groups of four, and a large welcome sign adorned the blackboard along with my pre-written notes. I removed lesson plans and materials from my soft leather briefcase and placed them on the desk, next to a photo of my two grown children. First impressions were crucial to bonding with your students.

"All set?" A voice from the doorway startled me. "I thought I'd come down to see how you're doing." Olivia entered, her eyes sweeping across the room. "Looks great!"

I appreciated the compliment. If my best friend, with her expectations of perfection, saw the room in a favorable light, my efforts had paid off. Olivia taught math classes on the second floor.

We first met when I joined the staff of Blue Water High, where my son, Brent, was entering Grade 9. Olivia had taken me under her wing when she learned I was a widow with two children to raise. "You're so brave," she had said. "Going on to build a good life for yourself and your children, in spite of what fate has thrown at you. Losing your husband, no parents, raising the kids alone, and getting your teaching degree. I don't know if I could have done that." Olivia confided that she herself had become pregnant at a very young age, but Cliff's well-to-do family welcomed her with open arms, providing childcare so she and Cliff could complete their education. "I've been very lucky," she had said, placing her arm around me. "I'm not sure what I did to deserve it. I admire you for taking care of your family on your own. You're a strong woman."

From the very first playdate we arranged for our nine-year-old daughters, the kids, and Olivia and I formed a special bond. The boys went off and did their own thing, too old for their moms' constant supervision, but we girls stuck together like glue. While Twyla and Jamie splashed in the Walker's pool, Olivia and I lounged on the patio, chatting about everything and anything. When the weather cooled down, we relaxed in the hot tub with a glass of wine while the girls played on the swing set. In the winter, we sat by the fireplace with a cup of tea and homemade scones, watching through the glass patio doors as the girls played in the snow. If I'd been lucky enough to have had a sister, this is what it would have been like.

Accepting the compliment about my classroom decor, I said, "Thanks. How about you? Ready for all those teen hormones?" I didn't doubt Olivia's room and lesson plans were as polished as she was, with her navy blazer overtop a crisp white lace-trimmed blouse and knee-length pencil skirt covering her tall, svelte figure. Olivia managed to walk effortlessly despite the heels she wore, a feat I abandoned after Jim's death.

"As ready as I can be," Olivia answered, lowering her eyes, "considering I didn't get much sleep, with the guilt of what I've done hanging over me all weekend."

I looked expectantly at my friend, but Olivia didn't elaborate. She looked her usual elegant self, chestnut-brown hair cut in a stylish medium-length bob and makeup expertly applied. Such a contrast to me with my short, straight, bleached blond hair, glasses, and makeup-free face, dressed in black slacks, a pink slouchy sweater over a slightly plump frame, and black flats.

"I'll tell you about it later," Olivia promised, her eyes still not meeting mine, as she turned toward the door. "The hall's starting to fill up with kids. See you in the auditorium." As lockers clanged open and locks snapped shut, Olivia's heels clicked down the long hallway and up the stairs, leaving me wondering what exactly was going on with her.

* * *

Principal Doug McLaren welcomed back the students and staff of Blue Water High at the school assembly in the auditorium twenty minutes later. After a few back-to-school announcements, he paused and seemed to consider his words before continuing.

"Maybe some of you have already heard the news," Principal McLaren said. "Police are investigating the discovery of a body down by the lake. They haven't released the victim's identity or any details surrounding the death."

A wave of murmurs rolled through the crowd of students and teachers. Olivia and I sat side by side, behind our homeroom classes, mouths popping open as our eyes met. The principal waited till he regained the attention of the crowd. "Our thoughts and prayers go out to the victim's family and friends."

I imagined everyone, like me, was hoping the drowning victim wasn't someone they knew. In a small community like Port Ripley, population of five thousand, where people waved at passersby, it was an unrealistic hope.

* * *

"I've done something I regret," Olivia confessed during lunch break. We were eating in my room, at Olivia's request, with the door closed. "I should have told you about it sooner. I'm so sorry."

My curiosity piqued, I watched my friend's expression. "Why? Does it have something to do with me?"

"Don't be mad."

"Why would I be mad?" Did Olivia betray my trust? Did this have something to do with work? Or maybe it was about our kids?

"A personal ad was posted on our online writers' group." Olivia took a deep breath and exhaled. "And I know I shouldn't have, especially not without talking to you about it, but I responded."

"You *what?*" My mouth flew open. Surely, Olivia wasn't thinking about cheating on Cliff. And with some stranger? "I thought everything was great between you and Cliff. Are you having problems?"

"No. Why?"

Olivia's furrowed brow told me I was way off track. But you never know. Turning forty-five this year was a major deal for us. Plenty of people went through an identity crisis long before turning forty. Maybe Olivia was looking for more excitement in her seemingly perfect life.

"This has nothing to do with me and Cliff." Her face reddened as she understood. "Oh, no, not *that* kind of ad. I would never...Sorry, I wasn't clear."

"Exactly what kind of ad was it then?"

"Actually, I'm surprised you didn't see it yourself."

"I don't usually read personal ads." After Jim's accident, I'd been content to be single, raising our children and teaching. Besides, no man could ever live up to my husband. "Why would you...?"

"It was a new literary agent, soliciting clients."

My mouth formed an O as Olivia's words finally registered. "I get it— you're querying a book. But you must know that's not the way it usually works. Are you sure it's legit?"

Olivia raised her eyebrows. "Well, I did wonder, of course. But I thought I'd take a chance. What's really bothering me is that I kept something from you that I shouldn't have. I know murder is your passion, but..." Olivia hesitated, looking around the room as if searching for a way to divulge her secret. "Yes, I've written a novel. A mystery novel."

"Well, that's great. Why would you keep that from me?" I set down my egg salad sandwich.

"I just thought…that I'd be stepping on your toes. You know, with you having written an entire mystery series and hoping to get an agent. Writing is nothing more than a hobby for me. But I wanted to see if I could get published. I'm sorry." Olivia acted as though she had committed a major crime, writing a mystery novel.

I worked as a reporter years ago and recently published a book of short stories. But even though I had been writing all my life, I had yet to find success with the novels I aspired to publish. That was no reason to stop Olivia from trying.

I assured Olivia she wasn't stepping on my toes at all. "You shouldn't feel that way. You've got as much right to write a book as I have."

"It's not just any book, though, is it? It's a mystery. And I submitted it to an agent. I don't want you to think I'm copying what you do."

"Of course, I don't think that. If you want to write mysteries and send them to agents, you should. I don't have a monopoly on writing mystery novels."

"I feel like I'm intruding on your life-long dream to be a writer. But nothing will come of it, anyway. I know I'm not good at writing, especially murder."

I suspected Olivia was being modest. She was good at whatever she chose to do. Olivia might have even written a bestseller. It would be just like her to pull it off. "Well, I want you to know that I would be absolutely thrilled for you if you got an agent and your book was published." I tried hard to ignore the twinge of envy pushing its way forward.

"I should have told you, though. Not try to hide it. I think I was jealous that you'd submit your work, too, and get accepted and I wouldn't. But I'll show you the ad tonight. You can still send your own work in. I'm sure it's a thousand times more likely he'll accept your submission."

"There's no reason to think I can write a better novel than you. I'd really like to read your manuscript. That is, if you want to share it." Olivia was my alpha reader, the first person to go over my unpublished work and offer feedback for improvement. I valued Olivia's input and wanted to return the favor. Not to mention, I *was* curious.

"I'd love that. I'll bring it with me tonight to Murder Club."

"I can't wait to read it. You know I love a good murder." We broke into an uncontrollable fit of laughter at the way that sounded.

Then I sobered up, remembering the body on the beach.

Chapter Two

Wouldn't you know it?

All day long, the sun shone through my classroom windows. By the time I finally had a chance to enjoy the lovely late summer day, it had clouded over. As I jogged to the parking lot, laden down with schoolwork, cold drops plopped onto my head.

A nice walk after school would have been refreshing, but instead, after saying hello to my cat, Tom, I retreated to my home office with a cup of peppermint tea. For my personal writing, I found the desk constricting. Ideas came to me during walks or sitting by the lake—when my mind was a blank slate. Inspiration came as I lay in bed trying to sleep or waking from a dream—when my brain was receptive to imaginings. The writing happened anywhere, anytime. I couldn't control it. It was always with me.

As for lesson plans and marking, I could concentrate better at my desk than on the living room couch or at the dining room table. It was too easy to get side-tracked by the view outside or by the television or radio. During my spare period, I had marked some of the papers from our twenty-minute creative writing block, yet there were plenty more waiting. I loved teaching, but the paperwork could be overwhelming. Right from the first day.

The rain drumming on the roof distracted me. Wandering into the living room, I glanced through the droplets streaming down the bay window. If the weather had cooperated, I would have walked down the one hundred and seventy-six steps from the park across the road to the beach below and strolled along the raised wooden boardwalk, watching the waves roll in from the endless expanse of Blue Water Lake. It always brought me peace.

As I returned to the office and tried to concentrate on grading papers, I considered Olivia's revelation about her own writing. Why hadn't Olivia told me she was working on a mystery novel? Asked me to critique her work as she wrote? I could have offered her some advice. I might even have told her not to bother. The chances of securing an agent, and then a publisher, were next to none. Surely, Olivia understood that.

Teaching, on the other hand, provided a sense of satisfaction, helping young minds develop. And it certainly wasn't boring. I ran a daycare out of my new apartment in Oakridge the first year after Jim's death, looking after a handful of kids along with my own till I could decide what to do with the rest of my life. My only reason to continue living was our children. I was thrifty with my parents' inheritance, spending only what was necessary, saving the bulk for Brent and Jamie's future. It was my love of children and reading that prompted me to use some of the proceeds from the sale of the house I owned with Jim in Lake Kipling to attend teacher's college the following year. When I received the offer to teach English Lit in the quaint town of Port Ripley, on the shores of Blue Water Lake, I found myself genuinely excited for the first time since Jim's death.

Time for supper. What's quick?

Scanning the inside of the refrigerator, I decided to make a ham, cheese, and mushroom omelet. Going through the effort of cooking for one simply wasn't worth it. With a sigh, I assessed my small kitchen, which was in desperate need of renovations. As much as I would have liked a new kitchen, I was saving money for an early retirement. If all went well, I would retire a few years down the road to pursue my passion for writing full-time. A minimal teacher's pension and interest on my investments would be supplemented with some writing income, although I doubted I'd make much as an author. My cold queries to literary agents had been met with rejections. No personal responses. Just form letters saying I wasn't a good fit and suggestions to submit elsewhere. What exactly did 'a good fit' mean?

The timer dinged, signaling that the omelet needed flipping. I always set the clock, an ingrained habit resulting from anxiety since Jim's death. I worried the house might burn down if I didn't. You never know when your world will come crashing down. It's just a matter of time. It's bound to happen.

After feeding Tom and taking my simple meal to the living room, I tuned the TV to the evening news. The headline on the local station was the body found washed up on the beach in the early hours. According to the media, the victim was a local resident, a middle-aged male, named Wendall Collins. My fork dropped onto the floor.

Wendall was a Murder Club member.

* * *

Murder Club was held from seven to nine p.m. at Alice Reading's house. My friend, Alice, owned Worth A Read, the largest book and games store in Blue Water County. I suspected there would be a lot more to talk about that evening than the bestselling thriller that was slated for discussion.

Normally, I would have walked fifteen minutes to the meeting, but a fine drizzle discouraged me from an evening stroll. After cleaning up the supper dishes, I climbed into my older model Jeep Cherokee and drove to Alice's house to meet with the book club.

The first part of the evening was somber, with no one knowing what to say. The group members greeted each other with a nod, then fidgeted and avoided eye contact. We were seated in the large basement family room, some on sofas and chairs, others on the carpeted floor. Alice took a deep breath, clasped her hands together on her lap, and began the meeting, her eyes scanning the group. Clearing her throat, she said, "I assume you've all heard about Wendall?"

People gasped, hands covered mouths, heads shook, and eyes closed as though hearing it from Alice made it real. Never mind that it was the big news story on the local station and on social media.

"Such a tragic accident". Alice's voice shook. "I picked up a sympathy card at the bookstore. If you want, we can all sign it and perhaps pitch in, and I'll order a flower arrangement sent to his wife from our group."

The other members nodded, and the card made its way around the circle as we honored Wendall's memory with a few moments of silence. We were more than happy to let Alice take charge. It was, after all, *her* Murder Club. She was the one who started it almost two years ago, gauging interest by displaying a poster in her bookstore. Although there was already a book club at the town library, run by her daughter, head librarian Valerie, this one was geared toward mystery, suspense, and thriller readers. At first, several dozen people signed up, and meetings were held at the town hall, but attendance quickly dwindled until there were twelve die-hard murder fans. That was when Alice opened up her own home to the weekly meetings, and things became cozier and more intimate.

Once the card made its way back to Alice, she asked, "What do you think? Should we go ahead with our meeting?"

"We may as well," said Dylan. "We're all here, and I think Wendall would have wanted us to go on…" He paused as the words caught in his throat. "What the *hell* happened to him?"

Tongues loosened as his question led to a discussion about how Wendall might have ended up dead in the water. There was speculation that he couldn't swim, that he was out on the pier alone at night and slipped. One wrong step…Or perhaps he was out for an evening swim. The undertow was dangerous. Maybe he jumped off the pier intentionally. Had anyone noticed he seemed a bit off lately?

Alice coughed into her sleeve and shifted the focus of the meeting to our novel. "Since it was Wendall's turn to lead the discussion, how about we raise a glass to honor him and continue with our book study? Dylan, can you pour the wine, and I'll get the conversation started?"

"To Wendall," Dylan said after glasses were filled. He lifted his glass, tipped it, and downed his wine in a flash, then poured himself another. "May he rest in peace."

Alice sipped her wine, set it on the table and picked up her copy of the thriller. "How important do you think the setting is in creating suspense in these last few chapters we've read?"

In between sips of wine and mouthfuls of cheese and crackers, we discussed the murder scene, setting aside Wendall's untimely death by Blue Water Lake.

"It's creepy, that old house with antique furniture. Makes you think a ghost might jump out at any time," Celia said.

"Especially with it being nighttime and the rain beating against the windows," Gabby added.

"You could almost hear the wind howling as you were reading." Dylan looked toward the window, where rain streamed down. "It was the standard dark and stormy night in an old mansion trope. But effective."

"I thought so, too. And all those rooms," I added. "So many places for the murderer to hide. I was constantly on edge. Every time Macy stepped through a door, I was expecting something terrible to happen to her."

The book reminded me of Olivia's house, and how it would be the perfect place for a murder. A beautiful old estate out in the middle of nowhere, with the lake several hundred feet below the property. But Olivia's house was full of love and laughter, with three generations living there and all the friends Cliff and Olivia entertained. Nothing bad would ever happen there.

At the end of the evening, Olivia and I followed everyone up the stairs. Rain hammered the windows, and the wind howled through the front door. Olivia had the farthest drive. The rest lived either in town or just on the outskirts. "Sounds like a nasty storm. It won't be a nice drive home. I've got a copy of my manuscript in the Jeep," she said.

The wind whipped our faces as we ran to Olivia's brand-new Jeep Grand Cherokee, and it tore the passenger door wide open. Olivia reached in to pull out the brown envelope tucked between the seats, shielding it from the rain under her jacket. "Here it is. Take your time reading. There's no big rush. And don't hold back on your criticism. I want to know what you *really* think."

"Okay, thanks for letting me read it. Text me when you get home." I slipped the envelope under my own jacket and hugged Olivia. Not being a fan of driving in bad weather, worried when the roads weren't perfectly dry, I wished her a safe trip.

The short drive home brought me to the last street in town before the cliffside sloped to the beach and lake, my white brick and stone bungalow second to the last house on the opposite side of the cul-de-sac. The streetlights were lit and the porch light on, but I removed the house keys from my purse before exiting the Jeep so I wouldn't need to fumble with them at the doorway, another habit I'd developed years ago. It was always best to take precautions.

Across the road, the park provided a spot for relaxing and picnicking with a couple of benches and picnic tables, as well as a playground for kids. The far side of the park overlooked the lake and the beach area, trees and shrubs covering the steep incline. From my front lawn, the lake was usually visible in the distance, its blue hues becoming one with the sky. Tonight, though, it was dark and menacing. Except for the warning posts and chain rope barrier separating the parkland from the cliff, one wrong step could send a person tumbling off the edge, several hundred feet down toward the beach road along the black lake.

Grabbing Olivia's manuscript, along with my purse and book club novel, I scurried to the front door, house key in hand. A sudden barking caused me to lose my grip on the keys, and they fell onto the wooden porch. I bent to pick them up and turned to see my eighty-year-old neighbor, June, on the sidewalk, walking her small dog.

Surprised to see June out in this weather, I shouted, "It's a bit rough for a dog walk, isn't it?"

"Thought I'd better take Clarence out before things got worse," June yelled above the wind and rain. Some of the leaves had fallen from the maple tree and swirled around her. "Just awful about that Wendall fellow, isn't it?"

"Tragic. His poor wife."

"I saw him at Larissa's place not long ago. He seemed in good spirits then. But the lake's taken more than a few lives in the time I've lived here." At the crack of thunder, Clarence pulled June toward the safety of their house. "I guess he's had enough." She waved goodbye.

Once inside, I organized my clothes and packed lunch for the next day before getting ready for bed. As the kettle boiled for tea, Olivia's text came through telling me she got home safely. Eager to read Olivia's manuscript, I settled on the couch.

Pulling out the thick wad of white sheets from the envelope, I read the title on the cover page—*Watch Your Step*. Olivia had printed the personal ad and clipped it to the top of the stack:

Agent desperately seeking mystery writers. New local agent is looking for novels in the mystery, suspense, and thriller genres. Please send your full manuscript, along with a detailed bio and complete contact information.

Following was an address, a PO Box on Richmond Street in Oakridge.

I turned to the first page of the manuscript. Partway through the first page, it struck me as odd. It didn't read like fiction. First of all, Olivia wrote in the first person and used her real name and the names of her family members. Second of all, it began with a scene I knew had really happened to Olivia. It was about the first time she met Cliff and how she fell for him—literally, face down in front of him, having tripped over her shoelaces the first day of Grade 9.

I jumped as my phone rang. "I've done something really stupid!" Olivia's voice came across in a frantic whisper. "You haven't read it yet, have you?"

"I just started. Why? What's wrong?"

"It's the wrong manuscript," Olivia's voice quavered. "I sent in the wrong book to the agent."

"There's more than one book?" Olivia never mentioned she authored more than one novel. Why was she so upset about that? Did it matter? If she got a call from the agent, she could easily explain she had two completed mystery novels, not just one. Even better.

"I can't believe I wasn't more careful. Usually, I double-check everything, well, triple-check. But I was in such a rush Friday afternoon, I didn't notice the papers got mixed up. My desk was full of school stuff, and I had just printed out two copies of my book, but it wasn't what I thought it was. You know how I worry about losing things, especially on my computer. I clicked on the wrong file and printed out two copies of something no one was supposed to read."

I still didn't understand why Olivia was so upset.

"It's my memoir. More of a diary, I guess. It's not something I want anyone to read. Ever. It's personal. I wrote it a long time ago to help me deal with something, like a kind of therapy. I should have destroyed it. I don't know how I managed to print it instead of my mystery novel. I should have thrown it out right away, as soon as I realized. Instead, I printed copies of the mystery book and left all four manuscripts sitting in neat piles on my desk. I can't believe I sent in the wrong one." She sounded like it was the end of the world.

"Just send in the correct manuscript and let the agent know you want the other one back right away. How did you get them mixed up, anyway?"

Olivia explained that the doorbell rang while she was organizing her mystery novel pages to put them into envelopes, one of which was going to the post office and one for her own records. Olivia chatted with the woman who brought some garden tomatoes from her neighboring farm, then excused herself saying she needed to get to the post office before it closed. When Olivia returned to her office, the wind from an open window had blown some of the sheets around. In her rush, she scrambled to collect the pages, stuff them into an envelope, and drove into town to mail her manuscript. "When I got home tonight, I decided I'd better shred my memoir copies before someone saw them. I took them out of my locked desk drawer and realized my mistake. The pages seem to be in order, but the title pages of the manuscripts got mixed up. I have two copies of my mystery novel with my memoir title page, which means the agent and you have my memoir. I have no idea how I didn't notice. I guess I was flustered and in a hurry. Now my memoir is no longer private. And I'm scared it might become public, and Cliff will find out... What am I going to do?"

Now, I understood why Olivia was whispering. She was keeping something from her husband. I wasn't about to judge, being an expert at keeping secrets myself. But I had to ask. "Why wouldn't you want Cliff to read it?"

"Because it would destroy my marriage, my family, and the life I've built. I wrote about some things I did a long time ago that I don't want anyone to know. Can you *please* destroy the copy I gave you? It's important. That's all I can say."

"Of course. I would want the same done if it were me."

"What should I do about the other copy?"

"Agents are busy. I doubt he'll have had time to read it. Contact him and ask for it back."

"I can't. There's no phone number or email or anything, just the post office box number. I have no idea who this agent is." Olivia sounded like she was at her wit's end.

I advised Olivia to send a letter to the agent explaining her mistake, along with the correct manuscript, and calmed her as much as possible before ending the conversation.

She's done something awful. Keeping it a secret. What is it?

For a moment, I seriously considered finding out exactly what my best friend was hiding. I even went so far as to flip through the pages, looking for something incriminating. But I stopped myself just in time.

How would I feel if it was the other way around? What if Olivia held my secrets in her hands? Could I trust my best friend?

Poor Olivia. I couldn't imagine having my life, with all the mistakes of the past, in print for someone else to read. Returning the manuscript to its envelope, I carried it to the gas fireplace. With the fire roaring, I tossed in the memoir. The flames consumed it, along with all traces of Olivia Walker's secret life. I texted Olivia to assure her the manuscript was gone, thankful I had the integrity to resist temptation.

As the manuscript burned, I caught the start of the local evening news.

"Police are investigating the death of a fifty-three-year-old local man. Foul play is now suspected in the death of Wendall Collins, whose body was found early this morning, washed up on the main beach next to the pier. According to a police spokesperson, drowning was not the probable cause of death. Police are asking that people stay away from the lake while the yellow tape is up. Anyone in the community with information relevant to the investigation should contact the local station."

I stared at the fire, reflecting on an extraordinary day—how innocently it began, and how wickedly it ended. Before bed, I popped a sleeping pill to calm my nerves.

Yes, the first day of school was tough, all right. Sometimes, the first day of school could be murder.

Chapter Three

Blue Water Writes:

What is wrong with some people? I just got a one-star review from an anonymous reader saying they've read all my stupid books, and my newest release is the stupidest yet. They wanted to give me a minus rating, but one is the lowest they're allowed. How do you deal with bad reviews?

The next day passed as smoothly as possible as we all settled into the new routine of school life. It *was* different from previous years. Murder was a rare occurrence in Port Ripley. Not that it had *never* happened. No community was completely without crime. But Port Ripley came as close as any.

The kids in the hall appeared not to be bothered by Wendall's death, laughing and goofing around, eyes glued to their screens. I envied their ability to carry on as usual.

The teacher's lounge buzzed with theories about a tourist passing through, high on meth or some other illegal substance. It had to be a tourist, everyone agreed. People came from all over to enjoy Blue Water Lake. City people mixed with locals during the summer months. Usually, that wasn't a problem. They supported the local businesses.

"I won't be jogging along the boardwalk till they find whoever's responsible," said Lily, the school's secretary.

It hadn't occurred to me that the beach could be a dangerous place, but the consensus was that it was best to stay away from the lake as requested until the police concluded their investigation.

"Do you think the town will go ahead with the Arts and Crafts Festival?" asked Doreen Morris, our music teacher. Her students would be providing entertainment for the event in two weeks' time, at the Harbor Park above the main beach.

"This should all die down by then," Doug McLaren declared. "Although the police consider it an unusual death, it will probably turn out to be accidental."

Chapter Four

A week later, Olivia phoned after school. "You'll never believe what happened. I got a call from that agent about my mystery novel. He offered to represent me, and he's emailing the contract," she said all in one breath.

"That's great. That happened quickly." I had sent close to a hundred cold queries over the past year for my novel, *Secret Lives, Secret Lies,* and received *no* offers. "What about your memoir?"

"He sent it back, saying he hadn't gotten to it yet, but he wasn't interested in memoirs. He read my mystery, though, and loved it. His name is Justin Newark. He's starting his own agency, so he's eager to sign up clients."

"Where is he from?"

"Somewhere in Oakridge. I'm not sure exactly. But he's got his website up and running, so you can check him out. You really should send your novel to him. If he's interested in my writing, he'll definitely want to sign you up."

After completing the call, I opened my laptop and typed in the web address Olivia had given me. Justin's website seemed legit. On the Homepage, a paragraph explained what the agency was looking for; a Submissions Guideline page and a Contact Us page provided details of where and how to send a query. No email was listed. The only way to submit seemed to be through snail mail to a post office box in Oakridge, the closest city to Port Ripley.

When I typed the agency name in the search bar, nothing more came up. Neither did Justin Newark, literary agent. But then, Olivia did say Justin was just starting up. Everyone had to start somewhere. Deciding I didn't have anything to lose, I printed out a copy of the first novel in my series and prepared it for mailing.

Lying in bed later, I couldn't help but feel jealous. Olivia had a handsome, loving husband and an extended family, a gorgeous home, a successful career, good looks, money, and plenty of friends. Now, she was on her way to becoming a published author.

All my life, I had dreamed of being a writer. There was never a time I could remember wanting to be anything else, other than Jim's wife and a mother to our children. Teaching was great, but it was my second passion. As a child, I wrote in my diary. As a teenager, I wrote poetry and the odd short story. As an adult, I spent a few years working as a small-town reporter. But real life got in the way of my creative writing. Tragedy struck, and then it struck again and again. I busied myself with college, raising my family, making a home, and providing for myself and the kids. There was little time to indulge in a hobby. It was just the last few years, with the kids grown, that I returned to writing with a frenzy, a frantic drive to get my stories out of *me* and onto the paper. Somehow, they ended up being murder mysteries. I most certainly hadn't planned it that way. But life had thrown death in my path so many times, it seemed only fitting that was what came out when I set my fingers on the keyboard. My fiction resembled my truth.

Art imitates life. Or maybe life imitates art?

I grew up reading. I loved mysteries. I loved suspense. I loved the thrill of discovering the murderer. Murder, it seemed, was in my blood. Perhaps writing was a way of purging my sins.

Chapter Five

"Oh, thank God." Olivia rushed into my classroom the next morning, breathless. "Did you hear anything more? About the body they found?"

"You mean about Wendall?" That was a strange question. Why refer to him as 'the body'?

"No, not Wendall. There's been another death. I was worried about you, but assumed I would have been notified."

"Another death? Worried about *me*? Why?"

"It happened last night. Didn't you hear?"

"No, I didn't." Setting down the marker on the whiteboard ledge, I gave Olivia my full attention.

"It was on the car radio this morning. I thought maybe you would know more about it since it happened on your street."

"*What?* On *my* street? What happened?"

"They found a woman in her home at the bottom of the stairs. Apparently, she tripped and fell all the way down, hitting her head when she fell. Isn't that odd?" Olivia stared at me in an almost accusatory manner, as if I should have witnessed it.

"Oh, no! Who?"

"I didn't catch the name. So, you didn't notice anything going on last night? No police cars around?"

"I didn't go out last night, so no, I didn't see anything." I explained I was busy skimming through my own manuscript so it would be ready to send in the mail at lunchtime. "Although, now that you mention it, this morning there were orange cones blocking off my street at the first corner. I couldn't see past the bend, but I assumed there must be some road repair going on. But another death? Oh, my."

"And it's just like in my book. Don't you think?"

"In your book? Oh…I'm sorry, I haven't had time to start it."

Olivia opened her mouth, but the bell silenced her, and kids' voices resounded through the hall. She lifted her hand in a wave and dashed off to her first class.

* * *

After the end of the school day, I strolled down the sidewalk to see if there was any indication where the accident had occurred. I didn't have to look far. A couple of blocks down from my place, yellow police tape blocked off the front yard. I knew the woman who lived there. Or used to live there.

On the way back home, I walked on the grassy area bordering the bluff, thinking how awful it was that Larissa would never again see the sun set over Blue Water Lake. I hesitated at my house, gazing over at my neighbor's bungalow. Should I knock on June's door and offer my condolences? I never knew what to say to people in their time of grief. Although I had experienced more than my share of it, I was at a loss when it came to consoling other people.

"Ohhh, June." I hugged the short, thin, silver-haired woman who answered the door, Clarence tagging along. "I heard there was an accident. I'm so sorry." How I hated the word 'sorry.' The number of times I had heard it when my parents died, when my husband died. It just seemed to be the wrong word, but I knew of no other that was more appropriate.

June's red face and puffy eyes showed without a doubt that her niece, Larissa, was the victim. "It's just awful. I don't know how it could have happened," she said, motioning me inside.

"She fell down the stairs?"

"Yes, that's the way it looks. The police are still investigating."

"So, they're not sure what caused her to fall?"

"They said it was standard procedure to ask questions. But I didn't know what to tell them. Larissa was fit and active. I don't understand how she managed to fall."

Larissa was about fifty, divorced, and lived alone in her large two-story home. I had never met her ex-husband. Their three children had recently moved out, one of them still in college, the other two married. Larissa often jogged along the boardwalk down by the lake or up and down the street. Sometimes, we met up and chatted about the weather, or our jobs, or about June.

"Was she feeling unwell? Dizzy? Could she have lost her balance?"

"No, not that I knew."

"Maybe something was left on the steps, and she tripped?" Although my home was a bungalow, I worried about the steps leading to the basement, especially with a basketful of laundry. It would only take one misstep.

"There was nothing. She must have caught her foot on the carpet and taken a tumble." Tears flowed down June's cheeks as she trembled, and my arm instinctively went around the old woman's shoulder, even though it made me uncomfortable. Grief had a way of doing that. It was contagious, too. I fought without success to keep the tears in the corners of my eyes from streaming down my face. The tears were shed for Larissa and June, but also for the loved ones I myself had lost. Especially Jim, the love of my life. I blamed *myself* for his death.

"How did you find out about the accident?" I asked.

"I was there."

I kept my face neutral, disguising my horror that she witnessed her niece's death. "You were there when she fell? Did you tell the police?"

"No. I mean, I was the one who found her. She'd been there for a while, lying like that." June sobbed without restraint while I patted her back. "Maybe if I had checked on her sooner."

I rubbed June's arm to soothe her. "It's not your fault. I'm sure there was nothing you could do. These things happen." I recalled being told that when my own parents died instantly in a car crash just before my thirtieth birthday. I had no choice but to accept it, even though I suspected my homecoming led to the accident. Grief mixed with guilt had a profound effect on a person. It changed who you were and robbed you of your ability to forgive yourself. Irreparably.

"I should have been there for her. I could have called for help and saved her."

"You can't blame yourself. What happened wasn't within your control."

"I hadn't heard from her for a couple of days. She didn't answer her phone. I thought maybe she was too busy to answer. Last night, I walked to her place, and her car was parked in the driveway, but she didn't answer the door. We have each other's keys in case of an emergency. I unlocked her door, and there she was." June blew her nose and added the tissue to a pile on her coffee table.

"How awful. So, you called the police?"

"Yes."

I asked if there was anything I could do for her, but of course, there wasn't. I understood that better than anyone. "I assume her children are taking care of the arrangements?"

"Yes, they're coming tomorrow. Poor dears. And her parents—how awful to have to bury your own child."

Before leaving, I hugged June again and told her to call or come over any time she needed to talk. Settling into my evening routine of doing schoolwork and preparing supper, I thought about the two visitations within the space of just over a week. I hated funerals. I avoided them if at all possible, making excuses for not attending when I should have made an appearance. Murder in fiction, I loved. Death in real life, I couldn't cope with. But I had made a short, quick visit to give my condolences to Wendall's widow, and I would do the same for June.

What are the odds of two people I know dying accidentally, one on the heels of the other?

Chapter Six

Saturday was a big day. My very first book event. I was invited by Alice to participate in the annual Worth a Read Book Festival along with other Port Ripley authors. Most of them had either published with a small press, like me, or gone the self-publishing route. There were nine of us set up in the lower level of the store. Alice had moved some of the shelves and displays holding games to make room for the event. Tables were set up for authors to display their books and sign copies, and thirty folding chairs were crowded together for guests. I shared a table with two other authors, a few copies of my book laid out, with more stacked on the sales counter, along with the other authors' books, waiting to be purchased after the readings. I hoped to sell at least a couple of my books.

Alice organized the entire event, with the help of her librarian daughter, Valerie. At 1:45, the room started to fill and, with the bodies surrounding me, I became increasingly nervous. Claustrophobia was kicking in, along with anxiety about speaking in front of a crowd of people. Although I had no problem speaking to my students, I developed stage fright when asked to do any other kind of public speaking.

Each author was allotted ten minutes to read an excerpt from their book. I had chosen "A+ For Murder," one of my favorite stories in the collection. I would have preferred to be the second reader, with an opportunity to see how the first author handled themselves, with the luxury of relaxing for the rest of the readings. As luck would have it, the number I picked out of a hat was nine, leaving me to the end. Waiting would feed my anxiety. Then again, maybe not everyone would stay till then, and I'd be reading to an empty room.

"Welcome to the sixth annual Worth a Read Book Festival," Alice announced. "It's a bittersweet day. As you all know, we recently lost one of our town's citizens under tragic circumstances. Wendall Collins was one of us. Please join me in a moment of silence to honor our fellow book lover who is with us in spirit."

Heads turned in all directions as though searching for the person responsible for Wendall's death before lowering out of respect for the man.

Alice continued. "We have a variety of genres for you today. The afternoon will be spent listening to our authors read from their books, after which we invite you to make your purchases and have them signed and personalized by the author. First up is mystery author Eugene Forsythe, reading from his new book, *Beach Bodies*."

Eugene strode to the portable presentation stand, set down his book, and opened to the first page, gracing the audience with his smile. They were enthralled with his dramatic reading and emitted a collective moan, indicating they hadn't heard enough. How was I going to compete with that? Eugene had already published two other mysteries in the series and had a large online following.

The romance author read a steamy excerpt from her novel, grabbing everyone's attention and eliciting some gasps. She was followed by the reading of several poems from a collection, a children's storybook, and a non-fiction book. After the fifth reading came a break for refreshments and an opportunity for mingling of writers and readers.

Olivia approached my table. "I'm afraid I'm going to have to leave right after the readings," she said. "We're having a barbecue. But I didn't want to miss your first public appearance."

"Thank you for coming. You didn't have to take time out of your family day. I know Twyla's home for the weekend. But I'm glad you're here." I hugged my friend, grateful to have her support.

Alice and Valerie manned the counter, ringing through sales and bagging books. I stretched my legs, walked along the tables, examining my fellow authors' books. Of particular interest was the non-fiction book about

Blue Water County, outlining its history and its current draw as a tourist attraction. There were photos of the lake area and of the towns dotting the shoreline, along with stories about the buildings and residents, one of which the author had read to the group. I spent a few minutes chatting with the writer of the book, Riley Patterson, owner of the local hardware store.

When I returned to my seat, a piece of folded notepaper protruded from under my author's copy. Pulling it out and reading it, I gasped. Someone had written a question for me. The note was handwritten in red ink and unsigned.

Where do you get your ideas for your murder mysteries?

That seemed like a legitimate question. It was the next part that shocked me.

Have you ever killed anyone in real life?

How did they know?

Fingers trembling, I stuffed the note into the pocket of my purple hoodie hanging over the back of the chair. The note must be someone's idea of a joke. Still, it left me feeling unnerved. That, on top of the butterflies in my stomach, made the room seem smaller, and as always, when the walls closed in on me, I looked for the escape door and focused on it. At the back, stairs led to the main floor. My eyes, however, fixated on the emergency exit, behind the portable stand where authors stood for their readings. If I had to, I could make a run for it. Not that I would have the courage to run. I'd stand and gawk at the crowd like an idiot.

A man's voice asked what inspired me to become a writer, forcing me back to reality. My eyes shifted to the good-looking guy in front of my table.

"I've always read a lot," I answered, glad for the distraction. "When I was young, and the other kids were playing sports, I had my nose in a book. Then, I started writing down my own ideas and found I really enjoyed it."

"Why mysteries, in particular?"

"That's a hard question to answer. I don't really know. I've always enjoyed the suspense of mysteries and the excitement of turning the pages to get to the end of the book. It's the fun of trying to put the puzzle pieces together to figure out what's happening. A challenge of sorts." I didn't add that I loved getting into the mind of the killer, understanding what drove them to such heinous acts.

"Well, I look forward to reading your stories. I'm going to buy your book after the readings are done. I'll be back later to get your autograph."

My nervousness was partly replaced with the excitement of knowing someone was interested in my book. When Alice asked everyone to take their seats again, I took a deep breath in an attempt to put the note out of my mind. It took great effort to be attentive to the fantasy writer's excerpt, then to the reading of part of a memoir. It was almost *my* turn to read. Right after the science fiction novelist.

"And now, for our final reading of the evening, Ivy Rose will read a short story from her book, *Murder Collections*. Afterwards, everyone is welcome to chat with the authors again, who will be happy to sign a copy of their book for you. Thank you for supporting our local Blue Water authors."

I toddled to the stand, my legs rubbery, everyone's eyes on me. My stomach was queasy, and my mouth dry in spite of the sips of water. For a moment, I stood frozen, staring back at the crowd. When I opened my book, the characters came to life, standing next to me, and my nervousness dissipated. "It was the perfect crime. No one would ever suspect her."

Ten minutes later, I finished the story. "She was the perfect student. A+ for motivation, A+ for method, A+ for opportunism. A+ for getting away with it." Closing my book, relieved it was over but pleased to hear the applause, I returned to my seat.

The sales counter was swamped again, and readers formed lines at the authors' tables, three of them in front of me. I signed each of their books as more potential buyers descended the stairs to browse the featured authors' books. By the end of the afternoon, I nearly broke even, selling fourteen books and purchasing the Blue Water non-fiction book, the children's book, the book of poetry, Eugene's mystery, and the romance novel.

By six o'clock, everyone had cleared out. I stopped at the pizzeria to pick up a pepperoni and mushroom pizza. Parked in my driveway, a touch of guilt overcame me. I really should do something more for my elderly neighbor in her time of sorrow. With the pizza left on the passenger seat, I knocked on June's front door.

"Hi, how are you holding up?" I asked. June answered the door in a lilac sweatshirt and matching sweatpants. Her eyes were dry, but her face was drawn. I wondered if maybe she was cried-out for the day.

"Oh, you know, best I can."

"Have you had supper yet? I was wondering whether you'd like to come over for pizza."

"That would be lovely, dear, thank you."

June accompanied me to my place and we ate our pizza on my couch, watching the news on television. I asked about the funeral and visitation times.

"The police have asked the family to hold off for now."

"Oh, why is that?"

"They did an autopsy and found there were drugs in Larissa's system when she died. They think there might be more to her fall. Maybe an overdose."

"An *overdose*? Of what?"

"Crystal meth."

My mouth flew open. "Crystal meth? I didn't know Larissa was using drugs."

"She wasn't. The police think someone may have drugged her, and that's why she fell down the stairs, or maybe she was pushed." June's hand shook as she set down the pizza slice. "Why would someone do that to her?"

"Oh, June, I'm so sorry to hear that. I can't imagine who would do such a thing. Poor Larissa. You're trembling. Let me get you a cup of tea."

In the kitchen, I plugged in the kettle, put two tea bags in the teapot, and set out two mugs along with cream and sugar. Usually, I drank herbal tea; some calming chamomile would be just what June needed.

The phone rang as the kettle whistled. Olivia was checking to see how many books I sold.

"I actually sold quite a few."

"That's great. Listen, did you happen to catch the news today about your neighbor?"

"No, what did they say?" I wondered whether the media had already reported Larissa died of a drug overdose.

"It's the strangest thing. They think her death wasn't accidental. What are your thoughts about that?"

"Actually, June, Larissa's aunt, is here, and she said the police think she was given an overdose that contributed to her fall."

Olivia gasped.

"You don't suppose her death is related to Wendall's, do you?" I whispered.

"As in, someone wanted them both dead?" Olivia sounded incredulous. "*Murder*? In our small community? It's impossible. I don't understand this. How can it be?"

My voice low, I agreed it was odd that two suspicious deaths had occurred so close to each other in a small town where everyone thought they were safe. "I think I'm going to keep my doors locked, just in case."

After the phone call, June and I sipped tea and ate biscuits while June reminisced about her niece and how she missed her. "It's been so nice having Larissa close by. She's the only family I have in town."

I made a mental note to invite June over more often in the future. I had never considered how lonely elderly people could be. For years, I lived next to June without getting to know her that well. Although I was alone since the kids moved out, teaching and writing kept me busy. Brent and Jamie visited now and then, and my furry friend, Tom, kept me company. Olivia and I spent a fair amount of time together, as well.

After June left, I settled in bed with Eugene's novel. It seemed morbid, reading a murder mystery in light of the two recent deaths.

Chapter Seven

His new-found critique partner had a sob story. Didn't everyone? She went on and on about the struggles of being a writer. Getting beta readers, even friends and family, to be enthused was tough. No agents were interested. Never mind publishers. It was pointless. There were just too many people who wanted to be writers. Not enough people who wanted to read. Way too much competition for the available market.

"Ever since I can remember," she had said, "books and writing have been a big part of my life. I'm so tired of hearing about other writers' successes. The contest wins, the awards, the arts council grants."

"Maybe you need a change," he had suggested. "There's more to life than writing."

She stared at him as though he had lost his mind. "Life *is* writing. Ever since I was born, writing has been there."

Wrapping an arm around her shoulder, he said, "Maybe you should concentrate on living. You're letting this consume you."

Chapter Eight

Blue Water Writes:

Had a blast at Worth A Read this afternoon, reading from my latest mystery and autographing books for my fans. I'm signing a stack of leftover copies, but hurry in and grab one before they're gone. Full of twists, you'll never guess whodunit.

A string of selfies were attached to the post.

The Writer

Honestly, writers are so full of themselves. Especially mystery writers. They put themselves on par with homicide detectives. Think they're experts at puzzles. As if life would make sense if you could just fit the pieces in the right spot. If only it were that simple. I love a good murder, but I hate mystery writers—always knowing whodunit and why they did it. And the reality is, they don't know anything. They simply create some convoluted story and a contrived unbelievable ending the reader has to live with. God, they're *pathetic*.

How did I get to be one of them?

It was tough being there today, with other authors proudly displaying their books, reading excerpts to the interested crowd, and autographing their precious creations. There's way too much competition. Good competition. No. Better competition. Better than me. It's like everyone has a book in them, dying to come out and be read by the world.

Why do I even bother? I hate events like the book festival. No. That's not true. I actually love them. It's the writers I hate. But what can I do? Even here, in this small community, I'm surrounded, lost in a sea of Blue Water wannabe-the-next-great-writing-sensation hopefuls.

What I need is validation. But after having secretly queried every agent under the sun, and having submitted to every small publisher out there, it just doesn't look like that's going to happen. Ever.

When Eugene read that excerpt from his latest book, I realized it would be only a matter of time till Eugene found himself an agent to represent his work. It was that good. In no time, Eugene would have a bestseller on his hands.

All the work I've put in over the years and so little interest. And someone like Eugene, with his murder mysteries, just seems to attract readers like a magnet. What do I have to do to get noticed like that?

Murder's obviously the way to go. Give people what they want.

My phone rings as I flip through the posts and photos from the book festival.

"Did you hear what happened?" The caller pants. "To Eugene?"

"No, what?"

"He lost control of his car…on the bridge heading out of town after the book festival. It broke through the guard rail and plunged into the river."

"*What? Are you sure?* Sure it was Eugene?"

"The police closed off the road. I'm out for a jog on the trestle bridge, and his Corvette's in the water below. Do you think this could be connected to the other two accidents in town?"

"I'm sure it's just a coincidence. Poor Eugene. I hope he's okay."

"Ohhh! They're pulling him out of the river now," the caller gasps. "I can't tell if he's moving."

Three accidents in town these last couple of weeks. Two suspicious deaths. And now Eugene? This is Port Ripley. Things like this don't happen here.

It's like something out of a mystery novel. But whether the local police solve the mystery of whodunit and why, that's yet to be seen.

Chapter Nine

"Have you heard? It's just awful what happened," Alice sputtered over the phone. "Poor Eugene."

"What? What happened to Eugene?"

"There was an accident. On his way home. His car went off the bridge and into the river."

"Oh, my! Is he okay?"

"I'm afraid not, Ivy. He's dead."

This couldn't be happening. Eugene's mystery novel was about a body found on a beach. The parallel to Wendall's death was uncanny. And now Eugene had a car accident.

Two mystery fans from our small town are dead. And so is my neighbor's niece. This can't be a coincidence.

I put Eugene's novel away in the night table drawer, no longer in the mood for murder. Three people I knew were dead. The last one, a victim of a car accident. I thought about Jim and the car crash that killed him thirteen years ago, leaving me alone, which always led me to think about the accident that claimed my parents' lives two years before that.

* * *

I had returned to my hometown of Hamilton to visit Mom and Dad after being in hiding for eleven years. Haley, my childhood best friend, asked me to attend our high school's twenty-fifth reunion weekend.

As I sat in my old math class, reminiscing about the time I met Jesse, instantly in love, I was called down to the office. Seeing the police in the principal's office, I naturally assumed they were there to arrest me. But it was worse than that. My parents' delivery van had gone over the embankment and struck a tree, bursting into flames. Their bodies were unrecognizable. A couple of months before my thirtieth birthday, I lost both my parents.

I didn't believe it at first. It had to be a mistake, somebody else driving my parents' van. Then, I thought someone had deliberately killed them. I was in denial. To make matters worse, when I went through their personal belongings after the funeral, I discovered my parents had been keeping secrets from me. It was a traumatic time and a major wake-up call in my life. My parents weren't who they said they were. And neither was I.

* * *

I couldn't sleep. Thinking about all the deaths. All the murders. My parents, Jim. Wendall and Larissa and Eugene. All gone. Victims of apparent accidents. Yet the police suspected foul play in two of the deaths. Would they find Eugene's death suspicious as well? Could all these deaths be connected? As these thoughts rolled through my head, I remembered the note someone left for me at the book festival. Who wrote it, and what did they mean? Did they know what I had done?

Have you ever killed anyone in real life?

After taking a sleeping pill, I fell into a fitful sleep and woke up in the middle of the night with thoughts of murder still on my mind. Something caught my attention—the click of a door closing. Sitting bolt upright in the dark, I listened. Someone was shuffling around in the living room.

Hand clamped over my mouth, I quietly reached into the drawer of the night table, withdrawing my gun. I had never used it but kept it for protection. Waiting, holding the gun firmly with both hands, I swallowed the lump in my throat. The floor creaked as someone approached along the hall. They were getting closer. I could sense them stopping outside my door. I reached back into the bottom drawer to retrieve the bullets.

As the light switch from my daughter's room shed a sliver of brightness through the slit in my slightly open door, I relaxed. Jamie was home.

My bedroom door swung open, and Jamie stood in the doorway, turning on my overhead light. She screamed. "Oh, my gosh, Mom. Put that gun down. Honestly, you need to get rid of that thing. You're going to kill someone. Why do you keep it?"

"It's not loaded. You know that." I tried to calm my daughter, while my own heart thumped in my chest. Keeping the gun next to my bed provided some measure of security, even though I knew it was unlikely I would use it. "It's just to scare off intruders, which I thought you were. What are you doing, sneaking in here at this hour?"

"It's not that late. My roommates had a bunch of people over, and I couldn't take the noise anymore, so I went for a drive. The next thing I knew, I was heading home. Why are you so wound up?"

Jamie attended school in Masonville, an hour and a quarter away, and she was expected home tomorrow for a visit. Her best friend, Twyla, was one of her roommates.

"I told you about Wendall and Larissa. Now Eugene, one of the authors from today's book festival, has died. I don't know what's going on, but I don't want to be next. Did you lock the door behind you?"

Jamie confirmed she did. "That's terrible. What happened to him?"

"Car accident. You look exhausted. Get some sleep, and we'll talk in the morning."

Chapter Ten

Blue Water Writes:

What a tragedy! Such a talent! I was there for his final reading yesterday. He will be missed. RIP, Eugene.

"Who were you talking to?" Jamie asked once I got off the phone. "One of the people in my book club. She was checking to see if I'd heard the news about Eugene. Did you sleep well? What would you like for breakfast?"

"How about our famous full brunch?" Jamie suggested. "I'm starving."

As we shared the small kitchen, Jamie asked, "So what exactly has been going on here? Three people you know had an accident within the last couple of weeks? That's more than a little weird, isn't it? I remember when I left for college two years ago, how worried you were about me being alone in the big city. Sounds like it's more dangerous to be here right now."

"Well, it's certainly not as safe as it used to be." I fried bacon in the microwave and prepared pancake batter for the griddle, while Jamie scrambled eggs in a frypan. Hash browns were in the oven, and bread sat in the toaster. We worked well together, having perfected this Sunday morning routine many years ago.

As Jamie poured orange juice and coffee, I filled our plates, and we sat at the dining room table to eat our breakfast feast. "I haven't heard anything more than what I've already told you about Wendall and Larissa. The police are looking into their deaths. And I don't know about Eugene. I agree it *is* strange that all three of them would have accidents so close together."

"And you knew all three of them personally. That's such a coincidence. Do you think there's some connection between what happened to them?"

"Wendall was in my book club, so I saw him every week for our book study. As for the other two, I wouldn't say I knew them that well *personally*. Larissa, of course, is June's niece and lived on our street. I knew her, but it's not like we were good friends or anything. Eugene, I barely knew. Just that he was a fellow mystery writer, and I'd see him around town sometimes. He was one of the authors at the book festival yesterday, and the crowd loved him. The next thing I knew, he drove his car off the bridge. But you're right. It is definitely odd that three people I knew had suspicious and fatal accidents in the last two weeks. Let's hope it *is* just a coincidence."

We spent the next hour discussing Jamie's classes, her roommates, and her social life. Since both the kids went off to university, a big hole had opened up in my life, one I tried to fill with writing. Until a couple of years ago, my life was full, though lonely, without Jim by my side. I missed him every day. Every moment.

Jamie reminded me of my husband. She had inherited Jim's mannerisms along with his good looks. Jamie constantly pushed back her wavy chestnut hair off her forehead, unintentionally drawing attention to big brown expressive eyes. She had Jim's dimples and a smile that lit up her face as she talked a mile a minute. Jamie's lack of awareness of her own beauty only served to make her more beautiful. Every time I looked at my son and daughter, I marveled at how I had managed to create two such smart, good-looking kids with hearts of gold.

I observed my daughter now as she talked about life at Western.

"There's something else I wanted to tell you," Jamie said, after stopping to take a breath. "I've met someone I really like."

"Oh?" I raised my eyebrows. Jamie brought home very few young men for me to meet. She hadn't seriously dated anyone; male companions were more friends than boyfriends.

"He's in one of my Sociology classes. We've walked together between classes and gone for coffee a couple of times." Jamie sounded excited, a dreamy look on her face as she stopped talking and sighed.

"What's his name?"

"Ben. He's really nice. You'd like him."

"Are you planning on bringing him home to meet me?" I wanted to see for myself whether he was worthy of my precious daughter.

"Maybe. It's a bit early to say. But I hope so." Jamie's eyes sparkled. "Like I said, I really like him, Mom."

"Well, don't jump into anything too quickly," I warned, not wanting her to fall for the wrong man. Then I remembered how I hadn't appreciated my own mother giving advice about boys. "But you're certainly welcome to bring him home anytime. I'd love to meet him. If you like him, I will, too." Surely, Ben was a nice young man. Jamie was a good judge of character and had a good head on her shoulders. All I could do was hope that my daughter didn't make the same mistakes I had made. The same mistakes my own mother had made. History had a way of repeating itself.

The sun shone through patio doors off the dining area, warming the room. "It looks like it's going to be a nice day," I said. "Do you want to go to the beach? Maybe have a picnic later? We can skip lunch and get takeout chicken for an early supper. It might be one of the last nice days of the season."

"Sounds good. I don't think I'll be back till Thanksgiving, and it'll be cold by then. I could use a good, long walk right now to burn off this breakfast."

"Better put on your hoodie." I opened the front door, and the cool air wafted in. "Hopefully, it'll warm up in the afternoon."

We strolled across the street to the park, then descended the long flight of wooden steps. Crossing the beach road, we stepped onto the boardwalk and headed toward the pier. I zipped up my hoodie, arms around my waist as the wind blew in from the lake.

"Good thing it's sunny," Jamie said. "It makes a lot of difference in the temperature."

We met others who were out enjoying the cool, sunny morning. I waved and greeted several of them, the usual board walkers. As we stepped onto the concrete pier, I stopped to admire the water. "I love the changing colors of the lake. The near-green along the pier." Although it was beautiful, I knew there was a dangerous undertow. Looks could be deceiving.

"I never get tired of the lake," Jamie agreed. "It's always changing." The crystal blue water on the other side of the pier, waves lapping against the wall, confirmed her observation.

The long stretch of concrete led out into the lake. With the sun beaming down on us, we ambled past the freighter docked along the side. The pier was nearly empty, apart from a middle-aged couple holding hands.

"I just love being out here," I said, looking past the breakwater. Shaped like an upside-down V, the gap in the middle accommodated freighters. "So calm and peaceful."

At the end of the pier, we stood watching the few boats that sailed in the distance as white waves crashed against the rock wall. Turning to look back at the sandy beach to the right of the pier, I watched people stroll along the shore.

"I wonder what Wendall was doing out here the night he died." I voiced my thoughts out loud. "I guess the police either don't know, or maybe they aren't releasing it to the public yet."

Jamie nodded. "They probably wouldn't want to let the killer know if they were onto him."

"Or her." I gazed out over the water, then surveyed the entire area. "I wonder if anyone saw what happened to him."

Turning to the freighter, I focused on the top railing where someone stood looking down. Were they watching us? I didn't want to alarm Jamie.

"Hey, let's head home," I said casually. "We'll come back later. Hopefully, it'll warm up this afternoon, and we can sit by the water." Spotting something in the sand as we strolled along the shore, I stopped and pointed. "What's that?".

We wobbled toward it, sandals sinking into the beige sand. "It's a book," Jamie said. "It must have fallen out of someone's bag."

Picking up the hardcover book, I examined the front of the jacket. It was in good condition. "Not just any book. It's one of Eugene's novels. *Beach Bodies*." I opened it. "And it's autographed by Eugene."

"Beach Bodies? That's weird. Wendall's body washed up on the beach, and now Eugene's book is in the sand? Where exactly did they find Wendall?" Jamie surveyed the shore, where a few people dipped their feet into the water.

"I don't know, but I heard it was close to the pier." I turned the book over to the back and flipped through the pages, then scanned the area, holding up the book in case someone was searching for it. When no one came forward, I removed the phone from my pocket and looked up the number for the local police station.

"What are you doing?" Jamie asked.

"I think the police should know about this. If they think there's something suspicious about Eugene's death, maybe this being on the beach where Wendall was found is important. Maybe not, but still…" I got through to the station and explained the situation. "They're sending an officer to have a look."

Fifteen minutes later, a police car cruised down the beach road, and an officer stepped out. After explaining my find, I asked, "Will you still be able to get prints off it?"

The book was placed in an evidence bag to be taken to the station. "Possibly," the officer answered. "If you find anything else on the beach, though, leave it be and call the station right away."

"Of course. I should have thought to leave it in the sand." I showed the officer the exact spot where I picked it up. He took a photo of the area, thanked me, and drove off with the evidence.

Jamie and I continued toward the stairs and climbed to the top of the cliff. I scanned the beach area. "You can see everything from up here. Too bad it's so far down. It's all miniature. If anyone was watching from here…"

"What are you thinking, Mom?"

"I'm sure there was a freighter along the pier a couple of weeks ago. I'm wondering if it was docked the night Wendall died. Or maybe a different freighter. Could someone have seen something? Could there be a witness on one of the freighters that left the harbor?"

"I'm sure the police are interviewing possible witnesses," Jamie said. "Leave the sleuthing to them, Mom. I don't want you putting yourself in danger by sticking your nose in this."

"Who me? Stick my nose in?" We burst out laughing at the thought. My curiosity often got me into sticky situations.

"I'm serious, though, Mom. I don't want you going around asking questions, not if someone's responsible for the recent deaths."

"Don't worry. I'm too busy with school to be an amateur detective." As the words came out of my mouth, it brought back memories of the happiest times of my life—when Jim and I were together in Lake Kipling. I had worked as a reporter for the local paper, always on the lookout for a big story. With that thought came memories of the time I had spent solving crimes with the man who became my friend when Jim's receptionist went missing. Detective Scott Evans. I wondered what he was up to these days. I hadn't seen him in years. Not since Jim's death.

* * *

"I love you," Jim had said as he kissed me, picked up his briefcase, and headed out to his new Jeep.

"Don't forget—we're switching vehicles today. So, when you go out to the parking lot, don't panic thinking your Jeep's been stolen and call the police," I joked.

Jim laughed. "Scott would have a field day with that."

I had plans to take my Toyota in for an oil change and service at a garage close to Jim's real estate office. "I'll drop by to get the Jeep, and you can pick up my car at the garage after work." I had an interview scheduled for a news article I was working on, and didn't want to waste time waiting around for my car to be done.

"Sure, no problem." Jim pulled me close for another kiss. "One more for the road."

And that was the last time I saw my husband alive.

He lost control of the Toyota on his way home and hit a tree, dying at the scene. Just like that, in an instant, I became a thirty-one-year-old widowed mother of two. The worst part of it was I didn't even get the chance to properly grieve Jim's death. Early that same evening, about the time of the accident, Brent was kidnapped from the park where his baseball team was playing. He was there under the supervision of his best friend's mom, who lost sight of him when he went to buy a hotdog at the concession stand.

I don't know how I managed to get through the funeral. The whole thing was a complete blur. My shell of a body functioned on auto-pilot without me.

It was my fault. The police investigation showed that the brakes on my Toyota had been tampered with as my car sat waiting to be picked up after being serviced at the garage. I took matters into my own hands. I was the one who should have been behind the wheel, the one to die in the car crash. My husband and son were victims of bad choices I had made in my previous life.

I knew exactly who had taken Jim and Brent from me, and I knew exactly what I needed to do. A mother will do whatever is necessary to protect her child. Whatever it takes. Regardless of the consequences.

* * *

By mid-afternoon, it warmed up sufficiently to return to the beach with a blanket, a cooler of water, and a couple of books. We sat on the sand and read, watched the waves, then walked barefoot along the edge of the water.

"I'm getting hungry. Why don't I go pick up supper, and you wait here?" Jamie suggested. "The usual?"

"Sounds good. Grab my debit card from my purse."

Jamie jogged up the steps back to the house. The fast-food restaurant was a five-minute drive from our home. I expected her back in half an hour.

I returned to my romance book, glancing up occasionally as people ambled by on the boardwalk, and families played in the sand and water. As time passed, I worried Jamie was taking a long time.

Maybe the restaurant is busy today. Or maybe there's more traffic since it's one of the last nice Sundays to go out.

After an hour, I texted Jamie to make sure she was okay. As I hit the Send button, my daughter approached.

"Did they have to go out and catch more chickens?" I joked.

"Sorry," Jamie said, carrying a bag of takeout food. "I met up with Valerie at the park on my way. She was out for a walk."

"So, what did you two talk about?"

"Valerie's worried about her mom because she often works alone in the store. She thinks there could be a killer in town going after random people. I want you to promise you'll be extra careful, Mom."

As we ate our supper of chicken, fries, and coleslaw, the few people left in the area packed up. Jamie threw a few fries to a seagull who circled us. "Hey, Fred! I've missed you."

When we moved to Port Ripley, Jamie and Brent made friends with a seagull, feeding him bits of food as we lounged and played along the shore. He showed up every time we did, stalking us, begging for food. I wasn't convinced it was the same seagull, but he always scrutinized our faces before venturing close and was bold enough to snatch food off our blanket.

"Too bad Fred can't talk. Maybe he saw what happened to Wendall." *Someone* had to have witnessed it. "Well, hopefully, the police will figure it out soon. I need to head out, but I want to watch the sunset over the lake first." Jamie wrapped her arms around herself, shivering in the cool breeze.

Together, we watched from a bench on the clifftop while the sun dipped below the horizon, as we had done thousands of times before.

After Jamie left, I organized myself for the next school day, got ready for bed, and settled in to watch television. Only when I received Jamie's text that she was safely back in Masonville was I able to relax.

As the late evening news report came on, I was nearly asleep. It was the mention of Eugene Forsythe's name that jolted me awake.

"Police are now considering the fatal car crash was not an accident. This is the third suspicious death in town in the last few weeks. Police are cautioning the public to keep their doors locked, travel in groups after dark, and to report any suspicious activity."

So, they think someone caused Eugene's death, too. I wonder how long it will take them to catch who's responsible.

That was my last thought as I drifted off, with Tom curled up by my side.

My eyes flew open as I remembered something from that afternoon.

What if someone saw something from the freighter? Is there a witness out there?

Chapter Eleven

Scott Evans was up for the challenge. The detective staff sergeant from Northern Ontario sometimes consulted in unusual homicide cases outside his area. Pulling into Blue Water headquarters, he stepped out of his Camaro, stretching his long jean-clad legs after the eight-hour drive that began in the early morning.

He surveyed the rectangular, single-story building. It didn't look much different than the detachment up north he called home base the last twenty years. Scott climbed the stairs and announced himself at the main desk from where he was escorted to Detective Mike Juliano's office.

"Nice seeing you again, my friend. Hope you had a good drive. Thanks for coming down to our neck of the woods." Mike extended his hand. "This is a small town. You know what it's like. Things like this don't happen here. I'm short-staffed at the best of times, and with my best man off on paternity leave and a couple of new hires, none of my officers are experienced in homicide. I could really use your expertise."

"I'm more than happy to help out. The case sounded intriguing on the phone. What have you got so far?"

Mike gestured to the chair in front of his desk, sliding a file across to Scott. "The first victim, Wendall Collins, washed up on the beach two weeks ago. His wife reported him missing when he didn't return from a drive to the lake. The body was found early the next morning, his car parked in the lot across from the main beach. At first, it looked like he might have fallen off the pier or jumped intentionally. The coroner's report indicates he suffered a blow to the head. According to our coroner, Will Jenkins, he was hit with a blunt instrument, perhaps a hammer. The lack of water in the lungs indicates he was probably dead before he hit the water."

"Someone hit him on the head and pushed him off the pier?" Scott leaned forward.

"Possibly. We haven't located any witnesses yet. Then there's the second victim. Last week, Larissa LaMante fell down the stairs in the home where she lived alone. She was found at the bottom of the stairs by her aunt, who lives just down the street. There was a lethal dose of crystal meth in her system, but the amount of blood loss indicates the fall was fatal. She cracked her head on the hard tiles."

Scott nodded. "So, someone gave her crystal meth, which would have killed her, but she fell down the stairs as a result of being drugged."

"Or she was groggy and pushed to make it look like an accident."

"So, you're thinking both of these cases were made to look accidental?"

"Three cases, now. Eugene Forsythe's car went over the bridge into the river yesterday. According to our initial investigation, the brakes were tampered with."

"So, within two weeks, you've got three deaths occurring that appeared to be accidental, but aren't," Scott said, examining the files. "Any relationship between the victims?"

"Apart from the fact they're all from the same small town, you mean? There is one thing," Mike said, sitting back in his chair, fingers steepled. "Two of the victims are mystery buffs."

Scott raised his eyebrows. "Mystery buffs?"

"Wendall was a member of the local mystery readers book club, organized by Alice Reading, the bookstore owner. They meet once a week at Alice's house. Eugene was a mystery writer. He was killed heading home from a book festival at Alice Reading's bookstore," Mike explained, watching Scott's reaction.

"That's quite a coincidence," Scott said, skeptically. "Both men have a connection to Alice Reading. What about Larissa?"

"We haven't found a connection yet." Mike suggested that would be a good place for Scott to enter the investigation. "Why don't you have another look at the statements and interviews of family members and friends? A fresh set of eyes might help. Maybe you'll notice something we overlooked."

"I'm not feeling very fresh after the long drive. Right now, I'm desperately in need of some sleep. Any suggestions for a motel?" Scott stood and stretched his neck from side to side.

"There's the Port Ripley Hotel, if you want to stay in the center of town. It's nice, and they've got good food. Or there are a couple of motels on the outskirts." Mike's forehead creased. "Listen, Scott. There's more to this than I indicated during our phone conversation."

"How so?" Scott asked, suppressing a yawn as he sank into the chair again.

"Over the last months, Blue Water County has had more than its share of accidents. Not *all* fatal, but I've got a feeling the three in Port Ripley are part of a bigger picture. I think the other deaths and near misses in the county weren't thoroughly investigated because they appeared to be accidents. But our local coroner, Will, was a close personal friend of Wendall's. He knew he was a strong swimmer, so accidental drowning didn't fly with him. Then there's Larissa."

"What about her?"

"Will and Larissa had been seeing each other for several months. He said she was a very fit woman, had perfect eyesight, and was health and safety conscious to the point of being obsessive about it. And there was no way she was on drugs."

"The coroner personally knew two of the victims? What's Will's connection to Eugene?"

"He didn't know him personally, from what I was told."

"And you suspect there have been others, in different areas of the county, whose deaths were mistakenly ruled accidental?" Scott asked, stroking his stubble.

"Yes, that's exactly what I think."

"And you believe the deaths may have been caused by the same person? As in a serial killer traveling around Blue Water County?" Scott pushed the point, checking Mike's reaction.

Mike nodded and clasped his hands under his chin. "This kind of thing doesn't happen here. Port Ripley is one of the safest communities in Ontario. People know each other, apart from the tourists who visit during the summer season. But, yes, and I hate to say this. I think we have a cold-blooded murderer blending in with our unsuspecting citizens." He rose and patted Scott on the shoulder. "Get some rest, my friend. You look beat. We'll discuss our next course of action bright and early tomorrow."

Fifteen minutes later, Scott checked in at the counter of the old yellow-brick building on the corner of Main and Beachside. After lugging his suitcase and bag to the second floor, he deposited them on the wooden luggage rack in his room. "Getting out of shape," he muttered to himself. "Good thing I'm not on the third floor." Years of fast food had added the beginnings of a paunch to his once-lean body. He headed downstairs to the pub for a bite to eat.

Scott sat by the window with a view of the main street, quickly working his way through a beer, watching the sports network on one of the mounted screens. The warmth and crackling of a fire in the stone hearth, along with softly playing country music in the background, caused his already heavy eyelids to close. As the waiter set down a double-beef burger with thick-cut fries, Scott's eyes shot open, he sat up straighter, thanked his server and asked for another beer. The first bite told him why the place was so busy.

Catching movement out of the corner of his eye, Scott turned to watch maple leaves swirl along the sidewalk as a few passersby strolled through the town's business section. Most of the stores had closed for the day, but people were window shopping. Traffic moved at a slow pace along the tree-lined street, though not because of volume. On the other side of the street, he noticed stores housed in the century-old commercial block—a hardware store, a drugstore, a women's boutique, a shoe store, and a bookstore. Something there seemed familiar. A typical scene from any town, much like the town where he spent most of his life. A perfectly charming slice of small-town Ontario.

Except...there's a killer amongst the residents.

Scott polished off his meal with apple pie a la mode and paid his bill, leaving a generous tip. He stepped out of the hotel restaurant onto the now mainly deserted street. To his left, the sun peeked through a background of pink and purple as it set above the lake. Glancing at the bookstore across the street, he read the sign: Worth a Read Books. Eugene was last seen there before he drove his car off the bridge. The lights were still on in the bookstore.

Scott crossed the street and pulled on the locked door. He could have sworn he saw movement inside. Hands up to shield his eyes, face against the glass door, he peered inside.

Maybe just security lights.

Banging on the door anyway, he was rewarded with a vision of an attractive woman in her mid-twenties hurrying toward him.

"We're closed," she mouthed through the door, indicating the sign.

Scott pulled out his badge and held it up to the glass. An expression he couldn't quite read came over her face before she unlocked the door and allowed him in.

"I'm Detective Scott Evans of the provincial police, looking for Alice Reading," he announced. "I'd like to talk to her about Eugene Forsythe."

"Oh, poor Eugene." She pushed her long blond waves out of her face. "What a terrible thing to happen. Just brutal. He was so happy with the reception he got from his fans at the book festival yesterday."

"Are you Alice?" Scott asked.

"I'm Alice's daughter, Valerie. I help out at the store sometimes."

"Would Alice happen to be around?" Scott's brown eyes left her blue ones and scanned the bookstore, filled to the brim.

"No, she left. I stayed late to put new stock into inventory. Is there anything I can do for you?'

"Were you there, at the book festival?"

"I was. I helped Mom set up the authors and ring through sales. It was a good day." Her face clouded as she added, "Until Eugene's accident, of course."

"Did you know him well?"

"Not personally. But, of course, I'd see him around town and in the library where I work, and here in the bookstore. So yeah, I sort of knew him."

"Was Eugene his usual self? Was anyone acting strangely around him?"

"No. Everyone loved his reading. Why do you ask? I thought he lost control of his car."

"The investigation is still ongoing. Would you have a list of the authors at the festival?"

"Yeah, sure. It's downstairs. That's where we held the festival." Valerie led him to the back of the store, where they descended to the lower level.

Scott scanned the huge display of hobbies and games on shelves, pegboard, tables, spinning racks, in display cases, and stacked on the floor. It was a wonderland for kids and young-at-heart adults. The display of car model kits caught his attention. A dozen or more vehicles sat assembled in a glass case with kits for sale underneath. One of the vehicles on display was a Camaro. The kid in him wanted one of those.

Seeing the Not For Sale sign in front of a white Chevy utility van, Scott asked anyway. "Are these models for sale?"

"Let's see if there's a Camaro in stock." Valerie searched the shelves below.

"No, I meant the ones that are already built," Scott explained. "I don't have time to put one together myself. I wonder if you would sell the display model? I see the sign…" He pointed to the Chevy van.

"You can have the Camaro if you want. No problem." Valerie opened the display case. "My boyfriend's a Chevy man, too."

At the sales counter, Valerie pulled out a large spiral notebook. "Here's the information you asked for. We keep a list of authors, books, and sales. This was our sixth year of hosting the book festival. Mom gauges interest by tracking which types of books sell during and after readings."

Aside from Eugene, there were eight other names in the notebook. None were names Scott recognized. His personal reading choices gravitated toward mysteries and thrillers, but he hadn't heard of Eugene until his untimely death.

Removing his own notebook out of his jacket pocket, he recorded the eight names. "Thanks, that's helpful."

Valerie, whose blue eyes bore into his, was young enough to be his daughter. He wondered how she saw him. Probably as the aging, worn down by the nature of the job, stereotypical detective that he was.

"Is there anything else I can do to help?" she asked, as Scott held out his credit card to pay for the Camaro.

"What about Wendall Collins and Larissa LaMante, the other two accident victims? How well did you know them?"

"Wendall was in Mom's book club, so he was at our house every week."

"So, you live at home?"

"Yep, it's just Mom and me. Dad passed away several years ago, and I didn't want to leave Mom alone, so I never moved out after college. My brothers are married and live out of town. And Mom's got that big house to herself. It doesn't make sense for me to rent somewhere else."

"What about Larissa?" Scott was sure there had to be a connection between the victims.

"I've seen her at the library and bookstore and around town. She worked at the post office."

"Did the three victims know each other?"

"No idea," said Valerie. "But I'd assume they all knew each other somewhat. It's a small town. Everyone's really friendly." Her expression changed abruptly from a gentle smile to a wide-eyed look of horror. "You don't think someone wanted them dead, do you?"

Chapter Twelve

By the time he returned to his hotel room Sunday evening, Scott could barely wait to flop onto the white goose-down duvet covering the queen-sized bed. He needed to be alert tomorrow. Too bad he couldn't shut off his mind. Thoughts of a serial killer followed him into his dreams. Scott had dealt with killers before, but never a serial killer. He recalled several cases of multiple killings in larger regions of the province. Why *not* the small communities? There was no law that stated psychopaths had to be restricted to the cities.

The buzzing woke him at eight o'clock, and his eyes surveyed the room, not comprehending his situation. Then he remembered where he was—working a murder case.

In the shower, Scott allowed the warm spray to caress his body for a long time, hoping to get the kinks out of his shoulder and neck muscles. Leaving the short stubble on his face, he brushed his teeth, ran a comb through brown hair with touches of gray, and took out a neatly folded shirt from his suitcase along with a fresh pair of jeans. Donning a leather jacket, he hopped into his Camaro and roared off to the police station.

Mike was in his office when Scott arrived minutes before nine. Sporting dress pants and his sleeves rolled up, the thirty-something detective greeted Scott amicably and handed him a large fresh cup of coffee. "Didn't know whether you still like it black and strong," he said, indicating the cream and sugar packets on the tray.

"I like it anyway I can get it." Scott sipped the black liquid.

Mike handed over the files of the Port Ripley victims along with another thick folder. "These are my notes on the recent fatal accidents from our other detachments in Blue Water County."

Scott flipped through the files, stating he'd begin with the local cases. "I want to try to establish a connection between all three victims and see if I can find a possible motive before we jump to the conclusion that there are random killings taking place all over the county."

Mike agreed. "So, where do you want to start?"

"I'd like to talk to the families and friends of the victims myself, see what my impressions are. Then compare our notes. Maybe someone will divulge information they didn't think was important before or something they forgot about till now."

"Sounds good."

Scott's first stop was Wendall Collins' widow, whose older two-story red brick home was close to the downtown area.

Claire Collins answered the doorbell on the second ring. Scott introduced himself, and after he showed his credentials, Claire asked, "Is there anything new?"

"Not at this point. I'm sorry for your loss. I know you've already talked to the police, but I'd like to speak with you firsthand. Do you know why your husband was out at the lake that night?" Scott asked as gently as he could.

His eyes scanned the room, finding an old wedding photo but no pictures of children or grandkids. Newspapers cluttered the coffee tables, along with used tissues, empty mugs, and glasses. The carpet needed a good vacuum. He related to the mess, living alone. What he couldn't relate to was losing someone close to you as a result of murder. From Wendall's file, Scott knew he was married for thirty-two years.

Thirty-two years till death do you part is a long time.

Scott's own marriage lasted eight years until his wife asked for a divorce.

"Wendall said he wanted to go for a walk. It wasn't unusual for him to do that. He went out on his own all the time. But he always came back." Tears welled in Claire's blue eyes, silver-blond hair falling across her face as she lowered her head. Scott waited for Wendall's widow, a not unattractive woman of about fifty, to continue. "I didn't want to question him because I was afraid."

"*Afraid?*" Scott pounced on the word. "Afraid of what?"

Claire wiped her tears. "No, that's the wrong word. Not afraid. The truth is I didn't want him to get upset with me for tagging along if he needed time to himself. We used to go for walks together, but lately—"

"Was there some reason he needed time to himself?"

"No, I don't know of anything in particular. He'd just been kind of distracted lately. I thought maybe he was going through a midlife thing or something." Claire looked down at her hands as though they held an answer for her husband's unexplained death.

"Did he say anything out of the ordinary before he left to go to the lake that night?" Scott knew Wendall left his house at 6:15, just after supper, still daylight.

"No, just that he'd be back in a while. The usual. Sometimes he walked for twenty minutes, sometimes he'd be gone for two hours. When it got to be ten o'clock, I was really worried. I couldn't reach him on his phone, so I drove down to the lake. He wasn't there. At least, I couldn't see him anywhere around the pier area. Or anyone else, for that matter. I thought maybe I'd missed him and he'd already headed home, but then I saw his car parked in the lot. I called the police just before eleven, after walking along the boardwalk for a while. It was really eerie being down there at night by myself."

"Did Wendall usually go to the lake for his nightly walks?"

"He often did. Wendall loved the lake. He especially enjoyed walking to the end of the pier and looking out on the lake," Claire sniffled.

"What did he do for a living?" Scott wondered whether it was as stressful as his own job.

"He's an insurance salesman. Was." Mrs. Collins stared blankly at the empty Lazy Boy recliner by the fireplace. "He loved his job."

When Scott inquired about their financial situation, Claire Collins said they were comfortably well off.

"What about life insurance?"

"Yes, we both have a half million in life insurance. I just never thought I'd have to collect it," Claire sobbed. "I thought we'd get old…" She apologized and lowered her head into her hands.

Scott left the Collins' house with three words rolling through his brain—afraid, distracted, and insurance. What exactly was Claire Collins afraid of? Scott recorded his thoughts in his notebook.

The late morning sun shone through his windshield, heating up the leather passenger seat. He appreciated the warmth as he pulled down the visor, drove into the business district, and turned right onto Beachside, toward the lake. The different hues of blue, lake meeting sky dotted with clouds, were mesmerizing as he descended the curving road leading to the main beach. At the bottom, a parking area on the left was bordered by grass, trees, and flower beds. To the right was the lake, the clouds above masquerading as glaciers in the distance, against the light blue background of the sky.

Leaving his car amidst a dozen others, Scott crossed the wooden board-walk to the sandy beach, waves gently rolling to the shore to meet him. Across the great expanse of lake, a few sailboats were splayed against the horizon, and Canada geese floated on the water's surface. To his left, the beach stretched out a fair distance before meeting what appeared to be a curved breakwater. Seagulls landed on the beach, beaks wide open, screeching. On the right-hand side, the concrete pier stretched into the lake, almost meeting the rocky breakwater. As Scott followed the nearly-deserted shoreline toward the pier, a few walkers and joggers passed on the boardwalk, which extended the length of the beach. An occasional car toured the beach road.

Scott buttoned his leather jacket against the lake's breeze and headed down the pier. To his right, a channel for freighters shimmered turquoise. A ship was in dock, towering several stories above. He noted the stairs and railings devoid of crew members and wondered where the ship's occupants were. To the left, a short concrete wall stood between the pier's pedestrian walkway and the rolling waves of the crystal blue lake. The water turned a darker hue of blue the farther he walked. Once he passed the freighter, there was nothing between him and the channel except a curb warning the concrete ended, water swelling over it. A leisurely stroll and Scott stood at the end of the pier, far from the shore, and stared out at the breakwater. Feet firmly planted, Scott peered down into the water. A steel ladder descended into the frothy depths, one of several along the length of the pier.

If you fell over, you could climb back up. Unless you weren't a swimmer.

He eased one foot up, let it hover above the water, and imagined taking the plunge off the slightly raised rusty iron curb.

It was mesmerizing. Hypnotizing. You could just float away. The ripples beckoned.

Except it's too friggin' cold. No one in their right mind would take the plunge, especially at night.

Was Wendall in his right mind when he came down to the pier and didn't return? White waves crashed against rocks not far from where Scott stood. He stepped back and turned to watch the waves roll to shore.

The grumbling in his stomach told him it was time to return to the hotel for a bite to eat before his next meeting, with Eugene's fiancée, who lived in his ranch-style bungalow on the outskirts of town.

No beer at lunch for Scott. He needed to be as focused as possible. Forgoing the usual burger and fries, Scott ordered butternut squash soup and a gourmet grilled gruyere and ham sandwich, along with coffee. The chill of the lake was still with him, and it wasn't simply the cool breeze that had lodged itself in his bones. The image formed in his mind of Wendall's lifeless body caressed by the waves and deposited on the sand, stayed with him.

As he enjoyed his meal, the foot traffic in front of the bookstore caught his eye. Now and then, someone stopped to look at the display windows. A few shoppers ventured inside, while others exited with a small cloth shopping bag. From where he sat, he could distinguish the Worth a Read logo on the bags.

I need to talk to Alice Reading.

Chapter Thirteen

Tossing his jacket into the car, Scott crossed the sidewalk to Worth a Read. The smell was the first thing he noticed. Strange how he wasn't aware of it last night. He inhaled it. It wasn't a bad smell. Scott thought if you could smell ink and paper, this is what it would smell like. Kind of woodsy. Underlying that was a sweet, smoky, almost musty, smell. It was an old brick building, probably dating back more than a century. That could account for some of the smell.

Strolling through the store, he took a good look around. The shelving and the counter were real wood, as was the banister leading to a lower level. Then there were the books, old and new, in every nook and cranny, from floor to ceiling. Shelf lighting illuminated the titles. A couple of wooden rocking chairs sat next to the stairwell, flanking a wooden electric fireplace, a braided rug between them, creating a cozy reading nook. Shadows cast by floor and table lamps loomed across the walls and wooden floor. Scott noticed the incense burner on top of the fireplace.

Books and burning incense, not a good combination.

"Hello, is there anyone here?" Scott called out, louder than he intended.

"I'll be right with you."

Scott searched for the source of the voice. A modern computer system sat at the unmanned sales center. Scott glimpsed the video baby monitor and realized the store wasn't unattended. Security in a small town wasn't exactly high-tech.

A few minutes later, an attractive middle-aged version of Valerie Reading emerged at the top of the stairs. "Oh, hello. Sorry to keep you waiting."

She was followed by a young woman carrying a board game. Alice rang through the sale and gave Scott her full attention. "So, what can I help you with today? Looking for a special book for yourself or as a gift? Or maybe a game for the family?"

Pulling out his credentials, Scott said, "I know you've already given your statement to the Port Ripley police, but I'd like to ask a few more questions about Wendall and Eugene."

"Certainly. I don't know if I have any other useful information, but I'm happy to help. Such an awful thing to happen. They were both very nice men. I can't imagine who would want to harm them." The smile on Alice's face faded as she talked about the fate of the two victims.

"How well did you know them?"

"I knew Wendall well from our mystery book club. And my online writers' group as well. I didn't know Eugene personally, just as an author whose books we promote through the store."

"Would you be able to give me a list of the book club members?"

Alice sighed as she wrote down names on a piece of paper. "Eugene was over the moon about his latest book. It was next on our book club list. He was confident it was the one that would get him a big book deal. I guess maybe that's why he was so…" Alice stopped abruptly.

"So…" Scott urged her to continue.

"Well, I shouldn't really talk. It's nothing." Alice turned away. "Wendall, on the other hand, was obviously happily married."

"What's nothing? What did you mean about Eugene?"

"It's just that he seemed to be flirting, I guess, with some of the women at the book festival. Maybe he was just trying to drum up business, but he is, I mean *was*, engaged to be married. I didn't think it was entirely appropriate, especially at that venue, but…" Alice waved her hand in the air. "I'm probably making too much of it."

"Was he flirting with you?" Scott inquired, thinking she was an attractive woman, although older than Eugene, who was thirty-seven when he died.

"Oh no, not me." Her cheeks reddened. "Although…he didn't seem to be picky about the women he flirted with. Older. Younger. *Married.* I'm not sure what his fiancée would think about his behavior." Scott made a mental note to ask her.

"Thanks, you've been helpful." Before leaving the bookstore, Scott asked Alice to recommend a good book. He needed something to entertain himself in between thinking about this case.

"Any particular genre?"

"Yes," Scott grinned. "I do love solving mysteries."

"Who doesn't?" Alice directed him to the mystery section. "What about one of Eugene's books?" He took her suggestion and purchased Eugene Forsythe's first novel, *You're Killing Me.*

As Scott drove to Eugene's country home, he pulled over before entering the bridge that separated the town from the countryside and stepped onto the concrete sidewalk which ran along the steep, inclined curving road. Across the road, pylons marked the spot where the impact of Eugene's car broke through the guardrail.

Scott waited for the traffic to thin out and ran across the highway to gaze down at the river, water rippling across the rocks. Eugene's Corvette took quite a plunge. According to the police report, he was traveling at a high speed when he entered the curve.

Scott pulled up in the driveway of Eugene's house, admiring the sprawling gray brick bungalow with several acres of land surrounding it.

The woman who answered the door looked to be about thirty. Although she wore no makeup, she was strikingly beautiful, with long, straight black hair pulled into a high ponytail.

"Willow Patterson?" When Scott introduced himself, she nodded and invited him in.

Once they were seated in the living room, Scott expressed his condolences. "I'm hoping you can offer some insight into what might have caused the accident. Perhaps a mechanical problem?" Scott surveyed the room, wondering who was the beneficiary of Eugene's estate.

"I never pay much attention to car maintenance. Eugene always takes care of that." Willow regarded Scott with red-rimmed eyes.

"Would he have procrastinated in getting brake work done?"

"He loved that car. Drove it like a maniac, though, reliving his teenage years." Willow paused, with a sigh. "But he loved his writing more. He'd get so absorbed in it, sometimes he didn't notice much of anything else. So, I guess the brakes could have been needing repair and he put it off."

"I heard Eugene was well-received at the book festival Saturday and excited about his latest mystery. Did you drive to the bookstore in your own vehicle?"

"No, I didn't go."

"Was it usual for him to attend book events without you?"

Willow sighed. "I supported Eugene's writing. It was important to him. But my dad was reading at the book festival, too. They hadn't been getting along, especially the last week or so. Dad never liked Eugene. I didn't want to be caught in the middle of their drama in a public place, so I told them I was staying home."

Scott considered that her decision not to attend the festival saved her life. Apologizing for being blunt, he asked, "Would I be correct in assuming that since Eugene had no children, you inherit this house?"

Willow didn't hesitate to tell him she was the main beneficiary in his will. "Eugene's parents left him very well off when they passed away. It gave him the freedom to pursue his love of writing full-time. But I don't want his money. I never did. I just wanted Eugene."

Willow's comment seemed to be a good segue for Scott's next question. "I've heard some rumors, unsubstantiated, of course, that Eugene was quite a ladies' man."

Willow shook her head and raised her hands to her mouth, closing her eyes. "He was. He definitely had his share of women before me. But then we met last year, and he asked me to move in with him soon after. He said it was time for him to settle down, and I was the one he wanted to have a family with. He promised it would be only me from then on." Willow hesitated, then added, "But I suppose old habits are hard to break." She looked out the window at the landscaped front lawn.

Scott recalled the first woman who made him think about settling down, fourteen years ago. The woman who was his best friend. The woman who was happily married with two kids when he met her. The woman who walked out of his life and disappeared, leaving him wondering why.

"I know he was a bit of a flirt. But he was a good man. He didn't deserve this. Who would want to hurt Eugene?"

Scott assured Willow that everything was being done to find the reason for Eugene's tragic accident. Before driving off, he made a few notes about Eugene's flirtations and Willow's inheritance.

The warmth of the midday sun coming through the car windows as he drove back to town had a dual effect on him. He felt lazy, wanting to close his eyes and bask in the warmth, forgetting work for a while. At the same time, the sun invigorated him, its brightness reminding him to seize the day. As he approached the turnoff to Larissa Lamante's street, Scott kept his eyes on the road ahead and made the descent to the lake. No point in wasting a perfectly beautiful fall day.

This time, Scott drove down the full length of the beach road, to where it ended in a cul de sac at the sandy cove. Choosing one of the angled parking spots facing the beach, with the intention of walking the full length of the boardwalk for exercise, he stepped out into the fresh air.

The breeze from the lake blasted him, and he reached back into the car for his jacket. Locking up, he set off down the long strip of raised wooden boards that followed the shore. For a while, the lapping waves and the screeching seagulls were the only sounds he heard apart from his shoes hitting the boards. A few vehicles cruising by interrupted his solitude, some with music blaring. Now and then, people passed by, greeting him with a nod or a 'hello.' He didn't know them, but then, it was a small town. Much like the small town he came from. People were friendly, and he instinctively returned their waves.

Halfway down the beach, the shoreline changed. Rocks replaced sand, whitecaps thundering against them. He continued to where the shore transitioned back to a silky beach. As Scott approached the pier, he turned toward the water, his shoes squishing through the sand, and picked up a few pebbles. He skipped them across the lake, his eyes drawn to an older couple walking hand in hand on the pier, past the freighter, following the concrete out into the lake. Behind him, a man walked his dog. Farther up on the boards, a few others strolled in his direction. Cars continued to cruise up and down the road at regular intervals. There were lampposts along the boardwalk and some on the pier. This area would be packed with tourists during the peak summer season. But how many people would be out here in the dark, on a cool September weeknight? Was Wendall out here alone when he died? Or meeting someone? Did he have an unexpected encounter?

It was a brisk twenty-minute walk back to his car. Along the way, Scott's eyes followed the treed incline to the left of the road. At the top of the cliff stood the limestone lighthouse. When he reached his car, he noted the wooden steps leading up the steep slope. Scott wondered how well you could see from the top of the bluff. Crossing the road, he stood at the bottom of the stairs. They zigzagged through the treed incline, disappearing partway up.

More exercise will do me good, considering the way this jacket fits around the middle.

Ignoring the railing, Scott jogged up the first landing, pausing to catch his breath and peer down at the beach.

That was easy so far.

He huffed and puffed, but was rewarded with a postcard scene of sand, lake, curved breakwater, boardwalk, lampposts, parking lot, grass, trees, cars, and people. By the time he reached the second landing, trees and shrubs obscured his view. He climbed higher, looking backwards every so often, but only the lake was visible past the greenery.

The vibration along the steps warned him someone was coming down. Keeping to the right-hand side, he grabbed the railing. The woman he met on the steps looked down at her feet, brushing past him in a hurry.

"Excuse me," he called. "How much farther to the top?"

She halted and rotated her head, giving him a look as if to say, 'Are you talking to me?' Her mouth flew open, then she lowered her head and turned away.

Wondering whether she didn't understand him, he repeated his question, adding, "It's quite a climb."

"You're about halfway there." She rushed down the stairs.

Scott watched her back until she disappeared. Although he only saw her face for a moment, she was familiar. And her voice brought back old memories.

No, wishful thinking. It can't be her. Can it?

Scott descended after the woman, zigzagging through the greenery. At the final landing, he stopped to scan the lake area. There didn't seem to be any sign of the short-haired blonde wearing a long, bulky, cornflower blue pullover sweater and loose-fitting jeans.

Scott resumed his climb, trying to convince himself it couldn't be the woman he once knew. Although he held the railing, taking it slower this time, he was breathing heavily by the time he reached the top. The view *was* worth the climb. The lake below spread out straight ahead, the sky in the distance, dark blue against lighter blue, with a row of fluffy white/gray clouds between the two hues. Scott walked along the edge of the cliff, peering past the greenery.

Depending on where you stand, you can see everything.

The sun bounced off his silver Camaro, a miniature toy amongst the other scattered vehicles in the parking spots. If the blond woman with the cornflower sweater was down there, he couldn't spot her. And if someone was up here the night Wendall died, they wouldn't be able to identify him, unless they had binoculars.

Scott walked the length of the grassy, treed park area above the lake until he reached the end of the street, which went off in two directions. One led to the town's center, and the other down to the lake. He was about to turn back toward the stairs when he spotted the street signs, Beachside and Lakeview. Crossing the street to check house numbers, it didn't take long to locate Larissa LaMante's two-story home. Four vehicles sat in the cement driveway.

A tall young man with black hair and stubble on his face answered the door, his eyes moving from Scott to his ID. "I'm Glen, Larissa's son. Come in."

As Scott followed Glen through the hall into the large kitchen, he noted the long, curved staircase to the left and the hard white-tile flooring. Scott considered a fall all the way down could prove fatal, drugs or no drugs.

Two young women worked at the kitchen island, one peeling potatoes, the other breaking apart romaine. "My sisters, Emma and Steph," Glen said, pointing to the petite brunette, then to the taller, younger blond. "And this is my wife, Melanie," he added as a pretty, slightly plump redhead entered the room, carrying a baby. "Then there's Reggie, Emma's husband. He's out back cleaning up the barbecue."

Scott asked if the family could gather to answer a few questions, prompting Glen to holler for Reggie to get into the kitchen. With everyone assembled around the counter, Scott apologized for the intrusion on dinner.

"I know this is a difficult time for you. I'm afraid there's no easy way to do this. Did Larissa have a problem with drugs?"

Shock and outrage were obvious in their cries of protest as they shook their heads.

"No! Absolutely not!" Glen's voice stood out louder than the rest. "She never took anything stronger than a Tylenol."

"Mom was really health conscious," explained the youngest daughter, Steph. "If there were drugs in her system, she didn't take them voluntarily." Her eyes became wet as she spoke of her mother.

"Any idea how she might have got hold of crystal meth?" Scott asked. "Some family member, possibly? A friend?"

"Well, it certainly wasn't one of us who gave it to her," Emma said, indignantly.

"I'm not making accusations," Scott held up his hand. "I'm just wondering if anyone she knew would have access to meth. If there's any way she could have taken it, mistaking it for something else."

"None of us take drugs, if that's what you're insinuating," Reggie challenged Scott, narrowing his eyes. "If you're looking for who's responsible, maybe you should look at that coroner she started seeing a few months ago. He'd be able to get his hands on drugs, wouldn't he?"

Scott ignored the question and turned to Steph, "Do you still live at home?"

"No. Well, sort of, I guess. I'm going to Western, but I come home for weekends when I can."

"Do you know if Larissa's friends included Wendall Collins or Eugene Forsythe?"

"No, I don't think so. Oh, wait a minute!"

"Weren't they just on the news?" Glenn interrupted his sister before she could answer.

"That's right," Emma agreed. "Their deaths are being investigated. That's where we heard those names."

"Are you saying Mom's death is connected to them?" Steph asked, her eyes wide. "Oh, my gosh. Who would hurt Mom?"

Scott assured them he would do everything he could to find out. As Glenn showed him to the door, Scott asked whether there were any obstructions upstairs that might have caused Larissa's fall.

"You should ask Aunt June." Steph spoke quietly, coming up behind them and following Scott's gaze to the top landing. "She was the one who found her, the poor old woman."

"June?"

"Mom's aunt. She lives at the end of our street, overlooking the lake. It must have been awful for her, finding Mom."

"Maybe not that awful, though, is it?" Reggie's burly body blocked the kitchen doorway. "She'll get her share of Larissa's money."

"June loved Mom." Steph glared at Reggie, then turned to Scott. "She was more than an aunt to her. They were really good friends. And it was good for Mom to have someone close by after I went to Western."

"So, the estate is split between June and the rest of the family?" Scott asked, looking at the people who stood to benefit financially from Larissa's death.

"Unless something happens to June. She's elderly and never married." Glen replied. "When she dies, her money goes to us." Glen's voice broke, and his face crumpled. Steph put her hand on his shoulder.

After thanking the family, Scott walked briskly back down the sidewalk, looking at the gracious older homes next to him and the grassy parkland across from them overlooking the lake. He thought he wouldn't mind living there himself once the killer was permanently secured behind bars.

June's house, the last on the street, was a bungalow. Much like the one beside it, but smaller with white siding instead of white brick and stone. He pressed the button next to the burgundy door. When no one answered, he tried again a couple of times before turning away.

"Can I help you, young man?" a woman's voice called from the park. He wasn't sure she was talking to him. He hadn't been called a young man for some time. When the elderly woman and her small dog approached, Scott realized she meant him.

"Yes, hello. Would you happen to be June?" Scott observed that the woman, although several decades older than him, appeared to be spry and fit. He wondered if she could handle the stairs from the beach better than he could.

"Yes, that's me. What can I do for you? You're not selling something, are you? Because I'm not buying." She narrowed her eyes.

Scott explained he was looking into her niece's death, working with the local police. Once June examined his credentials, she became quite talkative.

"Poor Larissa. It's taken the life right out of my brother and his wife. And her kids, the poor dears. I couldn't believe it when I saw her lying at the bottom of the stairs like that, like a broken doll. If only I had checked on her sooner." June wiped her tears before continuing. "I'm sorry, it's just that she was so young, barely fifty. And she'd just started seeing that nice man, what's his name? Bill? Oh no, Will. She'd been lonely since her youngest moved out to go to school in the city. Just like my neighbor, Ivy. A lovely woman, but she's been on her own for years, since her husband died in that car accident. I know what it's like to live on your own. I'm single myself. Still looking for Mr. Right." June stopped talking to blow her nose and give Scott an appraising look.

Scott took the opportunity to ask a question. "Did Larissa know Wendall Collins or Eugene Forsythe?"

"Hmm…yes, those names sound familiar. Wait, aren't they the ones in the news?" When Scott confirmed they were, June continued. "She knew Eugene from reading his books. Larissa enjoyed a good mystery. She might have run into him in town now and then. And Wendall lived a few streets over. It's a small town, so everybody sort of knows everyone else. But I don't think she knew either of them that well on a personal level, no, at least I don't think she did. But…hold on. I saw him one night. And she did say…"

Scott lost track of the conversation as June droned on, and a woman emerged at the top of the stairs across the road. It was her. As Scott stared at the blond woman with the cornflower bulky sweater and jeans, she turned sideways, lowered her head, hugged her waist, and briskly walked away. June stopped talking when she noticed him staring.

"Oh, that's my neighbor, Ivy. Ivy! Ivy!" she shouted and waved. "I guess she can't hear me."

"I doubt that." Scott's eardrums were about to burst.

June unleashed her miniature black Schnauzer and said, "Go get Ivy, Clarence!"

Clarence took off, barking. Instead of stopping, the woman quickened her pace. Undeterred, Clarence ran in front of her, jumping up, almost knocking her down in his enthusiasm. June yelled, waving both arms in the air as Clarence yapped around Ivy.

When Ivy ambled toward June and Scott, June shouted, "I guess you didn't hear me. So I sent Clarence after you."

Ivy stopped on the sidewalk in front of her own house. "I'm sorry, no, I didn't hear you." Her head was down, her chin almost touching her neck, and her left hand was up on her forehead, shielding the sun from her eyes.

"I wanted you to meet Detective…what was your name again? He's helping to find out what happened to Larissa." June motioned for Ivy to join them.

"Sorry, I need to go. Nice to meet you," Ivy said to her feet and headed for her door.

"It's Detective Evans. Scott Evans," he shouted, jogging toward her. "I wonder if I could…" Before he got there, she slammed the door.

"She's not usually that rude," June commented, sidling up next to him. "I guess she really needed to use the bathroom. I know what that's like."

"What did you say her name was?"

"Ivy. Ivy Rose."

So, not the woman he once knew. Not Cheryl. But there was something familiar about that name, Ivy Rose. He politely turned down June's offer to come inside for a cup of tea but promised he'd visit another time.

Climbing down to the beach, Scott slid into his Camaro and pulled out the file on the three victims. As he moved his finger down the pages, Scott found the connection. Wendall Collins, mystery book club member. Eugene Forsythe, mystery writer. Larissa LaMante, mystery fan. And there on the lists of names Valerie and Alice Reading had given him, was the clue that tied them together.

Chapter Fourteen

I don't believe this. After all these years, for him to show up here of all places, right in front of my house.

After my encounter with Scott, I sat in my living room with the curtains closed and the door locked, trying to calm myself with a cup of chamomile tea and some chocolate biscuits. The kitchen phone rang.

Please don't let it be him.

"Hello, Ms. Rose?"

"Yes." I gripped the phone tightly. "Who is this?"

"It's Justin Newark from Newark Literary. I just wanted to let you know that I absolutely loved your book."

The phone slipped out of my hand, and I scrambled to retrieve it. I had been cold querying for a long time, sending letters and samples of my work out in hopes that it would catch the attention of a literary agent. Justin said he would send my novel to publishers right away if I was interested in becoming his client.

"I have a whole series, actually," I said, a rush of excitement preventing me from asking more questions. "Would you be interested in reading the other five I've written?"

Justin assured me he was interested.

* * *

The next morning, I visited Olivia in her classroom, eager to share the good news in person. "Finally. All the work I've put into this series, and now it looks like it may actually pay off. You're the one responsible for connecting me with Justin. I can't thank you enough."

"You deserve it," Olivia responded, hugging me. "Your work is better than most of the mystery books I've read. You're a master at building suspense."

"Speaking of suspense, did you get your reading done for tonight's book club?" I still had a few chapters to catch up on. Last night, I couldn't settle down and concentrate. All I kept thinking about was my new agent, Justin Newark, and my old friend, Scott Evans. It was the latter that kept me up most of the night, tossing and turning.

"I did. By the way, have you had a chance to read my manuscript?" Olivia watched closely for my reaction. "I want to discuss it with you. To see what you think."

"Sorry, I haven't. But I'll get right to it, starting tomorrow. Honestly, it's just been crazy with school starting, and my writing, and critique partners, and the book club, and the book festival, and trying to fit in walks, and Jamie's visit, and I've been trying to spend some time with June, the poor dear…"

Olivia raised her hand and laughed. "Stop. I understand. You're a busy woman. It's no problem. Whenever you get a chance. But I *do* want to know what you think. Whether you think it could be connected…"

"Oh no." I rushed to the door as the bell rang. "I'm late."

Students were already filing into the classroom. I opened my copy of Margaret Atwood's novel and slipped into my teacher persona with ease.

That afternoon, I noticed some students flipping through their phones during the discussion of the author's point of view, while others wildly moved their thumbs, sending texts, whispering amongst themselves. Setting down my book, I asked if they wanted to let me in on what was so captivating on their screens.

"Sorry, Ms. Rose," Toby apologized. "It's Gary Reese's dad." Gary was one of my Grade 9 students and a friend to several of the kids in the class. "He didn't come home last night. The police just found his body in the woods."

Chapter Fifteen

"A hunting accident," Mike Juliano explained, motioning for Scott to have a seat. "Ten miles north. Phillip Reese went for a walk in the woods last night. When he didn't return, his wife called the police. They found him on his property early this morning. Two shots with a 12-gauge shotgun."

"Why was he walking in a hunting area?" Scott leaned forward, palms face up.

"It's a No Hunting Zone, on his land, clearly posted."

Scott's eyebrows shot up. "Did they get the shooter?"

"No, no sign of anyone. Like I said, there have been a large number of 'accidents' in the county this past month." Mike sighed, using his fingers to show parentheses. "I've coined them accidental murders."

He pulled out the thick file folder from the cabinet next to his desk and removed sets of sheets clipped together, one at a time. "These are my notes on the recent deaths in the county. The three in town are just the tip of the iceberg, if you ask me. Floyd Weber, trapped in a manure holding tank he was cleaning out. Fumes overtook him. Lindsay Hollinger, shaving her legs, perched above the bathtub. Electrocuted. Clark Helmsley, hiking alone in a conservation area. Fell off the escarpment. Take a look. Victims didn't know each other. Different MO's, no clear motive, no witnesses."

"A crazed killer, then?" Scott flipped through the files, his forehead furrowed.

"I'd say about as crazed as you can get." Mike sat back in his chair, meeting Scott's eyes. "And they aren't stopping."

Scott clasped his hands together, put them behind his head, and stretched out his legs, deep in thought. "Someone's been busy."

"They've been getting around, all right." Mike drummed his fingers on top of the file.

Scott sat up straight. "Even crazed killers have an agenda. Somewhere, there's a connection, a witness, a reason. We just need to find it. I'm going to continue investigating the in-town deaths for now. If there's a connection between the victims, it'll be here where everyone knows everyone. Small town and all."

His first stop of the day was June LaMante's house. "Oh, Detective." June opened the door and fumbled with the sash on her robe while trying to keep her Schnauzer in the house. "I'm sorry, I'm sure I look quite a sight. Detective...?"

"Evans. But you can call me Scott. Sorry for dropping by unexpectedly, but I was looking forward to that cup of tea I missed yesterday."

"Of course. Come right in. Where are my manners? I was just watching my morning talk show and haven't had a chance to get dressed," June explained in a loud voice, competing with the volume on the television. "I'll just be a minute. Why don't you have a seat in the living room and watch the show while I make myself presentable?"

Before Scott could react, June disappeared down the hall and closed a door, leaving Scott with the talk show host discussing cheating spouses. By the time she reappeared, he was on the sofa, engrossed in the show, with Clarence on his lap.

"It's addictive, isn't it?" June entered the living room in a pair of dusty rose slacks and a floral print blouse, her wavy silver hair brushed neatly in place, rouge on her cheeks, pale pink on her lips. "Some days, I spend the better part of my morning watching the shows. Then there's the afternoon soaps. Do you follow any of those?"

"No, I can't say I've ever seen one," Scott answered, still listening to the cheating spouses air their dirty laundry on morning television.

"You don't know what you're missing," she chuckled. "I'll go get the kettle on."

Minutes later, June brought out a tray with a teapot, two teacups, and a plate of digestive cookies. "I haven't had a gentleman caller for a while. I hope this is okay."

Scott smiled, turning his attention to June. "It's perfect. Thank you. To tell the truth, I haven't had the pleasure of a lady's company for some time."

"Not married?" June indicated the finger on his left hand.

"Divorced."

"Just like my Larissa…" Tears formed in the corners of her eyes. "I'm sorry, for a moment…I…I forgot she…." Clarence moved to her lap.

Scott patted her hand, telling her that was perfectly normal. "Actually, I was hoping you'd be able to help find out who would want to harm your niece."

June shook her head and dabbed her eyes with a tissue. "No one. Why would *anyone* hurt her? She was a lovely woman, so kind and thoughtful."

"Did she have a lot of friends?"

June said Larissa wasn't exactly a social butterfly. "She loved her kids. She had a few friends from the gym and the post office where she worked. And she and I spent a good deal of time together. Until that man she started seeing, then she didn't have as much time for me. Bill? No wait, it was Will. She said he's a doctor. I was happy for her. She'd been alone for too long after that scumbag, Rick, left."

"Did she spend time with her neighbors?"

"She talked to them when she was out walking or jogging."

"What about Ivy Rose?"

"What about her?" June cocked her head.

"What can you tell me about her?"

"She's single, if you're interested." June raised her eyebrows. "But I don't think she likes men. I haven't seen hide nor hair of any man around her place since she moved in eleven years ago. Although she'd be a fool to turn *you* down." June winked at Scott.

Scott gagged on his tea, and shakily set down the teacup. The woman he used to know went missing around that time. Whatever happened to that gutsy, feisty, attractive, curly black-haired girl with the big brown eyes he would get lost in? Was the self-effacing, blue-eyed blond next door the same woman?

"She teaches high school English," June continued. "Has two grown kids, Brent and Jamie. Are you okay?" Scott couldn't control his sudden coughing fit. June patted him on the back and asked if he needed the Heimlich Maneuver. He managed a headshake. "Brent's a lawyer, lives in Oakridge. Jamie's at Western College, in Masonville."

"No husband?" Scott managed to croak.

"Died in a car accident before she moved here. Poor man never got to see his kids grow up." June continued to pat Scott's back. "Are you sure you're okay? You look positively white."

"And her name is Ivy Rose?"

"Yes. Have you heard of her before? She did publish a book of short stories. Or maybe you've read her work in a magazine?"

Always a writer. Used to be a very nosy reporter.

It was the woman he once knew as Cheryl MacGregor, his good friend and sleuthing partner, the woman he secretly fell in love with years ago. Now she was Ivy Rose, a person of interest in a murder investigation. He thought back to the lists of book club members and book festival authors. One name showed up on both lists. Ivy Rose knew Wendall and Eugene. *And* Larissa.

"No, I hadn't heard of her till you introduced me to her. I assume she's at school right now?" he asked. June nodded. "Maybe I'll pay her a visit tonight. What time does she usually get home?"

"She's busy tonight. She's got Murder Club." Seeing Scott raise his eyebrows, June added, "At Alice Reading's house, seven to nine. Do you like solving mysteries?"

"As a matter of fact, I'm really into them. It's more than a pastime."

"That's good. You'll have a lot in common, then. Ivy's really into murder."

Chapter Sixteen

After school, I packed my beach bag with *Watch Your Step* along with a tablecloth and a bag of takeout food, grabbed a blanket, and climbed down to the lake. I planned to multitask—read more of Olivia's manuscript, get some fresh air and exercise, and have supper. The snack bar was closed for the season, but the washrooms were open, and picnic tables remained scattered around the grass.

When I met Scott Evans on the stairs yesterday, the sound of his voice startled me, and I turned and froze, seeing his face. A few lines that weren't there years ago, gray hairs creeping into the brown, and some extra weight around the middle. After my initial shock, I scurried off, hiding in the washroom for an hour.

Spreading the tablecloth on a picnic table in the sun, I removed the burger, fries, and coffee from the paper bag.

A bad habit from my days with Scott Evans.

Facing the lake, where Canada geese bobbed on the water as waves lapped against the sand, I enjoyed my meal, eyes peeled for a certain detective. If I encountered Scott again, what would I say?

Can I trust him to understand and keep my secrets?

* * *

Scott came to the house the morning after Jim died in the car accident. I answered the door in pajamas, no makeup, hair and teeth unbrushed. He didn't need to tell me how sorry he was. No words were needed. It was etched into his face, in his eyes, the minute I opened the door.

Scott walked into the home he knew well, put his arms around me, kissed my forehead, and held me for the longest time. I finally pulled away, tears streaming down my face, nose dripping, eyes stinging. But I didn't care how I looked. Jim was dead. Nothing mattered anymore. I had no family or close friends to console me. Only Scott, the detective I met last year working as a reporter for the local newspaper, assisting him in solving a case. Jim's receptionist, Julia, had gone missing.

"I don't know," I blubbered, seated next to him on the living room sofa, the drapes drawn, the room dim. "What I'm going to do without Jim."

Scott rubbed my arm, still silent, letting me cry until I collapsed against him. He brought his lips to the top of my head and held them there a while, stroked my hair, and finally spoke. "I'm here for you."

I raised my head to face him. "I know. Thank you." I wiped my eyes and blew my nose, "You're a good friend."

His voice cracked. "The kids…how are they doing?"

"I asked an acquaintance from out of town to take them so they wouldn't have to face the funeral. I thought it was for the best."

"You could have sent them to me for a while."

I didn't respond. Brent and Jamie loved Scott. But involving Scott in my grief process would open a whole Pandora's box I wasn't ready to set loose. Not even for him.

* * *

After supper, I laid my blanket across the soft sand and pulled one end over my shoulders to shield myself from the cool breeze. Pulling the hood up on my hoodie, I cocooned into the warm wool blanket and pulled out Olivia's manuscript.

Tightly holding the pages, I settled in to read. An hour later, I tucked away the manuscript and watched the waves. *Watch Your Step* contained a scene that eerily described Larissa's untimely demise, with a body at the bottom of the stairs, blood staining the tiles. In Olivia's novel, the victim was assumed to have tripped, but it was discovered she had drugs in her system.

Why wouldn't Olivia have mentioned that? It's like she predicted Larissa's death.

I would ask her at Murder Club. As I gathered up the blanket, Olivia sent a text saying she wouldn't be attending the meeting.

I called Olivia following my stroll on the boardwalk. "What's up? Everything okay?"

"You won't believe what just happened." Olivia's voice quivered. "When I came home, I wanted to relax in the hot tub. And then…"

"*What?* What happened?"

"If I had slid right in, I would have been burned," Olivia continued, her voice rising. "Cliff says the temperature gauge was turned too high, and the filter cycle was set wrong."

"Oh my! How did that happen?"

"The thermostat must have malfunctioned."

"But you're okay?"

"You know me. I always check everything. When I dipped my toes in, the water was scorching. They're a bit red and throbbing, but Cliff applied antibiotic cream and bandaged them."

"Oh, wow. Thank goodness it wasn't worse."

"Yes. Anyway, I'm going to spend the evening at home."

After ending the call, I realized I forgot to ask Olivia about her character's fall down the stairs.

There's no point in bothering her now. She's just lucky it wasn't worse.

But it was so odd. Olivia's manuscript described Larissa's accident, just like Eugene's book foretold Wendall's body being washed ashore. Eugene died in a car crash, and now Olivia had a freak accident?

The kitchen clock spurred me to grab my book club novel and purse and run to the Jeep.

Alice welcomed me when I arrived at Murder Club. "I'm just getting the snacks ready."

"Do you need help?"

"If you want to grab the bowls of pretzels and nuts, that'd be great."

I carried the bowls downstairs and set them on the table behind the sofa, next to the bottles of ginger ale and wine, then grabbed a cushion and joined Celia and Gabby on the floor. The others were on the sectional sofa, engaged in a conversation about a sci-fi program they all watched.

"How'd your week go?" Celia asked. "Kids behaving?" Celia's two teenagers were my students. One of them, Toby, was a favorite of mine as he always questioned everything.

"It's all good. Except one of my students lost his dad last night. Hunting accident."

"*Another* accident?" Gabby exclaimed. "Do they think it's connected to the others? To Wendall?"

"I don't know. But it does make you wonder."

"Haven't there been more?" Celia asked. "Accidents in the county?"

"Accidents?" Dylan chimed in from the sofa. "I wouldn't be surprised if they were murdered."

"Poor Wendall," Celia said. Everyone nodded, and there was a moment of silence. "Do you think it's the same person who killed all of them?"

Alice descended into the family room, carrying plastic glasses and napkins. "Shouldn't we wait for the others before we start talking about the killer?" She set the tray on the table.

Seeing the confusion on everyone's face, Alice added, "You're not talking about the book, are you?" The sound of the doorbell took her back upstairs, and she returned with a couple of other club members. "Just waiting on Olivia, then."

"Oh. Olivia's not coming." I was about to say Olivia had an accident of her own but thought better of it. "She's not feeling well."

We settled in and focused on the identity of the killer in our novel.

"Probably Spencer's wife?" Celia guessed. "Isn't it usually the spouse who's the villain? Gaslighting, maybe."

"Yes, someone who wants to make it look like it's Spencer. That detective sure has it in for him," Dylan conjectured. "What if he's a dirty cop?"

"It's always the one you least suspect," I agreed. "But I'd say it's Spencer's best friend. He was being way too secretive."

Halfway through the evening, the doorbell rang. As everyone looked around, I counted ten people. Olivia was home recovering from her accident. Wendall was dead.

Valerie shouted down the stairs, "I'll get it, Mom." Alice's daughter didn't take part in Murder Club as she had her hands full leading the library book club. "Oh, Detective Evans. This is a surprise."

"Oh," Alice gasped, rising from her chair. "That's one of the detectives looking into the recent deaths."

The conversation changed from fictional murder to real-life murder. As Alice climbed upstairs to greet the detective, I leaned over and whispered to Celia, "I'm just going to sneak out. My stomach is upset. I should have stayed home." Grabbing my purse, I climbed the back stairs to the mudroom off the garage.

* * *

The conversation in the family room, which Scott caught snippets of, ceased when he joined the group. "So, this is our little book club," Alice said, waving her hand over the assembled mystery fans and introducing everyone. His eyes scanned the group as Alice offered him her chair.

"Sorry to interrupt your book study," Scott said, taking another look around, leaning forward in his chair. "I'm hoping someone might know why Wendall was down at the beach the night he died. Maybe he was meeting someone?" His question was answered with blank stares, head shaking, and shoulder shrugging. "Sometimes," he added, "the smallest bit of information can be important in solving a case."

"Like a clue? Like in the books we read," Celia said. "So Wendall was definitely *murdered?*"

Scott turned his attention to the attractive brunette on the floor. "That's what the evidence suggests." The woman, who was about ten years his junior, chewed her manicured thumbnail. "If anyone remembers anything that could be relevant to Wendall's death, you need to let the police know."

An uncomfortable silence filled the room, broken by Alice's comment,

"I'm sure we all want to find out who's responsible." Everyone nodded but kept quiet.

"Are there some members of your group missing tonight?"

Alice nudged Celia. "Is Ivy in the bathroom?"

"She went home. Stomach upset."

"Oh, that's too bad. She would have loved this, a real-life detective asking questions. She would have probably interviewed him about his job and written a story about him."

"And he's really hot," Celia whispered loud enough for Scott to hear.

"Maybe she's sick with what Olivia has," Gabby added. "Probably caught it from the kids."

"Who's Olivia?" Scott asked Gabby, the bleached blond, who looked to be in her forties. "What kids?"

"The kids they teach at Blue Water High," Gabby answered, stretching her plump legs in front of her. "A lot of us have kids that go there."

"Olivia's not here tonight. Ivy said she wasn't feeling well. And now she took off, too," Celia explained. "You're probably right; it's some bug going around the school."

"Anyone else missing?" Scott asked.

"Wendall," Dylan said. Everyone stared at him. "Sorry, wasn't thinking."

"That's okay. Sometimes it's hard to accept when someone we're used to having around is gone." Scott understood from personal experience what that was like. It had taken him a long time to come to terms with Cheryl's disappearance. He rose from his chair and said he didn't want to disrupt their night any longer. "You can leave a message at the station if you need to get in touch with me."

As he drove back to his hotel, Scott thought about Ivy.

She's really going out of her way to avoid me. Why is that?

Chapter Seventeen

"Okay, so your character's motivation. Is it becoming clearer to you?" She pulled out a tablecloth, drinks, paper plates, and plastic cutlery, setting their makeshift table on the sand in an unpopulated area of the lakeshore. Her partner helped her take the plastic containers out of the cooler and laid them down on the tablecloth. They ate their roast chicken sandwiches, potato salad, and coleslaw, talking about how the book was coming along.

"I think so. A little less competition never hurt anyone. She knocks off the local mystery writers, and it gives her a leg up in the writing community. Better chance of winning local contests and competitions, building a fan base, selling her self-published stuff at the local bookstores and other venues. More attention and recognition. And besides that, it gives her lots of ideas for writing. She steals the victims' manuscripts, makes copies, and no one's the wiser. With the writer dead, she uses some of their ideas, the ideas that never got published, and changes them up a bit. With all those unpublished manuscripts, there's bound to be a bestseller in there somewhere. More chance of going the traditional route with an agent and a major publisher. It's not just about getting rid of a few writing bodies; it's about gaining the deceased writers' body of work. You're brilliant!"

"I know."

"I really had a good time today," he said at the end of the afternoon. "I enjoy your company, and not just as a critique partner. Can we see each other again?"

"You mean, like a date?" She was hopeful that was exactly what he meant.

"Yeah, can I take you out for dinner, maybe?"

What started as a critique partnership turned into a romantic relationship. A couple of months later, they were making plans for the future. But he insisted on keeping things low-key, not announcing the seriousness of their commitment to each other. Not to their families. Not to their friends.

"It's more special this way, if only the two of us know," he said, kissing her passionately, his arms around her waist as he pulled her closer.

"You're right," she agreed. "It makes things a lot more exciting, too. But I love you, and eventually, we'll have to go public."

"Soon," he said, pulling away from her. "It's about time you focus on living your own life. It's a big commitment. Are you sure you're ready for that?"

"I'd say we're about as committed as anyone can be."

Chapter Eighteen

Scott checked in at the office of Blue Water High the next morning. Principal McLaren exclaimed, with a solemn look, "You must be here about the hunting accident. Shocking news. Of course, Gary's not here today if you were hoping to speak with him."

"Actually, no, I'm not here to see Gary. I was hoping to talk to a couple of your staff members, Olivia Walker and Ivy Rose."

Principal McLaren raised his eyebrows. "Olivia and Ivy? Of course. They're Gary's teachers. Did you need to speak to his other teachers as well? I'll just pull up the schedules…"

"Just Olivia and Ivy for now."

Two women connected to Wendall were also connected to Phillip Reece. Scott made a mental note to check if Olivia was connected to any of the other accident victims.

"Olivia has a spare next period," the principal stated, scrolling through his teachers' timetables. "And Ivy, ah yes, here we are. Ivy's not available until lunch."

Principal McLaren led Scott down the long hallway. "This is Ivy's room," he pointed.

A familiar voice drifted through the open door. Scott caught a glimpse of Ivy standing at the front of the room, animatedly discussing something with her students. Although she didn't look like Cheryl MacGregor from a distance, she certainly had her mannerisms.

They climbed the stairs and approached Olivia Walker's room as the bell rang and students streamed out of the classroom. After introducing Scott to Olivia, Principal McLaren left them alone.

The poised woman in front of him wrinkled her brow. "What is this about?"

"I'd like to ask you some questions about Wendall Collins. I've already spoken to the other book club members but missed you last night. Do you mind if we sit down?"

She sat at one of the student desks and indicated he should take a seat beside her. Olivia's tailored outfit was incongruous with her white running shoes. Scott had a momentary flashback to his last year of high school, sitting at the front of Math class, focusing his attention on the pretty girl next to him rather than the blackboard. Your past all came rushing back to you, given the right circumstances.

"I understand you knew Wendall from your book club." Scott looked at the pretty woman next to him now, who nodded in response. "May I ask if that's the extent of your relationship? Were you friends?"

"Apart from Murder Club, I'd see him around. With his wife, Claire, out shopping or down by the lake. But I didn't know him well personally. Our relationship focused mainly on books. He was a friend, but not a good *personal* friend, if that makes sense." Olivia turned her body toward him and met his eyes, removing one of her running shoes to rest her foot on the wire book basket under his seat.

Is she flirting?

He noticed the rings on her left hand.

"Do you know why Wendall was at the beach the night he died, or who he might have been meeting? Was he behaving strangely in the weeks before his death?"

When Olivia shook her head, he asked whether she knew Eugene or Larissa *personally*. Her response was she didn't know Eugene, but she read his books. "And Larissa lived on Ivy's street. She was her neighbor's niece."

Hearing Ivy's name, Scott leaned in closer to Olivia. "Ivy? Are the two of you friends?" His brown eyes searched hers, and she raised her eyebrows.

Abruptly removing her foot off his chair, Olivia turned away from him as though she just realized her behavior wasn't exactly professional. She slipped her foot into her shoe and sat up straighter. "My toes got burned last night, and they're still stinging. Sorry about that."

"No problem." Scott asked about Ivy once more.

"Ivy is my best friend."

As tempted as he was to ask more about Ivy, Scott asked about Phillip Reece. Olivia didn't know him, but his son was in her math class, and she had heard about the hunting accident. Scott thanked Olivia for her time, and out of curiosity, asked how she burned her toes.

"It was one of those freak accidents," she said. Scott's ears perked up at the word 'accident'. His eyes automatically went to her foot. "I'm fine. It could have been worse. The water was too hot. I thought it was a malfunction with the hot tub. But then my husband had a closer look and said the controls had been fiddled with. And to top things off, the chlorine level was ridiculously high. Cliff said I could have suffered chlorine poisoning, and he complained to our pool maintenance company. He said they're lucky we're not the suing type."

"He's sure it was the pool company that caused the problem?" It seemed too much of a coincidence in light of the recent deaths, even though Olivia escaped unscathed.

"No one else in the house has been near the hot tub in the last couple of days, so Cliff assumed it must have been them. They were there to close the pool for the season."

"Is it possible someone else may have been on your property?"

"We're out in the middle of nowhere. I can't imagine anyone driving all the way out there just to mess with our hot tub. No one's been in our back yard, as far as I know, in the last few weeks, except the immediate family. Oh, and Ivy was over a couple of times." Olivia's eyes grew wider. "You don't think someone wanted to hurt me or my family, do you?"

Scott assured her that was unlikely, but told her to be extra careful, anyway. "With all these accidents happening, it's best to keep your guard up. If you notice anything else strange, report it to the local police. The same if you remember anything that might be helpful in finding out what happened to Wendall."

"Of course, I will." Olivia tied up her running shoe and stood.

Scott rose as well. "There's just one other thing I'd like to ask, if you don't mind. It's about your friend, Ivy."

"Ivy? What about her?" Olivia sat back down.

"How long have you known her?"

"A long time. Why are you asking?" Olivia tilted her head up to Scott.

"I met her briefly yesterday. She looked familiar. And I thought I knew her, but she didn't seem to remember me. Do you know where she's from?"

"Oakridge. She said she wanted to move to a small town, and Port Ripley seemed perfect, being on the lake. Maybe you know her from there?"

"No, I don't think so. I'm from a small town up north. I don't care for cities," Scott said with a grimace. "She reminds me of someone I knew up in Lake Kipling."

"She's never mentioned Lake Kipling. Why didn't you ask her about it last night at Murder Club?"

"She left unexpectedly before I got there. I'll ask her directly when I see her today during lunch."

* * *

My phone rang during class. "Hello? Is everything okay?" Olivia and I sent each other silly little texts sometimes, but didn't disrupt each other's classes with a phone call.

"Sorry to interrupt. Just wanted to give you a heads up. A Detective Evans was here asking questions about Wendall. And about *you*. He's coming to see you at lunch. Really good-looking guy. Said he knows you from up north?"

"Okay, thanks. Gotta go."

"That's it for today." I dismissed my students. "Study period for the rest of the class, in the library. Read the next three chapters for tomorrow."

As the students headed out the door, I peered into the hallway. Scott Evans was walking toward my room.

I pulled open the supply closet adjacent to my classroom door and stood behind it, hoping he wouldn't notice me wedged between the doors.

"Ms. Rose? Hello?" Scott's voice sent goosebumps down my arms.

Struggling to keep my breathing quiet and steady, I hid till his footsteps resounded down the hall.

Ten minutes later, I pulled into my garage, locked the house, and picked up my phone to call the school secretary. "Lily, this is Ivy. Can you please have someone cover my classes this afternoon? I've suddenly come down with something." I paused and waited for an answer. "Oh no, not that serious. Just a bad stomach flu, I think."

Closing all the curtains and blinds, I retreated to the basement, curled up into a ball on the couch, a blanket pulled up to my chin as shivers coursed through my body.

And there I waited for the inevitable.

Chapter Nineteen

All those years of hiding. And he found me. Showed up on my doorstep. How was I going to move forward with Scott Evans back in my life, digging up the past? What should I tell him about why I left my old life behind?

Not the truth. He'll keep digging till he finds out everything.

The phone brought me out of my cocoon. After the fifth ring, I resigned myself to the fact that I would have to face him sooner or later.

"Help…help me…please…"

"Who is this?"

"It's me…June…please…I'm…" I could barely hear her. She faded away.

Springing off the couch, up the stairs, over to my neighbor's house, I tried the front door. June's screen door was latched with the window raised, exposing a section of screen. I rang the doorbell and pounded on the metal frame, heart in my throat. Was I too late? Running to the back of the house, I found the patio doors locked.

In the corner of the wooden porch, June's gardening gloves lay on a stool along with a set of gardening tools. Grabbing the pruning shears, I rushed back to the screen door, stabbed, and cut through it until I could access the lock. The mesh scraped my hand and arm as I shoved them inside and turned the latch.

"June! June! Are you okay?" Through the archway on the right, June's body slumped over, her head on the far side of the couch, one arm reaching toward the floor, where the phone lay on the carpet. She wasn't moving.

"Oh, no. June!" I dialed 911 and gave the operator June's address, checking for a pulse and listening for signs of breathing. June's heart beat rapidly under my palm. "Oh, thank goodness, she's alive."

I ran to the bathroom for a washcloth and knelt in front of the sofa, placing the cold compress on June's forehead, my ear next to June's mouth, fingers on her neck. I was so absorbed in checking June's vital signs that I didn't hear him approach from behind.

"Cheryl?? Stop!"

I turned as Scott Evans stood in the archway, both hands on his gun, pointed directly at me. I froze and stared, a memory flashing before my eyes of our investigation into the case of a missing woman fourteen years ago. Another time he had his gun aimed in my direction, Scott asking, "Where'd you get the gun, Cheryl? You can drop it now."

The past morphed with the present as we measured each other. "Stand up slowly, your hands where I can see them. Step away from her," Scott instructed, his face registering disbelief.

I locked eyes with him and spoke as calmly as I could, moving away, keeping my hands visible. "June needs help. I called 911. She's still alive. I found her collapsed on the couch. She called for help and lost consciousness. I had to break in through the screen."

The sound of a far-off siren confirmed my story. Scott returned his gun to its holster and hurried to June's side. "Did you check her pulse?"

"Yes. Is she going to be okay?" I stood back to let him examine June. His limited medical training was more extensive than my nonexistent medical knowledge. "Is it a heart attack or a stroke or something?"

Scott twisted the silver bracelet on June's wrist to expose the engraving. "She's diabetic. Do you know where she keeps her blood glucose kit?"

"No...I don't know...maybe her bedroom?" I was shaking, chilled to the bone, but sweating. I had thought June was dead. I had a gun pointed at me. I was face-to-face with Scott Evans. He called me Cheryl. Red seeped through the scrapes on my hand and arm.

I was vaguely aware of the darkness enclosing me as I stared at the blood, some long-buried memory of blood pooling in a parking lot flashing into my brain.

* * *

"Just great!" Scott exclaimed, leaving the two unconscious women. In June's bedroom, he removed the meter from the black case on the dresser. A small drop of bright red blood oozed from June's finger as he pricked it and dipped the test strip into it. The reading was 1.2. Dangerously low.

Scott propped open the front door and ran out, ready to meet the paramedics. Lights flashed, sirens blared. The ambulance stopped in front of June's house. As two paramedics rushed out of the vehicle, Scott shouted, "An elderly woman in insulin shock. Passed out. Her blood glucose is 1.2."

Ivy, having regained consciousness, sat on a chair, her face ashen. The paramedics worked quickly and efficiently, confirming Scott's diagnosis of June's condition.

"We're giving her a shot of glucagon to raise her blood sugar level," one of them explained. "Then we'll transport her to the hospital."

"Can I come with her?" Ivy asked, her voice trembling.

Within minutes, June was loaded into the ambulance. Scott told Ivy he'd meet her at the hospital. "I'll lock up. Where's her key?"

"Probably in her purse. Try her room. Can you grab my purse for me, too, and lock up? It's in my room."

"Okay. No problem, but we need to talk. You've got some explaining to do," he said, touching her arm. Ivy nodded, not making eye contact, as she slipped out of his grasp.

* * *

The five-minute drive took forever as I waited for June to wake up in the ambulance. My life flashed before my eyes. Seeing Scott brought back a rush of memories, both good and bad.

I vividly recalled the hospital in Hamilton after my parents' car accident fifteen years ago. The antiseptic smell, mixed with the scent of life and death, struck my nostrils upon entering the hospital now as it did that day long ago. The acrid taste on my tongue and at the back of my throat brought forth a gagging reflex.

The Port Ripley Hospital was more like the Lake Kipling Hospital, where they took Jim's body. The three-story red brick exterior reminded me of blood, while the mostly white sterile interior brought bones to mind. The day of my parents' accident, just like the day of Jim's accident two years later, I held out some impossible hope that they were still alive, waiting for me in one of the hospital rooms, recuperating. But there's no recuperating from the hospital morgue. That was a fact I was forced to accept as much as I denied it. Smacking me in the face with the horrific task of identifying Jim's body, Fate mocked my naivete. Death had attached itself to me the day I first picked up a gun, and now, we were inseparable.

The black leatherette chairs in the Port Ripley Hospital contrasted sharply with the white walls, ceiling, and floor. The near quiet was incongruous with the name of the room. Emergency. People perched in chairs, others stood at the reception window, medical personnel strode back and forth with steady reassurance, but the atmosphere was hushed, as though we were in a church or funeral home.

"Hey," Scott whispered as he walked up behind me and touched my shoulder. "Did they tell you anything?"

I shook my head as he sat down. "No, nothing yet." Having him so close was both comforting and disconcerting. I felt him boring a hole through me. Deciding to meet his gaze, I stared back. The same warm brown eyes, but with fine lines around them. The brown hair had touches of gray. He was the same, but different. Something was missing. My gaze lowered from his eyes to his mouth. That was it. The confident, arrogant smile I had grown to love. The same smile that could be charming, endearing, and used to put me at ease. Where was it now?

"Your eyes." He softly broke the silence, but the staring competition continued, his eyes questioning. "They're blue."

"Contacts," I whispered. "They're still brown."

"That's good," Scott murmured. "I loved your big brown eyes." And there was that same smile I remembered from so long ago. Caressing my arm, he added, "I see they bandaged you up. How bad is it?"

"I'll live." The words slipped out of my mouth before I realized how insensitive they sounded. "They're not deep cuts."

For the next hour, we observed the steady flow of people, our eyes meeting now and then. Finally, a woman in medical attire escorted us to the examination room.

"She's one lucky woman. It's a good thing you were there to call for help. Otherwise, she may have suffered irreparable damage," the nurse said, pulling back the curtain. June was awake and sipping juice. "We'll be admitting her for observation, but she should be set to go home tomorrow." With a kind look directed at June, she left us alone.

I grasped June's hand. "I'm so glad you're okay. You had me worried."

"I didn't think you'd be home, but with Larissa gone, I didn't know who else to call. I got feeling kind of strange, and then I was woozy."

"I'm just glad I was there for you. But if you feel ill again, I want you to promise you'll call 911 right away. I don't want you to take any more chances." I shuddered to think what might have happened if I hadn't left school early. "Now, you get some rest, and I'll pick you up tomorrow. And don't worry about Clarence. I'll take care of him." I hugged June. Scott touched her hand, saying he was looking forward to another tea date.

I raised my eyebrows. "Is there something going on between the two of you?"

"Oh, it's nothing serious," June replied, with a twinkle in her eye. "We're only sort of dating. So, if you're interested, young lady, you'd better snap him up quick before we start going steady."

Relieved to see June feeling more like her usual self, I chuckled. "I'll keep that in mind."

Once we exited the hospital, I realized I didn't have my car, but the exercise and fresh air would help clear my head.

"I'll give you a ride," Scott said as though he could read my thoughts. "We need to talk. Have you had lunch? How about a burger and fries? Like old times?"

"Are you still into junk food?"

"Of course. Can't you tell?" He laughed, patting his stomach.

Warmth crept up my face as my eyes scanned his body. "You look good. In spite of your eating habits."

He grinned at my embarrassment as I ogled him. "Is it a date, then? You'll have lunch with me?"

"I don't date. But I'll join you for a burger and fries."

Scott chuckled. "All right. No date, just fast food. I do need to stop off at the station first and report this incident of June's, given what happened to her niece."

My mouth flew open. "You think this is connected to Larissa's death?"

"Nothing should be overlooked or taken for granted as simply accidental."

He led me to his vehicle and opened the passenger door for me.

"Still driving a silver Camaro, I see," I said as I slid onto the leather seat, the memories flooding me with warmth.

"Is there any other kind of car? I've still got the old one, too. I keep it in storage, take it out for an occasional spin. Reminds me of the good old times. You remember those, don't you?" He started the engine, turning to me for confirmation.

Instead, I raised my eyebrows and asked, "You weren't actually going to shoot me, were you?"

Chapter Twenty

Ten minutes after Scott told Ivy to wait in the car, he spotted her standing outside Mike's office, listening to their conversation. He had told Mike he found Ivy in June's house and misunderstood the situation, prompting him to draw his gun. "It turns out I know Ivy. We were good friends years ago."

Scott sprang from his chair and pulled the door to Mike's office wide open. "What are you doing? I told you to wait for me."

Ivy took the opportunity to walk right in. "If this concerns me, and I think it does, since I heard my name mentioned, then I should know about it," she insisted, hands on her hips, her eyes daring him to kick her out.

She hasn't changed after all. She's every bit as nosy and pushy as she ever was.

Ivy's eyes left his and gravitated toward the whiteboard that mapped out victims and potential suspects.

"Why is *my* name on there?" she demanded. "Just because I found June? I saved her life! You can't seriously think I would hurt her." She walked over to the board, even as Mike blocked it and insisted she should wait in the lobby. The lines on her brow deepened. "And why is there a line connecting me to all the victims?" She turned back to face Scott. "Am I a suspect?"

Scott escorted her to the car, explaining that when he put her name on the board, he didn't realize she was Ivy. "Of course, I'll take your name off the board now. You're obviously not involved. Are you?"

Ivy shot him a dirty look. "Really? Are you kidding me? Yes, I'm the killer. You've got it all figured out. Do you want to put me in cuffs and lock me up now?"

Ignoring her sarcasm, Scott started up the car and said they had thirteen years of catching up to do. "But first—lunch." They drove in silence, Scott's eyes on the road and Ivy's eyes on Scott.

* * *

"I want to know everything," Scott restarted the conversation as he unwrapped his double cheeseburger. "You owe me an explanation. Thirteen years' worth." They sat side by side on a bench, as they used to do when she was Cheryl. The warmth of the afternoon sun in the park across from Ivy's house felt good through his leather jacket. He noticed Ivy was shivering. "Cold?" A light gray cardigan covered her ivory blouse. Before Scott could remove his jacket, she stopped him.

"No, I don't want you to freeze. I'll just pop in the house and get my hoodie. I want to check on Tom, anyway."

"Tom? I understood you live alone."

"We do. It's just the two of us."

"Two of you?"

Further questioning was futile as she was already jogging across the street. She came back wearing a navy windbreaker, zipped up to her neck.

"Couldn't find it, so I grabbed my jacket." She popped some fries into her mouth as Scott watched her, expecting answers. "Let's just enjoy the moment, okay?" she pleaded. "I'll explain later. I *will*. So, how did you end up here, in Port Ripley, of all places?"

"Probably good luck. Serendipity. This is where I was meant to be right now. I was sound asleep one morning, dreaming about you, actually, when my phone rang." Scott beamed, thrilled to be reunited with her, regardless of the circumstances. "It was Mike, an old colleague I'd mentored years ago in Lake Kipling. He wondered if I wanted to consult on an unusual homicide case." Scott took a moment to examine her. The hair and eyes were different. She'd put on some weight, looked more mature than the girl he first met. But underneath all that, he still recognized the woman he once loved. How could he forget her face? Heart-shaped, high cheekbones, slightly upturned nose. "I had discovered you moved down south, so I decided to come and help out with the case, knowing there was little chance I'd bump into you. But like I said—serendipity." He took her hand and gazed into her blue eyes.

Ivy returned his smile. "Well, I'm glad you found me, Detective. I should have known you would. What took you so long? It's so nice to see you again." They basked in the sun, making small talk about the town, the lake, and the weather, while enjoying their simple meal. Scott waited for an opportunity to broach the topic of the past. He recalled the first time they met, when she crossed the yellow tape fourteen years ago, the image fresh in his mind— that bold, sexy, young woman who intrigued him from the very first time he laid eyes on her.

"Stop right there! This is a crime scene!" he had bellowed as she approached the home of the young woman whose disappearance he was investigating.

"I'm aware of that," she retorted, not stopping.

He remembered how she showed him her credentials, so proud of herself, calling herself an investigative journalist, working as a small-town newspaper reporter in a town that had nothing worth reporting. She intruded on his investigation, but he made excuses to keep her involved in the case just so he could be near her.

"What's so funny?" she asked, crumpling up her garbage, bringing him out of his reverie.

He realized he was chuckling. "I wasn't," he said, shaking his head.

She drew her brows together and tilted her head. "You weren't what? Laughing? Something clearly amused you."

"I wasn't going to shoot you," he answered, still grinning like a Cheshire Cat. "I know it's not the ideal reunion, but seriously, Cheryl, it looked bad. There was blood on the broken screen, and you were leaning over June with your hands at her throat. With everything that's been happening in town the last few weeks..."

"You thought maybe I was a murderer? Are you *sure* you're still a detective? Your detecting skills seem to be lacking, if you think I go around killing people," she scoffed, heading to the waste receptacle. When she came back, she added, "And I do. Of course, I do."

Scott's mouth flew open. "Do what?"

"I do remember the good times we shared. Of course, I remember. And it's not Cheryl, it's Ivy. Please don't call me that again." Sorrow and regret showed in her eyes.

"Why did you run away from me?" He couldn't stop himself from asking. He had to know. Why had she disappeared after Jim's funeral?

"I don't understand. Run away from *you*?"

"After the funeral. I thought I'd give you some space, but a few days later, you were just gone. Then you put the house on the market, and I knew you weren't coming back." The painful memory of finding that she'd left without a word caused his voice to crack.

"I wasn't running away from *you*," Ivy insisted, shaking her head. "It was just too much, losing Jim like that, so suddenly. I couldn't handle it. I had to get away. So, I joined the kids at my friend Haley's cottage for a while, then we moved to Oakridge."

"Why didn't you come to *me*? I would have helped you through it." Scott touched Ivy's cheek, gazing into her blue contacts.

"I couldn't," she said softly. "I was afraid..." Ivy looked down at her lap. "...of my feelings. I didn't want to betray Jim's memory by going to you for comfort. I was grieving and...vulnerable." Ivy looked back up at him, biting her lower lip as though she didn't know what to say.

His finger brushed away the tear rolling down her cheek. "I would have given you time to grieve, Cheryl. I would never have pressured you..." Scott had struggled to keep his feelings for Cheryl purely on a professional level at first, then convinced himself he was content to be her friend. He didn't intend to get romantically involved with a married woman, especially one with kids. She'd made it very clear she loved her husband, and her family was her top priority. And he'd done his best to keep his feelings hidden. But he knew Cheryl saw through him. He even deluded himself into thinking she had similar feelings for him. "I thought we were friends. You should have come to me. Not run off and change your name to make it harder for me to find you."

"I wasn't running from you. I'm sorry. I never meant to hurt you. I just needed a fresh start for me and the kids. I couldn't face staying there, in Lake Kipling, in that house, the place where we were so happy. I needed to get away."

"So, you left those happy memories behind? Just like that?" He knew there was more to it but didn't want to press until she was ready to confess the truth. "What aren't you telling me?"

Ivy turned away, blowing her nose. "I need to get some work done for school tomorrow. I'd better get to it." Facing him again, she added, "I'm sorry, I really am. It was a dark time for me."

"Will you have dinner with me?" Scott asked, not wanting to let her go.

"I can't. Not tonight. I have other plans."

Taking Ivy by the hand, he asked, "You're not going to run off again, are you? What about tomorrow?"

"Maybe tomorrow."

He watched as she slipped out of his grasp and disappeared into her house. *Why did she run from me? Is she still running?*

Chapter Twenty-One

The Writer

"Hello. My name is…well, everyone here knows me. And I'm an addict. I admit that I'm powerless when it comes to murder—the planning, the executing, the unraveling—and I believe that a power greater than myself will bring me back to sanity." I force myself to turn up my mouth in a slight smile, as I survey the twenty or so members who are there to offer support to each other. They all think it's a safe place to be. No judgments, no recriminations. Just understanding.

"I had a really good week, kept myself busy with several projects." I share my experiences of the previous week, adding, "I did spend a few hours on my latest novel here and there, but I didn't let it pull me in. I was able to keep myself at a distance from my characters and the murders. So, yes, I'm pleased with myself. I showed a lot of restraint."

Restraint is something I'm good at. Unless it involves murder, of course. That's one thing I've become passionate about.

I began to attend these meetings only because I was pressured into joining by my family, who insisted I get professional help. They claimed my fictional worlds were spilling into my daily life. Too much time spent on reading and writing and not enough on living.

The weekly meetings, in a central location of Blue Water County, in the town of Cliffton, turned out to be just what I needed. AAW (All Addicts Welcome) accepts all genres of addictions.

Not surprisingly, an addiction to writing murder mysteries isn't a common problem. Because it's not an addiction. It's not a problem. So, I found myself surrounded by a bunch of people who can't control themselves. Their addictions run the gamut from alcohol, drugs, smoking, gambling, food, and sex to violence, self-abuse, depression, and more. I absolutely love it! These addicts are as much fun as a thriller series. Being in their company provides fodder for my writing. Real people with real-life problems—better than anything I could possibly dream up in my wildest imagination or my worst nightmares. I don't know why I ever protested about joining.

It's the 'sharing' part I come for. Not my own sharing. That's all fabricated—stories I create to appease the addicts in the room. It's so easy to invent a reality that isn't real. The sharing is supposed to be therapeutic, I guess. For me, it's inspiration. As I listen attentively to each of the addicts' 'stories,' I assimilate them into my own current WIP or jot them down as ideas for future novels. It's the perfect group for a creative artist like myself, blending right in.

I turn to the woman on my right as she speaks next. "I need to confess. I was in a singles bar a few weeks ago. I knew I shouldn't go anywhere near a place like that; it would just be too tempting. But I went anyway. So, I sat down at the bar and ordered a drink, took a look around, and..." The attractive young woman appears ashamed, her eyes downcast as she addresses the group. For a moment, I wonder whether she will continue. "And...I...I had another drink...and there was this good-looking older guy... he's a well-known author, and I wanted to meet him...sitting in a booth with two of his friends." She continues to stare down at her hands, which are clasped together, as though looking for inspiration. "Anyway, I swung my legs around and smiled at him. He came over and invited me to join him and his friends. And...well, the next thing I knew, I'd had too many drinks and..."

I surreptitiously watch the reaction of the others. Some nod in understanding, all sport the expected solemn and understanding facial expression. No one looks shocked; they know what's coming. It's the same every week. The poor girl uses one addiction to help her cope with the other.

"I ended up in a hotel room with the three of them." She wrings her hands. "I don't know who the other two were. I can't even remember everything that happened. It's all a fog. And now, with what's happening…I'm scared…my reckless behavior might put me in danger."

One of the members walks across the circle and hugs her. "You should have called me. I'm here for you, you know that. Always. Next time you feel weak, let me help. I can keep you safe."

Her 'partner' is a recovering smoker. He hasn't smoked in over a year. I suspect *she's* his real vice, the reason he keeps attending. He's old enough to be her father, but anyone can see what's going on between them.

Whenever one of us slips up, our partner is supposed to be there to get us through it. A buddy system. My buddy's a gambling addict. But that's just a drop in the bucket when you consider his other problems. He claims someone put a hit out on him. Mafia. But that's a whole other story. Or novel, actually.

After the meeting, the group socializes over coffee and cake, continuing our discussions in a less formal manner. If I must say so myself, I'm a sympathetic listener, and people confide in me. I guess it helps that I'm acquainted with many of them outside of our group and a trusted member of the Blue Water community. But what happens at AAW stays there. Totally confidential.

"I just don't know what to do," the sex addict confesses to me. "How am I going to tell my husband?"

I calmly assure her that her husband will be understanding, like he always is. "Remember, he married you knowing you had a problem. He promised to support you no matter what. As long as you always tell him the truth."

"I know, but sometimes I worry he's going to leave me. That I'll go too far and he won't put up with it anymore. Maybe this time, he doesn't need to know. This is worse than anything else I've ever done. What if he asks for a divorce? What if he takes the kids, saying I'm an unfit mother? Sometimes, I have nightmares where he's smothering me with a pillow, or he has his hands around my neck, choking me." Tears stream down her cheeks as she speaks. "I know he would never…but I wonder just how far I can push him before…"

You can only push people so far before they snap.

103

Chapter Twenty-Two

I addressed the Grade 12 students from the podium. "We are fortunate to have two local writers here to share their publishing experiences. We have a lot of fresh creative talent here at Blue Water High. Perhaps this will inspire some of you to pursue a career in writing. Our first guest is children's author Paige Thornton."

Tucking a lock of brown hair behind her ears, Paige focused her brown eyes on the audience. "My Mom's my inspiration. She's always been a writer. But she didn't get published or become rich and famous." Paige choked up. Then she chuckled. "And if you're thinking of writing as your ticket to money and stardom, you'd better look for another career, an easier one, like brain surgery." Laughter rippled through the assembly.

"From the time my kids were infants, I read to them. Then, I made up my own stories to tell. My husband said I should write them down. So, I did."

Paige talked about finding a publisher, working with an editor, an illustrator, and an artist to design an eye-catching cover. Her latest book, the second in a series, was about a shy orphaned girl, and it began the same way her first book began. Paige read aloud, stopping now and then to glance at the crowd. "Lucy always wore a chain with a Kit Kat chocolate bar around her neck because she read somewhere it would bring her good luck. The problem was she couldn't stop herself from eating the chocolate, and so her luck kept running out."

I felt a strong connection to Lucy. My luck always ran out. I was cursed. Always waiting for the other shoe to drop.

Forcing myself out of my glum self-absorption, I returned to the podium as the students applauded. "Thank you, Mrs. Thornton. I'm sure you've inspired many of these young people to consider writing children's literature." I glanced at the other guest, seated next to Paige. "And now, something a little different. Non-fiction. Most of you know Riley Patterson as the owner of Riley's Hardware. He's also the author of *Blue Water Discoveries*, full of local stories and photographs about our county."

Riley Patterson strode up the podium and began with a reading about an old hotel in Blue Water County that was purported to be haunted. He had the kids' attention right off the bat.

Riley closed the book. "The spooky happenings at the hotel can be traced back to the late 1800s when a guest was murdered in his bed. I stayed there myself one night. I won't go back. You probably wouldn't believe me if I told you what happened."

His comment was met with requests to continue. "I heard footsteps. At first, I didn't think anything of it. The sounds were coming from the ceiling, so I thought it must be the guests above. But they didn't stop. They just kept walking back and forth, back and forth. I couldn't sleep. So, I called down to the desk and complained."

The students sat up straighter in their chairs, leaning forward as Riley took a sip of water and paced back and forth himself. "I was told no one checked into that room. In fact, no one checked in on that floor."

The auditorium was silent. Riley looked up to the ceiling. "There was no one up there. Yet all the while I was talking to this person on the phone, the footsteps continued. I insisted the desk clerk go check upstairs."

Riley looked straight out at his audience and approached the edge of the stage. "That poor man. He quit his job that night. I don't know what he saw up there. But I'll never forget the look on his face when he came running down the stairs saying there was no one in Room 211."

Riley explained that was what prompted him to research the past of Blue Water County and write his book. After discussing some technical aspects of how he created his end product, Riley talked about the importance of self-promoting. "Which is why I'm here today, talking to you, trying to convince you to buy my book," he joked. "Oh, and by the way. Sometime after my stay at the haunted hotel, I learned something about the murdered guest from the late 1800s. He stayed in Room 211."

I watched him intently as he stepped back from the podium. He was a tall and physically fit man around fifty, still sporting a head full of dark hair. There was a sexy confidence about him.

"That was absolutely fascinating," I said later in the teacher's lounge. "Are either of you interested in murder?"

Riley spilled coffee on his shirt.

"Mysteries? Thrillers? Suspense?" I fetched a napkin for Riley. "There's an opening in my book club, Tuesday nights. You're both welcome to come."

Paige politely declined. "I don't think it fits my image very well, being a children's author."

"It sounds interesting," Riley said, wiping the stain on his shirt.

"So, you'll come, then?"

"I'd like to, but…" Riley picked up his cup again.

"Murder's not your cup of tea?" I tilted my head. "I thought maybe you'd be into it."

Riley's hand shook. "Why would you think that?"

"The way you talked about the murder and ghost at the hotel. I thought maybe you'd be a good fit for our club. Although now that Wendall is gone…I'm not sure about the future of our group. I just hope we don't lose any more members. Last week, Alice called it off because too many people said they couldn't come. This week, some suggested we should stop meeting, with all the, um, accidents in town lately."

"Yes, isn't it terrible? This happening in our small community?"

"You never think something like that could happen in a place like this," Paige added.

"I'm confident the police will catch the murderer soon," I said. "I happen to know a very competent detective is on the case. Nothing gets past him, trust me."

"I'm glad to hear that." Riley steadied his hand. "My daughter's fiancé was one of the accident victims."

"Oh! I'm so sorry. I didn't realize. I didn't mean to sound insensitive."

"That's quite all right. You had no way of knowing. It's his own fault. Driving like a lunatic in that sports car. A grown man playing with a toy car. And acting like he's the next Stephen King." Riley harrumphed. "Don't get me wrong, I'm sorry he's dead. But my daughter deserves someone better than Eugene Forsythe. Treated women like toys, too."

"Thank you both again for taking your time to talk to the students today." The ringing of the bell emptied the room as my colleagues returned to class.

I was only a few steps down the hall when I realized I'd forgotten to check my mailbox. Hurrying back to the teacher's lounge, I opened the door as Riley pulled Paige into his arms. "Why don't we go to the hardware store? We can use my private office. You don't need to pick up the kids from daycare for a couple of hours. And Matt's at work. Let me give you what you need."

Quietly closing the door and retreating to my room, I tried to forget what I had just witnessed.

Chapter Twenty-Three

I was packing up my school materials when my phone pinged.

Dinner tonight?

Without hesitating, I texted back.

Okay.

There was no point in putting off seeing him. He wasn't going to go away. Another text came through.

No burger and fries this time. Let me wine and dine you properly. Pick you up at 7?

I smiled as I replied.

Sounds good.

I scrawled lesson plans into my daybook, just in case I got home late from our dinner date. My first real date in recent memory. I left my plans on my desk, along with related books and materials, so I wouldn't need to worry about it later, then headed to the hospital to pick up June.

"All cleared for take-off?" I asked, seeing June dressed and looking out her window.

"Can't wait to get back home."

During the short ride home, I apologized. "I've got something to tell you. I'm really sorry about it, well, not *really* sorry because I had good intentions. But I broke into your house when you were unconscious. So, you'll notice your screen door's damaged. You can let me know how much it costs to repair, and I'll cover it."

"You silly girl. You saved my life. You're my heroine." June waved her hand in the air to dismiss the idea. "Do you want to come over later? Take out pizza?"

"I'm sorry, I would, but I can't. Another time." I pulled into her driveway.

"Not hungry?"

"I've got a date."

"You? A date? Since when do you date?" June narrowed her eyes as she exited the Jeep and motioned for me to follow her. "Who's the lucky guy?" Clarence came bounding up to her door, nearly knocking June over.

"Actually, he's the guy who helped save your life. Scott Evans."

"What? I'm in a coma for a few minutes, and you break down my door *and* steal my man? I should call the police," June laughed. "So how did this happen?"

"Well, it turns out, we knew each other years ago. So, we're just going to catch up, as old friends."

"Friends, my foot! I saw him looking at you! And I saw you looking, too. Don't give me any of that *friends* talk. Now go get yourself all gussied up and have a good time."

I promised to check in on her later.

"Don't worry about me. But I expect to hear all the juicy details. Thanks again for saving me." June hugged me. "You're my guardian angel. You can thank your boyfriend, too. Now scoot."

After getting out of the shower, brushing my teeth, and drying my hair, I rummaged through my makeup drawer. I rarely wore any since Jim's death, but fortunately, kept some on hand for special occasions. Pulling out some of the less ratty-looking products, I organized them on the counter and plugged in the curling iron.

Who am I kidding? He's already seen me without makeup. He's seen me wearing my old baggy clothes and my hair sticking up in all directions.

Still, I wanted to make a good impression. This was our first real date.

With a heavy sigh, I flipped through the hangers in my closet, wishing I had treated myself to a shopping spree sometime in the last three years. Resigning myself to the black skirt that fell just below my knee, a flowery blouse, and my black blazer, I took another look and spotted the black dress at the back of the closet.

Please, let it fit.

It was a simple cut, but elegant. The short sleeves were lace, it had a scoop neck and some ruching along the side that drew attention to the waist. I bought it for Olivia's son's wedding last year, and it had lain in my wardrobe ever since. I set out the two outfit choices on the bed, wondering whether there was a third option. There *was* the casual flowery purple summer dress. Perfect for a picnic, maybe not a dinner date.

I slipped the black dress over my head, struggling with the back zipper.

Too much chocolate.

I tugged the zipper and was surprised the dress didn't rip. The full-length mirror reflected my five-foot-six, curvaceous figure. I was pleased with how the dress defined my waist.

Not bad. As long as I'm careful how I sit.

After adding dangling fake pearl earrings, a faux-gold twisted necklace, and a solid gold-colored bangle, I returned to the closet and donned my sparkly gold bolero sweater. It struck me that something seemed to be missing in my closet.

My hoodie! Where did I put it?

When I looked for it in the front hall closet yesterday, it wasn't there. Nor was it in the bedroom closet.

Just before seven o'clock, I inspected my hair and makeup for the last time, dabbed on perfume from a dusty old bottle, slipped on my slingback black pumps with a bit of a heel, grabbed my black clutch, and waited on the couch.

Scott's Camaro purred into my driveway right on time. Seconds later, he rang the doorbell, wearing navy dress pants, a light blue shirt, and a tie, his face clean-shaven.

"Wow, you look great!" he exclaimed. "And who is this?" Scott bent over to rub my cat's chin. Tom purred against Scott's legs, giving him his seal of approval.

"Tom." My answer brought a huge grin to Scott's face. When I mentioned Tom earlier, I think Scott wondered if he was a male friend.

When we arrived at the hotel restaurant, Scott extended his hand as I carefully inched my way out of the Camaro, mindful of my tight dress. The sun was setting against a mauve and orange sky, casting shadows across the sidewalk. Scott's arm wrapped around my waist as we approached the entrance.

"Ivy? Is that you?" Celia called as she scurried across the street. "Ohh, Detective Evans. So nice to see you again." She appraised him and turned back to me. "You look different. I almost didn't recognize you. Are you two on a *date*? Wow, good for you."

Scott greeted Celia cordially, saying it was nice to see her again, too, but we needed to get to our dinner reservation. "Is she a good friend of yours?" he asked once we were inside. "I met her at the book club."

"A fellow mystery enthusiast."

Several people waved to me as we were escorted to a private booth at the back of the restaurant, and I acknowledged them, but didn't have an opportunity to stop to chat. Riley sat alone in the booth next to ours, finishing his dessert, an empty plate across from him.

"Riley, hi."

Riley's eyes darted down toward the back exit as he returned my greeting.

When the Maitre d' left us, I leaned toward Riley and introduced the two men. "This is Detective Scott Evans, an old friend of mine. He's in town to assist with the investigation into the deaths. Riley Patterson owns the hardware store in town, and he's a fellow writer. I bought his book about Blue Water County, and I loved it."

Riley stood and moved closer to extend his hand to Scott, his eyes still wandering to the back. "Nice to meet you."

I told Scott about Riley's visit to the school that morning. "Along with Paige Thornton, who writes children's books. Actually, here she is now."

Paige, exiting the washrooms located at the back, held her head down, but it jerked up as I called her name, her cheeks flushing. Riley motioned for her to have a seat. "Paige and I decided to get together for dinner to discuss our writing following this afternoon's presentation."

After I introduced Scott to Paige, Scott and I perused the menu. The Maitre d' returned with our wine orders, and Riley pulled out his credit card while Paige slipped out the back exit.

Once we were alone, Scott asked, "Riley *Patterson*? Any relation to Willow, Eugene's fiancée?"

"Her dad." I sipped my red wine, then set it back on the table. "I'm going to have a garden salad and filet mignon. How about you?"

"That sounds good. I'll have the same."

"I see your taste buds have matured somewhat," I teased.

"I still love burgers," he said, the corners of his mouth twitching up. "But I wanted to impress you tonight. Is it working?" His eyes held mine.

My face grew hot, my stomach doing flip flops, "It is. I'm very impressed."

"Good," he beamed. "So, how well did Eugene and Riley know each other?"

"I don't know, but they both took part in the book festival Saturday."

"Willow's father and fiancé at a book event, and she didn't make an appearance. Seems odd. Willow told me they didn't get along, though."

"No, she wasn't there. When I spoke to Riley this afternoon, it didn't sound like he was upset about Eugene. Said his daughter was better off without him."

"Hmm." Scott rubbed his chin.

The waiter arrived, taking our orders, and Scott changed the topic. "So, Ivy Rose, tell me what you've been up to for the last thirteen years."

I couldn't believe it had been that long. With Scott across from me, I was transported back to happy memories. The years I had with Jim were the best of my life. Jim helped me forget the trauma I had suffered and kept me safe from it. Until he was gone.

My troubled past, my parents' deaths, and finally, Jim's accident. I had filed it away in a part of my brain that I seldom unlocked. My kids were all that mattered anymore.

But have I missed out on something?

"Ivy?" Scott took my hand in his and gazed into my eyes. "Everything okay?"

He has no idea who I really am.

Scott Evans was once Cheryl MacGregor's best friend. There had been a spark of something more between us, but I had never allowed it to go further. We held back our feelings for each other. I was in love with my husband and refused to jeopardize our marriage. Scott understood that. After Jim's car accident, I went on the run, shedding my old life and leaving Scott behind.

Now I'm single and available. And here he is, back in my life.

That spark was still there; I felt it in the air between us. And I *knew* how he felt about Cheryl. But how would he feel about Ivy?

"Just thinking about the good old days," I sighed. I thanked the waiter as he set down a plate of salad and waited for him to leave before continuing our conversation. "Back in Lake Kipling with Jim and the kids. It's still painful for me. So, what about you? Did you ever get married? Or are you still flirting with every pretty woman you meet?" I recalled how he used to look at me, the way I'd get jealous when he looked at other women, even though it wasn't my business what he did.

Scott held up his ringless left hand and chuckled. "Guilty, as charged. But I *was* married. Two years after you left. Crazy story. You won't believe it."

"I like crazy stories. I'm a writer, remember? The crazier, the better." Scott had nothing on me when it came to unbelievable life stories. He had no idea. My life was worse than a pulp fiction novel.

"I ended up marrying Julia."

"Julia Brenner?" I dropped my fork.

Julia was the young woman who mysteriously vanished from her home fourteen years ago. Scott and I met when we investigated Julia's disappearance. "You're right. I don't believe it. How'd that happen?"

Scott explained he had asked around town when I took off after Jim's death. "I had some leads. Julia insisted on helping me find you. And we did."

I couldn't believe what I was hearing. "You *found* me? But I never saw you or Julia again after I left Lake Kipling."

"I talked to your neighbors and co-workers to see if they knew where you'd gone. Mavis Kaufman wondered if you had returned to Hamilton. She said it's your hometown. Why did you tell me you were from the west?"

"I...I...yes." I couldn't meet Scott's eyes. I wasn't sure how much to tell him. "I did go to Hamilton. It's where I grew up. I'm sorry I lied to you about that. But you *found* me?"

"We found news *of* you. We went to Hamilton, Julia and I. But no one seemed to know Cheryl MacGregor, or if they did, they weren't talking. Then we came across a news article from Scarborough. And I requisitioned the police report."

I felt the blood drain from my face.

"Are you okay?" Scott jumped out of his seat, cradling my head. "Cher... Ivy?" He dipped his napkin into the glass and applied cold water to the base of my neck.

"So, you...know?" My voice was distant, and I let the darkness overtake me as Scott caught me in his arms.

Chapter Twenty-Four

"Ivy! Ivy!" Scott called as the cold water, and memories chilled me to the bone.

The waiter's voice mixed with Scott's. "Do you need some help?"

My eyes flickered, and I forced them open. "I'm okay, just a bit faint. I'm okay now."

When Scott suggested maybe I needed something more to eat, the waiter scurried off, saying he'd be back shortly with our order.

"You had me worried," Scott said as I sat up straighter.

"It's just the shock of all this, going back to the past, the bad memories."

"Sorry, I didn't mean to cause you pain by bringing it up."

"What did you do after you found out about…Scarborough?"

"Nothing. We stopped looking. Julia convinced me if you wanted to be found, you would have come back yourself. I knew you and the kids were safe. It was clear you'd left and stayed away voluntarily. Letting you go was one of the hardest things…" Scott's voice cracked as he laid down his fork. "…I've ever done. But I decided she was right—knowing you, I figured you must have had good reasons for not wanting to come back or get in touch."

"I did." I prepared to confess part of the truth, knowing I couldn't tell him everything. The police and the media never did get all the facts. I shivered at the memory of the man who killed my husband and kidnapped my son as retribution for his own son's death.

"I wanted to put it all behind me. It was a nightmare. I went to Hamilton, looking for Stefan Markovic. He was a mobster." I paused before revealing the part no one else knew. "And Brent's biological grandfather."

Scott watched me intently, leaning forward, his palms face up on the table. "Are you telling me that Jim *wasn't* Brent's biological father?"

"He was his father in every way, just not biologically. Jim knew that. Brent doesn't. I don't want him to ever know his bloodline. I knew Stefan was responsible for Jim's accident and kidnapping Brent. When I found Stefan in Scarborough, he and I fought, and he went over the cliff. After the police determined that Stefan caused Jim's accident and Stefan's death was the result of self-defense, I wanted a fresh start. So, I took the kids and made a new life for us. Moved away and changed my name so reporters would stop bothering me." I laughed at the irony. I had once been one of those hacks, always after the next big story. When you *are* the big story, you see the media in a different light.

The waiter placed our steaks in front of us. After he left, I took the opportunity to switch the topic to Scott. "Tell me about you and Julia."

"She helped me get through it, losing you. She said I should be satisfied to know you were okay, and I should respect your decision to start a new life. We got married two years later. We were two broken people—she was still living with the after-effects of her abduction, and I was mourning you. Anyway, it lasted eight years, most of them fairly happy. Two kids—Jason and Sarah. They're ten and eight now. We've been divorced for two years, and Julia remarried, but we're all friends. She got custody, and I see the kids whenever I want." Scott's face lit up as he pulled out his phone and showed me a photo of Jason and Sarah.

"They're adorable. Why did you get divorced?"

"Mainly my job. The long hours, the stress…Julia didn't understand it wasn't the kind of job that ends when the clock strikes five. Too many late-night stakeouts. She expected more of my time and attention to be focused on her and the kids. And she was right. It should have been." His regret was obvious as he stared at the piece of meat on the end of his fork. "Maybe I was already too set in my ways when we got married."

I recalled how Scott loved his job. In fact, much of the time we spent together was work-related. "And what about now? Are you still obsessed with work?"

"Well, here I am, hundreds of miles away from home, working a case. Looking for a murderer." Scott shrugged. "It's in my blood, I guess."

As I cut into my steak, I realized I forgot to ask for it well done. It was red in the middle. The sight of blood made me queasy. Looking away from the plate, I brought my fork to my mouth, chewed, and swallowed. "Delicious. I haven't had filet mignon in…well, I don't remember when I had filet mignon."

A hand touched my shoulder, and I turned to find Alice Reading beside our booth. "Hi, Ivy. I didn't know you and Detective Evans knew each other." Alice smiled at Scott. "Are you staying at the hotel?"

"Nice to see you, Alice," Scott stood to greet her. "Yes, I am."

Alice was joined by a balding, handsome, middle-aged man. "Ivy, I'm not sure if you know Will Jenkins? Will, this is Ivy Rose, a friend of mine. And Detective Evans. A friend of Ivy's, I take it?"

"Um, yes…" I wasn't sure how to explain why I was in a clearly intimate situation with the out-of-town detective in the murder investigation. "It's nice to meet you, Will. And this is Scott Evans, an old friend of mine. We knew each other a long time ago."

Will shook hands with me, then Scott, as Alice's eyebrows shot up. She remarked, "What a coincidence! It's a small world, isn't it?"

"That it is," Scott agreed, placing his hand on mine.

"Nice to meet you both," Will said, his arm around Alice, leading her back to their booth.

"Oh, Ivy." Alice turned, pulling away from his embrace. "You forgot your hoodie at my place Tuesday night. You can stop by to get it after dinner, if you like."

"So that's where I left it."

When they were out of earshot, Scott remarked, "Will Jenkins? The coroner? Hmm…interesting."

"You know him?"

"Heard the name before. Anyway, let's get back to you. Tell me what happened after you ran off to Hamilton and Scarborough."

"Like I said, after the altercation with Stefan, I needed to break away from my old life. So, I moved to Oakridge, changed my name, and had a makeover. It was a struggle for the first while, dipping into our savings, and I ran a daycare out of my apartment the first year to help with the bills. Then, I went to teachers' college in Masonville and got my degree. A lovely young woman agreed to be my live-in nanny/housekeeper in exchange for room and board. With my lawyer handling the sale of our house in Lake Kipling and the payout of Jim's life insurance policy, it allowed me to buy a house once I accepted the job in Port Ripley. That's about it."

Scott was visibly impressed, his fork down on the plate, and his mouth slightly open. "Wow, just widowed, two kids, daycare, a new home…and teachers' college? That's a lot to handle."

"It was a really tough time for me." Tears welled in my eyes, and I stared at my plate, moving food around. "Staying busy was what kept me sane."

"I still don't understand why you left everything behind—your home, your job…*me*. You could have come back. Especially once the dust settled. I feel like there's more to the story." Scott tried to make eye contact.

"I guess you *would* think there's more. You're a detective, after all. But I don't want to talk about it now, not here."

We finished our meal in silence, topping it off with cheesecake and coffee. "My room's upstairs," Scott whispered after paying the bill. "I want to invite you up." He hesitated, seeing my reaction. "To talk some more. But I wouldn't want to damage your reputation. Half the people here seem to know you."

"We could go to my place." My voice was intentionally low. "To talk some more." I knew Scott didn't need to be asked twice.

As he escorted me to his car, I said, "I want to get my hoodie first. It's important to me. A gift from Jamie. When I attended teachers' college, I couldn't afford a school sweatshirt. Jamie's first year at Western, she bought us matching hoodies."

When I rang the bell at Alice's house, Valerie handed over my hoodie. Before she closed the door, I caught a glimpse of Alice and Will in the living room.

"Will and Alice seem to be pretty cozy on the couch," I commented when

CHAPTER TWENTY-FOUR

I slipped back into the Camaro.

"Didn't take Will long to get over Larissa," Scott said. "They were supposed to be an item, from what I understood."

"Will and Larissa? Yes, but maybe they weren't exclusive. Now that I think about it, I'm sure June mentioned seeing *Wendall* at Larissa's place one night. So, Larissa might have been seeing someone else while she was supposedly with Will."

Scott's ears perked up at the mention of Larissa and Wendall. "I was led to believe they didn't know each other."

"Maybe no one was supposed to know. Wendall *was* married."

As he pulled into my driveway, Scott remarked that maybe that's why Wendall went out for so many walks and why his wife was afraid to question him. Maybe she suspected he was cheating on her and didn't want to risk losing her husband by confronting him.

Scott locked the door behind us as we entered the house, then pulled me into his arms. His lips brushed mine, and he murmured, "I'm so glad I found you."

Chapter Twenty-Five

I squirmed out of his arms, and Scott bent to pet Tom, who was purring around his legs. "Tom likes you. He's a good judge of character. Make yourself comfortable while I go change. This dress is a bit constricting."

By the time I returned, dressed in jeans and a sweater, Scott was on the couch, his tie removed and his shirt partly unbuttoned. The lights were dimmed. I sat next to him, and he wrapped his arm around my shoulder. "You have a lot of friends," he said.

"Actually, I don't. They're more like friendly acquaintances. People I know from work and groups I belong to, neighbors, that sort of thing. I've lived here for a long time, and I know a lot of people, but I'm not close with anyone. Just Olivia."

"We used to be close," he reminded me, running his fingers along my arm. I responded with goosebumps as heat flowed through my body.

"Yes, close friends."

"Cold?" Scott asked as a shiver overtook me.

"No...yes...I guess, a little." I escaped his grip. "I'll just start the fire." Once the flames licked up behind the glass, I settled into the armchair beside the fire.

Scott watched me intently. "So, tell me."

"Tell you what?" What was he referring to? My friends? The sparks zinging between us?

"About the past. What *really* happened? Tell me about Darko Markovic."

My jaw dropped. I shouldn't have been surprised. Darko's name was in the papers after the Scarborough affair. And Scott was a good detective. I had no choice but to tell him. Because he was my best friend once upon a time and because I knew he wouldn't let it go until he got answers. So, I spilled the beans. Most of them, anyway.

"Do you believe in curses?" Shadows cast by the fire danced across the room.

"Curses? As in old gypsy curses?" Scott moved to the edge of the couch, closer to my armchair.

"Well, sort of. European curses, anyway."

"Ahh…no, can't say I do. Do you?"

"Yes. A Serbian one, in particular. I'm cursed."

Scott stared at me, mouth agape. "Are you serious? What kind of curse? Are you messing with me, Cheryl? Sorry. Ivy."

"It's not Cheryl. And it's not Ivy," I began my confession. "My real name is Svjetlana Babic. I used to go by Lana. But please call me Ivy; that's who I am now."

Scott joined me by the fireplace, on the opposite armchair. "I'm listening."

"It's a long story."

"I'm not going anywhere." Scott's soft tone caressed my ears.

And I told him everything. But not the whole truth.

The flames flickered between us. "A year before you met me, my parents were killed in a car accident."

Images flashed through my mind. Their catering van crashed through the guard rail, down the embankment, into a tree, bursting into flames—the bodies unrecognizable. "After they died, I found out they weren't who they claimed to be. They had changed their identities." Memories of birth certificates, forged IDs, and a mysterious past, assailed my brain.

"I went to visit my grandmother in Croatia after the funeral and learned their village had been cursed by a Serbian mobster. My parents tried to escape by moving to Canada. But I think the curse is attached to our family."

Scott looked incredulous, leaning forward, not saying a word, afraid to break the spell I wove.

"When I was eighteen, I met Darko. I thought he loved me, but after I got pregnant, he didn't want me anymore. I found out he was the son of a

Serbian Mafia boss. I wasn't sure what he planned to do about me and my baby, but I was scared." I paused to let that sink in. "And even if he *did* want me, I sure didn't want my child raised by the Mafia. So, you see, the Serbian curse was passed on to me."

I explained what happened to Darko. The heated fight between Darko and his father when I revealed the pregnancy. The accidental shooting in the alley behind their bar. Darko's father, Stefan, charged with the manslaughter of his son.

"Jesse—Jim worked part-time as a bartender at the bar owned by Stefan. Jesse and I had been together since Grade 10, but I broke up with him when we went to different colleges. We remained friends. When I told him I was pregnant by Darko and scared for my life, he offered to run away with me. We moved up north, changed our identities, fell in love all over again, and became a family. Jim got his real estate license, and I finished my schooling." I brushed away the tear tickling my cheek. "We were…we were…happy."

Scott nodded. He knew that part of the story—Cheryl and Jim MacGregor lived and worked in Lake Kipling, raising our children in our happy home. That was when Scott entered our lives and became my best friend and partner in crime-solving. "But…" Scott motioned with his hand for me to continue my story.

"But when I went to Croatia, I reawakened the curse. Stefan was released from jail. He blamed me for what happened to Darko. If I hadn't gotten pregnant, Darko would still be alive. I knew Stefan was the one who caused Jim's accident and then kidnapped Brent, but I had no proof. So, I decided to handle things on my own and get my son back. It was my curse in life, and I had to face it alone." A dark vision of the night on the cliff clouded my memory. The struggle with Stefan, his fall over the edge.

"So, Stefan died accidentally in the struggle, when you were trying to get Brent away from him. None of that was your fault, Cheryl…Ivy. Why did you leave your life behind?"

"I was afraid. I thought someone might come after us, someone from the family or the organization. So, I changed my identity again. I made a *new* life for myself and my kids."

"How did Stefan find you in Lake Kipling?"

"Remember the drug bust we made and the connection to the Mafia? I think it was his organization behind it. My photo was published along with the news story. He must have seen it and hunted me down."

"Oh, Cher...Ivy," Scott shook his head. "I'm so sorry. I let you get involved in the case. I'm responsible..."

"No, it had nothing to do with you. I insisted on being part of the investigation. My boss shouldn't have printed the photo without my permission, but he had no way of knowing..."

Scott rose and pulled me into his arms, steering me to the couch. Sitting me down, he drew circles on my back to soothe me. "You're not cursed, Ivy. You're blessed with two wonderful children and good memories of Jim. You just got yourself into some bad situations, none of which were your fault. Bad things happen to good people. It's just the way it is." His hands moved to my shoulders, and he massaged the knots out of my tense muscles.

"Bad things happen to me a lot. You know that." I reminded him of Julia's abduction and the connection to the Mafia. Julia was Jim's receptionist at his real estate office. "And now these murders here in our small community. What if they're connected to me, too?"

Scott stopped massaging and froze. "Connected to you? In what way?"

"What if it's the curse? People connected to me have terrible things happen to them. My parents, Jim, Julia. Darko." I gulped at the memory of Brent's biological father. Was he a victim of my curse, too? "It's bad karma. Maybe these Blue Water deaths are a continuation of the village curse in Croatia."

Scott assured me the curse was in my imagination and the current situation had nothing to do with me. "I do think you need a thorough massage, though, to work some of that bad karma out of you."

He maneuvered me onto the floor and turned me onto my stomach. Straddling me, he worked on getting the kinks out of my system.

"Scott...I don't think..."

"Don't worry, I'm a registered massage therapist," Scott stated, sounding serious. I snorted and burst into laughter, remembering how he tried that line on me fourteen years ago. "Now, let's get this sweater out of the way."

I protested again, but his strong hands and firm fingers moving rhythmically along my back and shoulders quieted me, and I allowed him to lift my sweater to my shoulders and place his hands on my bare skin. "Your hands should be registered as weapons of persuasion. You're making me drool."

He chuckled and continued with the massage. "Let me know when you've had enough drooling, and you're ready to surrender."

"Scott Evans, you are such a…" The right word escaped me. "Scoundrel."

"Scoundrel? Really? That's what you think of me?" He rolled off and sat cross-legged, searching my face.

"Not in a bad way," I drooled, trying to take it back. "But you have to admit you're a flirt. A relentless one." Although he flirted with me when I was married to Jim, there was a line he didn't cross. I wasn't sure he'd stop himself from crossing that line now. And I didn't trust myself to keep him in check.

"So, is it working? We're both unattached, Ivy." He sprawled beside me and smoothed a lock of my hair, kissing my forehead. "I held back my feelings when you were with Jim, had to stop myself from making a move on you then, but you must have known how much I wanted you."

I sat up, moving away from him. "You can't expect me to just fall into your arms. We've had one dinner date."

"Lunch and dinner. Actually, we've had *lots* of dinner dates."

"We had burgers and fries. Work dates. Pizza. You, at my house as my guest. *Friend* dates, not romantic dates."

"They were good dates, though, weren't they?" Pulling me back down with him, he smiled, his face nearly touching mine. "Don't worry—I'm not a scoundrel. You're safe with me. I can wait till our *second* dinner date."

"We did have some really good times working together," I agreed, putting some distance between us. "I've missed that. I've missed you." As Scott leaned in for a kiss, I sprang out of his reach. "What if we work together now? On *this* case."

"No."

"Yes. You know how good we were together. We can be good together again." I gazed down at him. It was all I could do not to give in to my feelings for him. But the last thing I wanted was to be nothing more than another notch on Scott Evans' bedpost. "I can help you gather information on potential suspects."

"No. You're not an investigative journalist anymore," Scott reminded me, his elbow digging into the carpet.

I scoffed. "I never was. I was just a pushy small-town reporter who worked for a weekly newspaper. I may have over advertised myself to you."

He shook his head. "Ivy, you're a schoolteacher, not an investigator."

"You'd be surprised how observant teachers are. You should see all the confiscated gadgets and notes in my desk drawer. Besides, I know the people in this town. You don't."

"It's too dangerous," he insisted. "A lot of people have been killed. You and I never worked a case like this. It's not happening. I won't allow you to become involved."

"You won't what? Won't *allow* me to talk to people?"

"Poor choice of words. You know what I mean." He seemed to consider something, then added, "You're not going to keep your nose out of it, are you?" We laughed, remembering how persistent I was in helping him find Julia, the first case we worked together. I wouldn't take no for an answer. I had a way of getting people to talk, and he knew it.

We spent the rest of the evening entwined on the carpet, discussing the past, bringing up one memory after another. "Do you remember when…?" It was like a game, turning over cards and finding a match as we nudged each other's minds. Working on cases, our easy rapport, the attraction we fought. The friendship that developed included my family—games nights with all five of us and weekend afternoon sports viewing with Jim. The times he brought a date to dinner, and I felt a spark of jealousy, joking whether he was finally going to settle down, and the one time he caught me alone and whispered in my ear, "The only woman who could ever tie me down is already taken."

The gap of thirteen years closed, and it was as though we had never been apart. He stroked my head, kissed my face, the corners of his mouth turning up. I caressed his cheek and gazed into his eyes. Tom kept pushing his way in between us to cuddle. Which was just as well because my willpower was waning.

"I'd like to stay all night," he said at one in the morning, peeling himself off the carpet and extending his hand to help me up. "But we'd better get some sleep."

"You're right. I won't be able to function at school if I don't get to bed." Scott pulled me close, and I added, "To sleep."

Grabbing his tie, Scott headed for the door, with me on his heels. "I'll let you go, then. This time." He turned, bent down, cupped my face in his hands, lifted it up, and kissed me goodnight, our first *real* kiss. "Goodnight, Ivy," he said huskily, one more gentle brush of his lips over mine. I closed the door on that cocky smile of his.

Locking up, I sighed like a lovestruck schoolgirl. You'd think I'd never been kissed before. Not in the last thirteen years, anyway. In bed, I relived his kiss over and over, wishing I'd let him stay. Then my eyes flew open.

What if he finds out the truth? What will he do?

Chapter Twenty-Six

Students and staff were ready to leave for the weekend. Buses lined up at the front of the school, and parents waited to pick up their kids. Teachers filed out one after the other, through the side door to their vehicles. Some kids headed to the student parking lot out back, others began their walk home. Everyone seemed intent on getting out. Only the killer was focused on being inside.

Walking with a purpose, the killer strolled down the hallway, glancing at the plaque on the door: Ivy Rose, Head of English. One thing they had learned was that if you acted like you had a right to be somewhere, no one took notice or questioned your presence. Just another school board employee or temporary worker.

Peering inside, the killer observed the blonde bent over at her desk. She appeared to be marking papers. Patience, that's what it took to do the job properly. Too many errors were made already; another one wouldn't be tolerated. The accidents needed to be more than just accidents—they needed to be fatal accidents.

If this occasion didn't prove to be conducive to getting the job done, there would always be another one. Better to wait and succeed than to rush and fail. If the school emptied quickly, if she kept working, if no one interrupted them…Slipping into the workroom down the hall, the killer laid a book on the counter and pretended to sort a file full of papers for photocopying. Just in case someone came along, it was best to look busy, as though you belonged.

Fifteen minutes later, an eerie quietness descended on the school. The students were gone, and most of the teachers had bolted for the door, with it being a Friday. The killer exited the workroom and checked to see if the woman was still in her classroom.

There she was, oblivious to the fact she was about to become the next victim. Sensing someone's presence, she glanced at the doorway.

"Excuse me," the killer said. "I wonder if you'd mind giving me a hand. I'm having trouble with the photocopier. I hope I didn't break it." A chuckle followed.

"Oh, sure, no problem. I'm no expert at technology, but I'll have a look."

"Working late?" the killer asked.

"I thought I'd get some of the marking done and tidy up a bit, just so I don't leave a mess for Monday."

"I know the feeling. I have a few pages I wanted to copy, so they're ready for next week, but the darn machine seems jammed or something."

The woman led the way to the workroom and examined the photocopier, which seemed to be fine, opened the lid, and asked, "What do you need copied? Let's give it a try."

While she placed a sheet on the top of the copier and pressed some buttons, the killer removed a black scarf from a pant pocket, pulled it over the woman's head, wrapping it tightly around her neck. Although she was caught off guard, the woman struggled, flailing about, kicking, her hands clawing at the scarf, then pulling and scratching her assailant's arms. The killer panicked that someone might hear the commotion. The woman was putting up more of a fight than the killer had anticipated.

Eventually, she stopped struggling, and her body went limp. The killer dragged her to the paper shredder next to the photocopier. Slipping one end of the scarf into the shredder, they turned it on. As the scarf fed into the machine, the woman's head was pulled toward the shredder.

Cautiously opening the door, the killer scanned the hall and found it empty. Luck was on the killer's side this time. Everything had gone smoothly. The only thing left to do was to exit the building before the body was discovered.

Straight down the hall, out the back door, the killer strode confidently from the scene of the crime. In a short while, the killer returned safely home and sent a text.

129

Chapter Twenty-Seven

Mike Juliano left a voice message for Scott. "We just received a call from the principal at Blue Water High. There's been another accident. Can you meet me there?"

Scott's heart raced as he rang Ivy's number, and she didn't pick up.

Please, please, please, let her be okay.

All day he'd been interviewing Phillip Reece's family, as well as families of the other victims in the county, and he found an interesting connection to the in-town cases. The out-of-town fatalities were *mystery* writers. It took Scott twenty minutes to race back to Port Ripley, his foot heavy on the pedal, his hands shaking.

A couple of cruisers were parked in front of the school. Scott ran up the stairs to meet Mike, and they slipped under the yellow police tape. "The custodian found the body after everyone had cleared out for the weekend. She opened the workroom to use a power outlet for the floor polisher when she found her."

"Her?" Scott's voice trembled. A sensation of dread crept up his spine. He couldn't lose her permanently now that he'd finally found her. Scott rushed into the school, stopping next to the principal and two uniformed officers.

Mike caught up with him. "Scott, it's not..."

"At first, we thought it was..." Doug McLaren broke down, his voice quivering. "Hers was the only classroom...with the door still open, the lights on. When Doris found her...she was sure it was Ivy."

The floor fell from underneath Scott. He braced himself against the doorjamb, a 'whoosh' flooding his ears.

"But it's *not* Ivy," Mike said, his hand gripping Scott's shoulder.

"No. No, it's not Ivy," Doug clarified, "Not Ivy." His eyes darted back and forth between Scott and Mike.

Mike entered the workroom and turned his head in the direction of the shredder.

"It's Connie Schultz. She's the substitute teacher who…took Ivy's place today. I'd forgotten Ivy was…taking the day off. She hardly ever misses school." Doug remained at the doorway, looking down the hall, avoiding the dead woman. "We have warnings posted about keeping loose articles of clothing away from the machine."

Relief rushed through Scott, bringing another round of dizziness, but he had to see for himself. Taking a deep breath, he stepped through the doorway and turned to the scene that had Mike's attention.

She was slumped over, head turned to the side on top of the shredder, short blond hair accented by a black scarf that pinned her to the machine. Scott approached the body, holding his breath. Her bloodshot eyes bulged; her swollen black tongue lolled to the side of her blotchy skin. Scott's breath came out in one big blast. The rational part of his mind took over from his emotions as he inspected the gruesome scene before him.

Will Jenkins, the town coroner, knelt beside the woman, partly hidden by her body. He rose to greet Mike and Scott. "Looks like another one. The red marks on her face indicate suffocation or strangulation." He lifted her sweater and blouse.

"But you don't think it was an accident," Scott stated, noting the disbelief on Will's face.

"I haven't seen anyone killed by a shredder before." He examined her torso. "There are red marks on the body as well. But…" He stood up. "It's the skin under the fingernails and the bruises on her arms that tell me she wasn't killed by the shredder. She put up a good fight against someone."

Scott scanned the workroom. Photocopier between the shredder and laminator. Shelves along the adjoining wall, containing supplies. Cupboards on the wall opposite the machines, along the top and the bottom, a shelf in between with some office tools. And something that was out of place in the midst of it. A hardcover book—*Murder Collections* by Ivy Rose. Scott picked it up with gloved hands. There was a bookmark in it. Turning to the selected page, Scott skimmed Ivy's story, "My Life in Shreds". It described the murder scene in front of him.

As Will arranged for the body to be taken to the hospital morgue, Mike and Scott questioned Doug McLaren and the school custodian. According to them, strict security measures were in place. No surveillance cameras on school property, but guests were required to sign in at the main office. Doors were locked outside of regular school hours and the alarm was set. Staff had keys and knew the alarm code, as did maintenance staff. "But it surely can't be one of our own who's responsible for this tragedy," Doug asserted. "We've never had anything like this happen at Blue Water High. No major accidents, no serious violence. It's a safe school."

The body splayed across the shredder belied Doug's claims. No one was safe anywhere in Blue Water County. When Scott's phone rang, relief coursed through him. But the display showed an unknown number.

"Hello, who is this?" Scott answered, his voice abrupt. If Ivy was trying to contact him, he wanted to be available.

"Hello. Is this Detective Evans? I've been told by my captain that you're investigating Wendall Collins' accident. I talked to Wendall a few times."

The man, a crew member on the freighter docked at the pier the night Wendall died, explained he'd been approached by Wendall a few months ago when they were unloading the ship. Wendall was working on a novel involving a murder on board a freighter, and he wanted to do some hands-on research. "He said he'd mention me in the acknowledgments. I love mystery novels, so I talked to him about life on a freighter, and with the captain's permission, I brought him on board."

"Did you meet the night he died?" Scott paced the hall. As excited as he was about this information, his mind was on Ivy.

"I did. We talked for a couple hours down in the gazebo. Then I returned to my quarters."

"Did you see anyone with him?"

"No, but he did mention he was meeting with someone else to do more research."

"Do you know who?" Scott sensed he was about to make a breakthrough in the case.

"No, he didn't say."

Chapter Twenty-Eight

Her text came through after he finished his call. He silently thanked God.

Busy tonight? Want to get together?

He had been thinking about her all day, hopeful for a romantic evening, just the two of them. A man could dream, couldn't he? But now, this new turn of events was going to affect the rebuilding of their personal relationship. Her life was in danger, and she needed his protection.

"Hey, I'm never too busy for you. How was your day?" Scott tried to keep his voice calm and steady when he called Ivy. He wanted to tell her the news in person, before the gossip spread.

"Actually, I did a terrible thing."

"What terrible thing was that?"

"I played hooky."

That was a term he hadn't heard in a while. Not since his days in high school when he sometimes skipped class just for the heck of it. He kept his tone light. "What do you mean you played hooky? You're the *teacher*."

"I know. Isn't it awful? You're a bad influence. I hardly ever take sick days. But I didn't think it would hurt if I missed one day." Her guilt came through on the phone. "I was just *so* tired this morning."

He shuddered at the thought of what would have happened if she hadn't allowed herself a mental health day. "It's my fault, keeping you up late last night. I should have left sooner, but…I'm *really* glad I didn't."

"So am I. But I spent the whole morning sleeping in."

Scott said he hoped she was well rested. He had some bad news for her.

"It's about the case. I'll tell you when I get there. And Ivy? Don't talk to anyone till I get there. Make sure the doors and windows are all locked, and don't let anyone in, except me. *No* one."

"Sounds ominous. What's going on?"

"We'll talk about it tonight."

"That's why I was texting you. I've got an event tonight. A writers' awards banquet, and I need a date."

Scott had been hoping for something a little more intimate. Still, he wasn't going to miss an opportunity to spend time with her. Besides, a writer's banquet was the perfect place to gather more information about the case. "What time should I pick you up?"

At 7:30, Scott exited his Camaro as June waved. "Detective Evans!"

"June, how lovely to see you again." He bent to pet Clarence, who jumped up on his dress pants. "How have you been feeling?"

"Better. Especially since I figured out what caused my little attack." The setting sun showed concern on her face. "Now I just need to worry about dementia."

"What do you mean?"

"My pills. I have a weekly pill organizer, so I remember to take my medication properly, but I still got mixed up."

"June, are you trying to steal back Scott from me?" Ivy teased as she joined them. "I'm afraid he's already taken for tonight."

"Are you two hooking up? *You* move fast. We barely broke up." June narrowed her eyes at Scott.

"We're going to an awards banquet," Ivy explained. "Just another dinner date."

"I know what's going on," June said. "I may be old, but I know the score. I saw him sneaking out of your place last night."

Scott cleared his throat. "If I was sneaking, you wouldn't have seen me. What was it you were saying about the pills?"

"I noticed it yesterday. My diabetes pill container had fewer pills in it than I remembered. And my new Vitamin C bottle is almost full. They're both white and oval. I take a lot of vitamins. All those pills look alike to me. I guess I got confused and doubled up on the diabetes meds. I'm going to be extra careful from now on." June bent to pet Clarence. "We need Mummy to stay healthy to look after her good boy, don't we, sweetie?"

Scott asked if he could have a look at her pills sometime. "We do need to get going now, but I'll come around on the weekend."

"I'll look forward to it. We'll have tea again. And you can bring your new girlfriend. We'll make it a threesome." June nodded toward Ivy.

As they drove off, Ivy asked what that was about. Scott explained he thought someone may have messed with June's pill organizer. "She doesn't strike me as the kind of woman who gets confused easily. And with the accidents that have been happening lately, I wouldn't be surprised…"

"Who would want to kill June?" Ivy interrupted, her voice high-pitched. "She's just a sweet little old lady."

"I don't know who would kill any of them. Wendall, Larissa, Eugene, Phillip…and…"

"And?"

Scott told her what happened at the school.

"Oh my gosh. That poor woman. How awful. I shouldn't have taken the day off. It's my fault she's dead. If she hadn't taken my place…" Ivy stopped abruptly.

As he pulled into the parking lot of the community center, Scott turned to Ivy. "Yes, it would have been you. Keep it to yourself, though. It hasn't been released to the public. Pretend nothing's wrong. I'm betting someone's going to be very surprised to see you tonight. Let's see if we can flush out the killer."

"We?" Ivy's voice was barely a squeak.

"The police."

"Oh. I thought maybe you were including me. This is all about me. It's the curse. It's my past coming back to haunt me. People are dying because of me." The light from the lamppost fell upon her face. She was pale, her mouth open, and she stared through him.

"None of this is your fault." Scott took her hands and leaned over to kiss the top of her head. He didn't want to alarm Ivy further by telling her that

"My Life in Shreds" was found next to Connie's body. Now, two deaths were connected to books.

"I've found a connection between the deaths, and it has nothing to do with your past. I think the killer is going to be at the banquet tonight, though, so I don't want you leaving my side."

They were so close, their noses almost touched. "Let me work with you on the case. We made a good team before," Ivy whispered.

"We did," he conceded. "But I told you…it's too dangerous. There is something you can do for me, though." She perked up at that. "I want you to call Brent and Jamie right now to let them know you're safe. I don't want them to hear about this on the news when it's released."

Ivy's hand flew to her mouth, and her eyes widened. "Oh!" She scrambled to get out her phone and called Jamie, who insisted on coming home. "No, it's okay. I don't want you here in harm's way. Besides, I have a detective to look out for me." Scott listened as she explained that he was on the case. "Yes, I will be very careful. Don't worry." She promised to text her daughter several times a day.

The conversation with her son went in a similar manner, but Brent wanted to hire a bodyguard. "No, I don't want somebody following me. I'm already on edge. I'll be fine. I can take care of myself. You know that better than anyone."

Scott motioned for Ivy to hand over the phone. "Hey, Brent. It's Scott Evans. I just want you to know your mom already has a bodyguard. I'm not going to let her out of my sight till the killer's behind bars. Trust me, no one's going to guard her better than I will."

"I know a lot of people," Ivy said after talking with her kids. There are people at this event who live in town, my neighbors, people from this community. Let me in on what you know, and we'll solve the case together. I'll bet I already have tons of information that could help you."

He had thought that part of the discussion was over. Apparently not. "Then I'll have to find a way to get it out of you," Scott said as he held the car door open. "And if you really want to help, then keep your eyes and ears open tonight and fill me in later."

"So, I can work with you?"

"Let's just enjoy the evening. I'm starving. I hope they have decent food at this place."

"I doubt it'll be anything as classy as burgers and fries." Ivy rolled her eyes, recovering from the shock of being an intended murder victim.

Chapter Twenty-Nine

Blue Water Writes:

Tonight's the night! Looking forward to seeing everyone at the banquet. Congrats to all the nominees. What an honor for me to be in the running! Thanks to everyone who voted!

The Writer

How am I going to get through tonight? Another event to glorify writers. Another event that doesn't recognize my talent. The Blue Water Writes awards banquet, organized by the Blue Water Library, is sponsored by bookstores in the county. This year, Port Ripley is hosting. It's a must-attend.

I don't know who you have to sleep with to get nominated. It's obviously rigged. We're *told* readers nominate and vote for local published authors through the library. Unpublished authors submit their manuscripts to be judged by a panel of so-called literary experts. I consider myself as much of an expert as anyone. The three top nominees in each category are honored at this ridiculous awards banquet and receive a trophy. The winner in each category is also awarded a small cash prize. Of course, I'm not among the top three nominees. As usual.

Still, I *have* to be here. Everyone who's anyone in the literary world in Blue Water County is going to attend. But, who to attend with? I'm sure people have seen us together before. There's nothing wrong with two friends hanging out, is there? But in light of the recent tragedies, tongues *will* wag.

Rumors run rampant in Port Ripley. But since most people have something to hide, gossip is generally considered to be speculation. Keeping secrets is something the people of Port Ripley excel at. You never know when you might need to have someone return the favor of silence.

Chapter Thirty

Scott scanned the generic-looking hall. White tablecloths covered about two dozen large round tables. To the right, people lined up in front of the bar. Along the far wall, a black podium took center place in front of a table holding several trophies.

"Table eight," Ivy said, looking at the seating plan posted by the entrance. "Looks like we're with Riley. And Paige, too." She headed in their direction.

"Hi, Celia," Ivy said, touching her friend's shoulder as she passed. As Celia glanced up at Ivy and Scott, her eyebrows raised, Ivy greeted the others at her table. Olivia caught Ivy's attention, waving at her from across the room. "I'd better go say hello to Olivia."

Olivia's eyes were on Scott as he accompanied Ivy, his arm linking hers. He overheard her whisper to Ivy as she hugged her, "I want to hear all about this."

"I wish we were at your table, but we're over at number eight," Ivy indicated with her head. Turning to the salt-and-pepper-haired man next to Olivia, she introduced Scott. "Cliff, this is an old friend of mine, Scott Evans. Scott, this is Cliff Walker, Olivia's husband. We'll stop by later to chat."

Leaving Olivia with unanswered questions, Ivy led Scott to table eight and greeted Riley and Paige, no one mentioning anything about seeing each other at the restaurant last night. "This is an old friend of mine, Scott Evans," she introduced him to the group at the table.

"This is my husband, Matt," Paige said, nearly knocking over her water glass as she indicated the clean-shaven man with glasses and wavy brown hair.

Riley introduced his daughter, Willow. She hesitated, then said, "Detective Evans and I have already met. He asked me questions about Eugene's accident."

Riley set his hand on Willow's arm. "Hopefully, you'll find the person responsible quickly so my daughter can have some peace."

Scott nodded, assuring them he intended to do so.

Alice and Will Jenkins joined them. "Detective Evans, how nice to see you again." Alice tilted her head toward Ivy and mouthed, "I'm so glad you're okay". Will caught Scott's eye and mouthed he was sorry, indicating he had told Alice about the murdered teacher.

"Hello, Paige, Riley," Alice greeted them. She acknowledged Matt with a smile, nodded at Willow, lowered her eyes, and sank into the chair Will pulled out.

Once the introductions were complete, the conversation turned to the writer nominees. "We're in for an exciting night. It was really close this year—the unpublished authors top pick—a tough choice for the judges. As a bookstore owner, I was on the panel." Alice boasted. "Such an interesting job. Lots of raw talent out there."

"How do writers get nominated?" Scott asked Alice, noting she pulled away from Will when he leaned close and put his arm around her.

Alice explained the process and how the winner was chosen. "It's all very subjective," Alice added. "That's the thing with writing. It's not always about the talent or the literary value of the work. Every judge has their own idea of what makes for good writing. They're not always right. But we were able to come to a consensus after some discussion." Alice pursed her lips. "It's all anonymous, until we've made our choice. To discourage favoritism."

"Does anyone smell that?" Willow asked, sniffing the air.

"I think it's probably the furnace starting up for the first time since spring," Alice suggested, prompting a conversation about the change over to fall.

The conversation stopped as a server brought a cart to the table and placed food in front of them. They were offered a choice of broccoli-and-cheese stuffed chicken breast with mashed potatoes and baby carrots, or baked salmon with rice pilaf and asparagus. The server poured a choice of white or red wine into glasses.

Scott resumed the conversation, cutting into his chicken. "So, who are the lucky nominees? Anyone here know them?"

"I know two of them," Ivy answered. "Not personally, just from our online critique group."

"Yes, the same here." Alice explained that she, Riley, Paige, and Ivy belonged to the Blue Water Writer's group. "We read each other's work and offer constructive criticism." She snorted, "Although sometimes it's not exactly constructive, is it, Ivy?"

"Everybody has their own opinion. You can't please everyone," Ivy agreed, fiddling with her napkin.

"You've got that right," Riley said. Scott noticed Riley's knee bump against Paige's, causing her to lean closer to her husband. "Some people are hard to satisfy. All you can do is keep trying. Isn't that right, Paige?"

Paige gasped and nodded, "Yes, everyone likes different things. Um, books."

Matt raised his eyebrows at his wife. Willow nudged her father. Will furrowed his brow at Alice, whose eyes flitted between Riley and Paige. Scott lost track of what they were talking about until Ivy brought everyone back on topic. "Like you said, Alice, it's all very subjective." Then she explained to the non-writers at the table. "It's not easy being a writer. Everyone's a critic. All you can do is write for yourself."

After a dessert of strawberry gelato, the tables were cleared while a crew checked the microphone. Paige whispered something to her husband and downed a pill with a glass of water. Matt put his hand on the back of her neck and massaged it. "Sorry, I've got a headache coming on," Paige apologized, saying she needed some fresh air.

On her way to the podium, Valerie Reading stopped by their table. She greeted everyone, but Scott noticed a slight twitch in her eye when she noticed Ivy's hand linked with his.

People better get used to seeing us together.

"Welcome to our annual Blue Water Writes awards banquet." The county's head librarian stood behind the podium, with her fellow librarians seated on either side. "Tonight, we will be honoring our six nominees, three authors of books published this year, and three authors of unpublished manuscripts. As you know, the unpublished authors are chosen by a panel, while published authors are selected by reader ballots. Unfortunately, one of our nominees isn't with us tonight." As the librarian named the nominated authors, Paige returned to her seat.

BEEP BEEP BEEP BEEP!

Riley marched to the podium and took charge as the alarm caused heads to bob in all directions, searching for the problem. "No need for panic," he assured the crowd, his voice booming. "It's the carbon monoxide detector. Calmly proceed to the exits, please."

As the crowd gathered in the parking lot, Riley advised, "We need to air out the building." He asked Scott to prop open the front door while he opened the kitchen emergency exit and the side door. "The fire department will be along soon," he shouted to the guests. "They'll get it sorted."

Scott commended Riley, who it turned out was a volunteer firefighter and had installed the alarms himself, for his quick action.

"This is exactly why it's important for people to check their alarms are in working order," Riley said. " Carbon monoxide is a silent killer. You can't see or smell it, but it can be deadly."

"So, what do you think caused it to go off?" Alice asked. "The gas stove?"

"Could be. Or the gas furnace. A leak somewhere. We're just lucky the alarm alerted us before anyone was poisoned."

The sound of fire engines cut through the crisp autumn night. Two fire trucks, an ambulance, and the fire chief's vehicle pulled up in front of the community center. Riley briefed his colleagues on the situation. The fire chief asked everyone to gather around. "Anyone with a headache, nausea, dizziness, any out of the ordinary feeling, should be examined." He indicated the ambulance, and Paige, Valerie, and a few others headed over to be checked out.

A light drizzle started to fall, but no one retreated to their vehicle, the crowd curious to find out why the detector went off. When the fire chief returned to the parking lot a short while later, he had an answer for them.

"We've found the problem, and it's been taken care of. There was a bird's nest in the furnace vent on the side of the building, causing carbon monoxide to build up inside. Just to be on the safe side, we're going to shut down the building for the rest of the evening."

A collective hum rippled through the crowd, a mixture of a groan at the inconvenience, and relief that no one was hurt. The head librarian gestured for everyone's attention. "We'll be continuing the awards ceremony at the town library. See everyone there in half an hour."

As they drove away from the community center, mist enveloped them. Scott said, "Well, this is certainly an exciting evening out."

"Not quite the way it was expected to go," Ivy agreed. "It's a lucky thing the detector was working. Otherwise..."

Scott kept his eyes on the road as he maneuvered through the fog. "It could have been a disaster."

Valerie welcomed people at the library door, directing them to the fireplace area. The comfy sofas and armchairs were already filled, and people had pulled up chairs from the computer tables.

"Over here," Alice beckoned, and Scott and Ivy joined the group assembled on the carpet.

"Everyone feeling okay?" Riley asked, paying particular attention to Paige. "How's that headache?"

"I'm fine now. The fresh air helped," she answered, avoiding eye contact.

"That was quite the excitement, all because of a bird's nest," Alice said. Everyone nodded. "We've never had anything like that happen at an awards banquet."

"If they hadn't turned on the heat, it wouldn't have been a problem," Will suggested.

"Just as well the issue was discovered and taken care of before someone's wedding," Riley said.

Olivia and Cliff entered the building, and Ivy motioned for them to join their group.

"That was certainly unexpected," Olivia commented after everyone exchanged greetings. "There's never been an alarm go off at the hall in all the time I can remember." She raised her eyebrows, seeing Scott's hand on Ivy's back.

"Celia, do you want to sit with us?" Ivy asked as her friend walked past, with Dylan's arm around her waist.

Celia's gaze fell upon the others seated next to Ivy. Willow glared up at her, and Celia's smile faded. "Thanks, but we'll just find our table group."

The head librarian got everyone's attention. "I apologize for this inconvenience, and I thank each of you for bearing with us as we improvise."

Once the authors completed their readings, the final part of the evening took place—the announcement of the winners.

"And the winner of Blue Water Published Author of the Year is…Gloria Holstein, author of the Science Fiction novel *A New Kind of Utopia*." Applause greeted Gloria as she accepted her award.

"And now for our unpublished winner…Carter Loewen. Unfortunately, Carter couldn't be here with us tonight, but we'll make sure he receives his trophy. And that concludes our annual Blue Water Writes awards ceremony. Thank you to all who submitted, and to those who came to support our local literary talent."

"That's strange. Carter not showing up," Alice remarked, and Ivy agreed. "He was in our online writers' group and was excited for tonight. I was rooting for him. No one from town was nominated this year. Not that there isn't lots of talent right here in Port Ripley. Like I said, it's subjective. Every year, there are different judges, so you just need to keep trying. That's what I've been told, anyway." Her comments seemed to be directed at Ivy. "And you, too," she added, glancing at Paige, then Riley. "Don't give up."

Riley winked at Paige. Paige lowered her eyes. Ivy sighed. Scott said he was glad he wasn't a writer. Their success was too dependent on the opinions of others. It had to be tough, trying to break into the profession.

The crowd thinned out quickly once the winners were announced. Alice spoke to her daughter in the lobby. "See you at home after you lock up." A tall, well-built man, around forty, with dark brown hair, had his arm around Valerie.

"Don't wait up," Valerie answered. "I'll be late."

Scott noted the look of disdain Alice directed toward the man. She obviously didn't approve of her daughter's boyfriend.

During the short drive to Ivy's house, the wipers swishing across the windshield, Scott asked, "Did you submit work to the competition? Is that what Alice was talking about?"

"Yes, not my first year, either." She told him about the mystery series she was working on.

"I guess that makes sense. You always were a writer. And you loved to solve crimes. I bet your books are realistic, considering the time we spent together working cases."

"So, did you figure out which one of them is the killer?"

"Not yet, but it was quite the evening," he answered, avoiding discussion of the case.

The streetlight in front of Ivy's house illuminated the shiny driveway through the fog. The street and park were empty. He figured it was too late, too wet, and too foggy for June to be out walking Clarence. As he accompanied Ivy to the front door, his hand on her back, his mind was on spending the night with Ivy. There was no way he was returning to his hotel.

"Do you want to…" Ivy asked as she turned the key in the lock.

"I do want to…" Scott walked her in, closed and locked the door, pulling her close.

"Come in for a coffee?"

"I do want to come in, but not for a coffee." His mouth found hers, soft and gentle at first, the kiss becoming more passionate. When he broke away, he searched her eyes for an answer.

"Okay, then, no coffee," Ivy said, her voice quiet. "Maybe some tea?"

He broke into a fit of laughter. "No, no tea," he said once he composed himself. Then he tilted her head and resumed kissing her, with an increasing urgency. She laid her hand on his chest and gave him a gentle push. He released her.

"I haven't…" she began. "I haven't…There's been no one since Jim. And only Darko before him." She backed away. "I'm sorry…I'm not ready to…"

"You don't need to be sorry, Ivy. I understand." He'd give her the time she needed. With an effort, he smiled. "So, how about that tea?"

In the kitchen, Ivy set two bags into two mugs. "I'm going to change into something more comfortable," she said, "if you can handle pouring the water."

Scott waited at the counter for the kettle to boil. The small kitchen was cozy and homey. Not as large as her kitchen in Lake Kipling, and not as busy. No husband, no kids. Things had changed. For both of them.

The kettle boiled, steam rising in the cool air. Pouring water in the mugs, Scott wondered if she had any cinnamon buns to go with the tea. He remembered her home baking with a fondness. Taking a look around, he found a package of store-bought cookies. They would have to do. In the living room, he turned on the gas fireplace, placed the tea and cookies on the coffee table, and waited.

She returned in a fluffy pink robe. "I thought I might as well get ready for bed."

There was something different about her. Not just the robe. She had removed her makeup, and her eyes...her eyes were no longer blue. They were the same beautiful pools of chocolate he used to drown in.

"Your eyes..." he said, staring into them. "I've missed looking into those big brown eyes of yours." He cradled her face and brought his lips to hers, gently once again, then more insistently. She responded, and he slipped his hand under her robe.

"Um, I..." she broke the embrace and pulled his hand out. "It's just...I'm not ready to..."

He touched his lips to her forehead. "You're killing me here," he murmured.

"Speaking of killing..." Ivy said, pulling away. "We really should solve this case before...well, before someone else gets killed." Her face was flushed, her breathing quick. "Cookie?" she thrust the plate of chocolate-covered biscuits at him.

He took one and settled back on the couch. She wasn't going to be easily persuaded, and he didn't want to push.

"So, tell me your thoughts about tonight. Did you pick up any clues at the banquet?" Ivy bit into a cookie.

"You mean apart from the near-death experience we just went through?" Scott had no doubt the bird's nest had been intentionally placed in the vent.

"That was odd, wasn't it?" She scrunched up her face. "You don't think someone caused that, do you?"

"I wouldn't be surprised. All those people in one spot like that. Kind of an easy target if someone wanted to get rid of several people at once."

"But the alarm went off, so no one was hurt," Ivy reminded him. "If the killer actually meant to kill us, wouldn't he have disabled the carbon monoxide detector?"

Scott suggested it might have been a warning, or part of a sick game. "Maybe the killer wants to let people know he can get to them anywhere, anytime. Even in a crowd. Fear mongering."

"Wow," Ivy exclaimed.

"Yeah, wow," Scott agreed, leaning in for another kiss, only to be rebuffed.

"Do you think the killer was there tonight?"

Scott recalled how they used to bounce ideas off each other in the past. They worked well together, although they didn't always agree. Ivy had a way of reading people and getting them to open up. "I think you have some interesting friends."

"What's that supposed to mean?" She sat back against the cushion and crossed her arms.

"Just that there's more going on than meets the eye."

Chapter Thirty-One

"I don't like the way this is going. It's not working."

He knew he'd made mistakes. But to be fair, this was his first experience with multiple serial killing. It's not like he was an expert in the field.

"We had a simple plan. There was an order and a method that had to be followed. Now, it's all out of sync. I don't like your revisions." Exasperated, she plopped onto the couch.

"I know, I know," he approached her cautiously and sat down, maintaining a safe distance. "But let's move forward. Everything will work out in the end. A bit of rewriting never hurt a story."

"You're the one who asked me for input. Now you're changing the plot."

"I'll make it right," he promised. "No survivors. No victims getting away. Give me another chance. Please." He pleaded with her to forgive him.

"You'd better get the next ones right. That's all I can say," she threatened. "Or else."

"Or else what?"

"I'll be looking for another critique partner. Which means you'll have to go."

Her eyes met his, and it was like staring into a pool of water with no bottom. He imagined the water was ice cold.

He attempted to assuage her by stroking her hair. "You know I love you. I'd do anything for you. Tell me what's next."

Chapter Thirty-Two

Scott spent Friday night at my place. On the couch. I was sure that wasn't what he had in mind when I agreed he could stay.

"I'm not leaving," he had said. "If you're in danger, I'm not leaving you alone. No way."

I had acquiesced but slipped out of his grasp when he pulled me into his arms again and brought him a pillow and blanket from the linen closet. I plopped them on the couch, keeping my distance. "Good night, then."

In the morning, Scott asked, "So, are there any more exciting events happening this weekend? Any place people might be hanging out? I'd like to keep my finger on the pulse of what's happening in town."

"Well, yes, of course. It's a small town. There's always something going on," I nudged him with my elbow. "The agricultural fall fair is today. Maybe you'd be interested in going to the demolition derby at two? Then there's fireworks at night. I'd love to see that."

"It's a third date, then. But right now, I'm starving. How about we go out for breakfast? Then it'll be our fourth date. Five, if you count lunch the day we met. And, I had a sleepover. We're practically engaged."

An hour later, as we drove into the downtown area, the main drag seemed eerily quiet. Usually, cars would be cruising around the business district, parking spots would be filled with eager shoppers, dog walkers would be strolling around the square. This morning, it was a ghost town.

In the near-empty lobby of the Port Ripley Hotel, I waited on a leather sofa in front of the stone fireplace while Scott headed upstairs to shower and change.

As he came down to join me, Scott's phone rang. He answered, put his hand up to his forehead, and shook his head. When I opened my mouth, he held up a finger to indicate he needed a moment.

I flipped through the tourist leaflets in the brochure rack while I waited, and as I picked up the Festival of Lights pamphlet, Paige Thornton and Riley Patterson walked toward the hotel counter. When I turned to say hello, Paige scurried to the exit door. Riley waved, then proceeded to check out, his back turned to me.

Scott startled me by placing a hand on my shoulder as I pretended to be absorbed in the brochures. Seeing the frown on his face, I asked what was wrong.

"I'll tell you later. I was told they serve a great breakfast buffet here. What have you got there?" He pointed to the leaflet in my hand.

"It's the Festival of Lights. I thought you could come back at Christmas."

The corners of Scott's face turned up, and his eyes regained their usual warmth. "I'd love to come back. This town has a lot going for it. If you can overlook the murders." Scott gazed into my eyes. "It has you."

He brushed a lock of hair behind my ear, then escorted me to the breakfast room. Scott reached across the table to run his fingers through my hair, which I had curled for him. I had also, for the third time in the last few days, made up my face, and I donned my flowery dress and earrings while he spent quality time with Tom.

"You said you were starving," I reminded him, my face hot as he moved his fingers across my cheek. "We should get some food." Pushing back my chair, I joined the few people at the buffet table.

"Quite a spread," Scott commented, as he piled his plate with a bit of everything: scrambled eggs, bacon, ham, sausages, pancakes, French toast, fried potatoes, along with fresh fruit and pastries.

I was a little more selective in my meal choice, reminding myself how I struggled to squeeze into my black dress.

Setting his overflowing plate at our table, Scott commented, "I noticed Riley and Paige were here."

"Yes, I saw them, too." I moved eggs around my plate. "I guess they're friends getting together for breakfast. Like Riley explained before. Fellow writers."

"I think it's a little more than that," Scott countered, leaning forward. "I saw them coming out of one of the hotel rooms." He raised his eyebrows. "So more than friends. And judging from last night, I have the feeling her husband knows, or at least suspects."

I nodded and said in a quiet voice, "Riley's a widower, so I guess he's entitled to seek company. But Paige is young enough to be his daughter. And she's married, with kids." A twitch in Scott's right eye had me wondering if he was thinking of our own friendship that remained platonic because of my marital situation. "Maybe they were, um, discussing their writing in private. I don't think she'd…well, you know…" I couldn't bring myself to say, 'cheat on her husband'. It hit too close to home. Although Scott and I were 'just friends' when I was married to Jim, I knew it could easily have escalated into a love affair if I had allowed it.

"All I know is they were pretty friendly when they came out of the hotel room," Scott insisted. "But I guess it's not our business. Discussing their writing, huh?" He smirked and picked up his fork with another raise of his eyebrows.

I decided to keep quiet about seeing Paige and Riley embrace in the teachers' lounge. I agreed—it really wasn't our business. I steered the conversation to Scott's earlier phone call. "Something was bothering you. I could tell. Who were you talking to?"

"Mike at the station. Bad news," he cautioned. "It's Carter Loewen."

"Carter Loe..? Oh, right. Last night's winner who didn't show up." I set my fork down.

"He tried to show up. Didn't get too far."

"What are you saying? He's not…?"

"Dead? Afraid so."

Staring at Scott, I waited for him to elaborate. When he didn't, my impatience won out. "What happened to him? Was he murdered?" My voice carried more than I realized. Heads turned in our direction.

"His neighbor came home last night and saw smoke billowing out of

Carter's garage. He called the police. They found Carter in his car. Carbon monoxide poisoning. It looks like an accident—he started up the car and lost consciousness before he could open the garage door."

"That can't be a coincidence! The blocked vent at the community center and this, at the same time? There's no way it was an accident."

"The killer wanted it to look that way, though. I need to go to the station after breakfast. But I can still make our date for the fair."

"That makes nine unnatural deaths in the county this past month. All suspicious, and who knows how many non-fatal accidents. A lot of the victims are people I know. Who do you think is behind this?"

Scott tactfully changed the subject to the demolition derby slated for two p.m. "I'm looking forward to it. As long as there aren't any Camaros being destroyed."

"Well, I...I don't know. I can't guarantee there won't be any."

"I'm kidding. It'll be fun. I'm going to drop you off at June's place while I'm at work. Lock the doors and don't let anyone in," he ordered, wagging his finger at me. "Text me every fifteen minutes. If I don't hear from you, I'm sending in the SWAT team."

"Haha. Yes, Dad." Hoisting myself off the wooden chair as Scott loosened his belt buckle one slot, I said, "That was quite the breakfast."

Leaving me at June's door and instructing her not to let me out of the house and no one into the house, Scott kissed me on the cheek and left.

Two minutes later, Clarence yapped around June's legs, wanting to go out. "No sweetie, not now. Mommy has to take care of Ivy."

"We can go out for a walk," I said. "I'm sure we'll be fine, especially with Clarence to protect us."

"But Detective Evans said..."

"He says lots of stuff. Sometimes, he acts like my dad, telling me what I can and can't do. It's not the first time he's done *that*, believe me. I grew up with a strict father, and I don't need to put up with that nonsense now. Let's go."

As we sauntered along the sidewalk, I noted the neighboring houses with closed drapes where normally windows would be open. I stopped in front of Larissa's house. "You told me you saw Wendall at Larissa's one night."

"Wendall? No, it was Bill. I mean Will. Oh…wait. Him. He's the one they found on the beach. That's right…he was at her house a few times when I stopped by. I don't remember exactly when. But he was sitting on her couch, drinking tea, reading." June stopped walking as Clarence sniffed around a tree.

"But what about *Will*? I'm just wondering because Will seems to be dating Alice, the bookstore owner. You gave me the impression he was *Larissa's* boyfriend."

"He *was*." June shook her head. "Maybe he's a two-timing rat, like Larissa's ex, Rick. You should talk to Steph. The kids are here for the weekend, going through Larissa's stuff. She probably knows more about her mom's boyfriends than I do."

"Could we stop in now, do you think?" I wanted to learn more about the Larissa/Will/Wendall triangle and how Alice was involved.

June tried to open the door of the two-story house. "That's odd. The door's locked." She pounded hard and rang the doorbell. Steph answered.

Clarence ran ahead, down the hall.

"Sorry, we're being extra cautious. Come on into the kitchen, Aunt June." Steph locked the door behind us. The women were packing dishes and kitchen utensils into cardboard boxes. They hugged June, their eyes puffy and red. "I'm so glad you're feeling better. You gave us quite a scare," Steph said.

"I hope you're checking your pills carefully," Emma chided. "You could have done serious damage to yourself, double dosing like that."

"Oh, I know, I know. I can't imagine how I managed to get mixed up," June said, waving her hand in the air. "I guess I wasn't thinking clearly. Too much on my mind."

"It's okay. It's not your fault," Emma said, patting June on the back. "We're all under a lot of strain, coping with Mom's death, especially considering the circumstances."

"Speaking of which, you just missed all the excitement," Steph announced. "The police were here this morning. When Emma and I were packing up the food cupboard, we found something." Steph stopped talking for a moment as if wondering whether she should share the information with me present.

"A contact lens—in the tea jar!" Emma exclaimed. She held up a ribbed glass jar with a silver lid.

"Larissa dropped a contact lens in her tea container? Why did you call the police about that?" I asked.

"Mom didn't wear contacts," Emma informed me. "Just reading glasses."

"The tea?" June scrunched up her face. "The night I found Larissa at the bottom of the stairs, there was a tea set on the coffee table. I thought that was strange."

Everyone looked at June with a puzzled expression, except Steph, who nodded. "Mom wouldn't use her good tea set for herself. She must have had company."

"But there was only one cup."

"Do you think the killer staged it that way?" Melissa suggested. "To make it look like she was alone?"

"But why? Why would someone do this to Mom?" Emma plugged in the kettle. I think we need a break."

As we sipped our coffee, I asked, "If we suppose that Larissa had a visitor before she fell down the stairs, could it have been Will Jenkins, the town coroner?"

Steph shook her head. "I don't think Will is a big tea drinker. He'd probably be drinking coffee with a shot of Baileys."

Since Steph still lived at home on weekends, I assumed she would know more about her mother's friends than the other siblings. "Was she seeing someone else?"

"Like that Wendall fellow?" June spoke up. "The one who drowned. He was here a couple of times when I stopped by."

Steph furrowed her brow. "Well, yes, she did tell me something about him. But it couldn't have been him. He was already dead."

Footsteps on the basement stairs caused heads to turn as Glen and Reggie entered the room. While Reggie grabbed a couple of beers, Glen kissed his aunt on the cheek. "Glad to see you're feeling yourself again."

"Thanks to my guardian angels, Ivy and Detective Evans, who got me to the hospital in time. Otherwise, I might not be here now."

Reggie gagged and coughed. "Went down the wrong way," he rasped.

"We were wondering who Mom had tea with the day she died," Emma said as Reggie joined the group at the table. "We've eliminated Will, her boyfriend. And Wendall, the guy who drowned. Apparently, Mom knew him."

"I never met him myself," Steph explained. "But I remember now. Mom said he was good friends with Will, but Will got jealous when he found Wendall here one night. They had an argument, even though Mom explained Wendall was just giving feedback on her writing. She was getting it ready to send to an agent."

"Her writing?" I interjected. "That's the connection! So, they met up in person to talk about their writing?"

"Yes, I guess so. Mom was also reading a manuscript. Paige Thornton, the children's author. She wrote a mystery about a hot tub murder. But..." Steph looked at me, as though a realization suddenly hit her. "Mom did say *you* were in the group. She said Wendall was critiquing another mystery novel—Alice Reading's, the bookstore owner. The one you told her needed a lot of work," Steph said, in an accusatory tone. "Wendall said Alice was upset about your comments, and she asked him for a second opinion."

I looked down at my hands. "I may have been a bit harsh with my critique of Alice's work. It was just meant to improve her writing, not to offend. You need to have a thick skin to be a writer. So, Wendall was seeing Larissa and Alice to discuss their writing? What type of writing did your mom do?"

"She just finished a mystery novel a while ago—her first attempt at writing a book. And she didn't think it was very good. But I liked it," Steph said with a sad smile.

"So did I," June added.

Steph sat back in her chair and tilted her head toward me. "Actually, it's kind of strange, now that I think about it. In Mom's book, one of the characters died in a car accident. The vehicle went off a bridge. It's like she predicted what happened to that writer—what was his name?" Everyone continued staring at Steph. "Eugene…somebody?"

I nearly knocked over my coffee mug. Steph had just made a connection between the deaths.

***

Wait till I tell Scott I have it all figured out. The accidents are connected to books.

Eugene's book, *Beach Bodies*, was found at the site of Wendall's accident. Larissa wrote a book describing Eugene's accident. Olivia's manuscript was about a woman who died from a fall down the stairs, after being drugged. And Alice's book contained a scene about a hunting accident, much like Philip Reece's death.

I was going through all the evidence in my head when June's muttering caught my attention.

"That good for nothing lowlife. I don't know what Emma sees in him." June waited for Clarence to sniff around a tree. "He'll be only too happy to get his hands on Larissa's money. Like mother, like daughter, I guess. Larissa never had any sense when it came to men. Marrying into the Mafia like it was some sort of royalty or something. I'm just glad she figured out what a piece of…excuse me…you know what…Rick was…and got rid of him…" June stopped talking. I stood frozen on the sidewalk, heart in my throat.

"Mafia?" I focused on Clarence, trying to control my hysteria.

"Yes, dear, the Mafia. Organized crime, the mob, gangsters. You've heard of them, haven't you?"

"I…I…yes. In movies and books." All this time, I had thought I was safe from the Mafia. And all along, in a cozy small town, just down the street, within a family home, lived a dangerous criminal. If he could go undetected, who else lurked close by?

I was right. These murders *were* all my fault. All this happened after the recent publication of my book of short stories. I'd exposed myself. Someone was watching, biding their time. They were taunting me, using mystery writers, mystery books, mystery fans. People connected to me were the accident victims—my neighbors, my best friend. That's why it all seemed so close to home. Who would be next? My family? Rick must have seen my photo and bio on the jacket cover of my book and matched it to the news article about Stefan, even though I had changed my looks and identity. He reported back to the organization, and they wanted to avenge Stefan's death. Maybe Rick suggested they get rid of his ex-wife as part of the deal.

There's no hiding from the Mafia. They'll be after me until I'm dead. But first, they'll make me suffer.

Chapter Thirty-Three

As Mike Juliano went over the physical evidence, Scott took notes in his spiral notebook. "We have several fingerprints on the book found at the lake. One set likely belongs to your friend, Ivy, who found it half-buried in the sand."

Scott picked up the evidence bag containing Eugene Forsythe's book, *Beach Bodies.* He considered the killer must be sending the police a message. "It can't be a coincidence this book was found on the beach where Wendall's body washed up a few days before. And then shortly after the 'drowning,' the author is killed? Have you read the book?"

"No. Do you think there's a clue in it?"

"Possibly. Maybe there's more to it."

"We'll take a closer look, then. We also found blond hairs in Eugene's Corvette. His fiancée has black hair."

"Eugene apparently had an eye for the ladies." Scott shrugged. "A cheating fiancé could be reason enough for sending a man off the edge of a bridge. Not to mention the huge inheritance."

Mike nodded. He held up a plastic bag containing a strip of white paper with colorful squares. "A search of Carter Loewen's garage came up with this."

"What is it?" Scott took a closer look.

"Litmus paper. They use it for testing water quality, but there's no pool or hot tub on Carter's property."

"Hmm…interesting. Hot tub?" Scott asked if Mike thought there was a connection to Olivia Walker's accident. Mike agreed there could be.

Scott's attention was diverted to the tiny object in another evidence bag. "Is that…a contact lens?" He held up the bag containing the blue contact. "Where was it found?"

Mike explained one of Larissa's children called the station a couple of hours ago, after they found it in a tea container. "Larissa didn't wear contacts."

Scott examined each of the pieces of evidence. There was also Ivy's book of short stories, found at the scene of her substitute's murder.

"Eugene was a published mystery writer," Scott pondered. "Olivia and Ivy, *intended* victims, are members of the mystery book club Wendall belonged to, and Ivy has also published mystery stories, one of which was murder by a paper shredder." He stopped to check Mike's reaction. Mike leaned across the desk, hanging on his every word. "Carter was an award-winning writer. Yesterday, I interviewed Phillip Reece's wife. Turns out he's been trying his hand at mystery writing. And Lindsay Hollinger? A self-published mystery author. Clark Helmsley and Floyd Weber? Mystery writers in the same online writers' group Ivy and Alice belong to."

"Hold on. You're saying the murders are all about mysteries?" Mike removed his hand from his chin and waved it in the air. "Is this about killing mystery writers with their own mystery novels? *Beach Bodies, Murder Collections*? But who would want to kill off a bunch of writers?"

"I'm going to the Walker's place to check on their pool maintenance company. See if there's any connection to the rest of this." Scott indicated the evidence on the table.

He drove out of town, the radio tuned to the local station, country music piping into his Camaro. He would have preferred the Lake Kipling station, with its mix of classic rock, contemporary pop, and country. At least up north, he'd get to hear something he liked now and then.

Trees lined the gravel road leading to the Walker residence, with an occasional clearing for farmland. As he approached the property with its long circular drive, Scott took in the manicured treed lawn and the gracious large red brick two-story Colonial home. Three vehicles sat in the driveway behind the partly open four-car garage—a BMW, a Dodge Ram truck, and a

Jeep. Scott marveled that some people could live so well. He recalled the tiny, boarded-up houses in the small communities up north, abandoned when their owners lost their jobs.

"Detective Scott Evans. Here to see Olivia," Scott flashed his ID to the middle-aged woman who answered the door wearing an apron. She ushered him in through the double-glass doors. In the center of the expansive entry hall with gleaming tiles stood a spectacular double wooden staircase.

"Detective Evans, how are you? It's nice to see you again." Olivia greeted him as she motioned for Scott to have a seat on one of the expensive-looking sofas in the living room. "I'm assuming you have more questions about Wendall or Phillip? Although I don't know what else I can tell you."

"There's been another suspicious death. Last night, Carter Loewen died of carbon monoxide poisoning in his garage."

Olivia gasped, her hand going to her mouth. "Oh, dear. How awful."

Scott nodded and took out the evidence bag from a folder. "Does this litmus paper look familiar? I wondered whether your pool maintenance company uses strips like this."

Olivia looked it over as he held it up. "No, ours are different." She gave him the name of their company. Intertwining her fingers, nicely manicured and polished nails contrasting with her jittery hands, she added, "There's something that's been bothering me, and I didn't know whether I should report it to the police or if it's just a strange coincidence. I was hoping to get Ivy's opinion, but she either didn't see any connection or hasn't read it yet. For whatever reason, she hasn't mentioned it."

"What is it?" Scott leaned forward.

"The way Larissa died—the fall down the stairs. I had a similar incident occur in a mystery novel I wrote called *Watch Your Step*. My murder victim suffers a fall, and her death is attributed to an accident. Until the coroner discovers she had drugs in her system. But it must be a coincidence. No one would know what happens in my book. It hasn't been published yet."

Scott asked what she meant about getting Ivy's opinion. Olivia explained she gave her friend a copy of the manuscript for feedback.

Scott decided he needed to let Ivy in on all the facts and get her to share everything she knew. They had always worked well together in the past. Maybe it was time to renew their partnership.

Chapter Thirty-Four

Scott escorted Ivy into her house to change for the fair. She dressed in jeans, white running shoes, and a white t-shirt with a gray cardigan. She wore her purple hoodie on top, unzipped. "I thought I'd better be prepared and layer, especially for tonight. It'll cool down quickly after dark."

In the car heading to the fairgrounds, they spoke at once. "Wait till you hear what I found out about..." Ivy said, as Scott said, "I've got some interesting new evidence..."

"You first," Scott insisted.

When Ivy told Scott she had been to Larissa's house, he stopped the car on the side of the road. "I don't believe this! I can't trust you for one minute. When I tell you to do something, I need you to listen. From now on, you don't investigate anything without me. Is that clear?"

"Yes, Dad." She rolled her eyes. "I'll do whatever you say from now on. Maybe you can get one of those child harnesses for me when we're out in public, so I don't run off and get lost. Do you want to stop at the baby store before the fair?"

Scott gave her a stern look, and she reciprocated. "This is no joke, Ivy. This is a murder investigation. And the killer is targeting mystery writers using plots from their books."

"Well, I had a similar thought. That methods from mystery novels were being used by the killer. And I'm glad you're letting me in on what's going on. I have lots of useful information to share with you. But we're both on the wrong track. The mystery writer angle is a red herring." She explained the murders were her fault. "Larissa's ex-husband is with the Mafia. What are the odds that a member of the Mafia used to live down the street from me? With my history? With Darko? Stefan? They're still out to get me. I don't know who it is, but there must be someone in their family, in their organization—someone who wants to implicate *me* in these murders, someone who wants me *dead* in the end. Killing Connie was just a way of taunting me. That poor woman."

"Your story, "My Life in Shreds", was left at the scene of her death. *You* were the target. Because you read and write mysteries." She needed to have all the facts.

"Oh!" She remained silent for a few seconds as she assimilated that information. "But...Don't you see? That's more proof that this is about getting to me. I'm the only victim who had their *own* book used against them. Right?"

"Why would they kill all these other people to get to you? It doesn't make sense. This is a complicated case, with one murder connecting to another," Scott argued. "If they wanted you dead, they wouldn't have messed around like they did, killing your substitute teacher. The Mafia know what they're doing. They don't make mistakes. They don't play games. That's why they get away with what they do."

"I disagree. They're human. And it's part of the curse," Ivy reminded him. "The Mafia's been part of my life since I was born. My parents, Darko, Stefan, the drug ring we uncovered when we were looking for Julia..."

Scott put his hand up to stop her. "I get it. The Mafia is a big part of your past. But I don't see how this case is Mafia-related. Not everything is about the Mafia, Ivy. And I'm sure they've got bigger fish to fry than you. Stefan's personal vendetta is over and done."

"But..."

"Let's just enjoy the day and see who we bump into today. I've got a feeling the killer's close to us, wandering around town with everyone else. Keep a watch out. She'll mess up sooner or later and give herself away."

"She?" Ivy whipped her head toward him.

"I meant they. It's just a pronoun."

"But you're obviously thinking it's a woman."

"I'm just saying it could be anyone." Scott wasn't discounting the possibility of a woman serial killer.

Cars were parked on all the streets surrounding the fairgrounds. "People take shelter amongst others, assuming it makes them safer. But after that attempt at the awards banquet hall, I'm not so sure that's wise," Scott said during our brisk ten-minute walk to the entrance gates. Scott's first stop was one of the food booths.

"How about hotdogs instead of hamburgers this time?" He was taken in by the smell of onions and mustard. Laden down with a tray full of drinks, fries, and hotdogs, Scott gestured toward the popcorn stand. "We have *got* to have caramel corn." He passed the food tray over to Ivy while he paid for a big bag, then headed toward the pizza booth.

"We'd better get going if we want to get a seat at the stadium. You can get more food later. Honestly, I don't think we're going to starve."

The stadium filled as Scott and Ivy climbed the wooden steps, finding an empty spot halfway up. Ivy squeezed in next to another couple while Scott stood, scanning the crowd seated in the stands. "There are a lot of people here."

Handing Ivy the food tray, Scott stomped on the wooden boards, bent to peer beneath the seats, and gazed up at the roof. When Ivy asked what he was doing, he explained. "I'm just hoping this stadium is sturdy. Do you know if any of your author friends wrote a book about a collapsing stadium?"

"I thought this was supposed to be a relaxing day out." Ivy sighed, shaking her head. "But you're looking for a murderer under every rock."

"The last date we went on could have turned out to be our *last* date," Scott reminded her. "You're connected to most of the accident victims. And there was an obvious attempt to kill you. You can't blame me for being extra cautious."

"That's exactly what I'm trying to tell you. *I'm* the one they're after. Using my story, ideas from other local authors I know. It all connects to *me*."

"Why would they go to this much trouble?"

"I don't know. To show they can kill people close to me? Maybe to *scare* me to death before they kill me?"

"I just might starve to death if you don't pass over the food." Scott grabbed a hotdog and bit into it. "Looks like the show's starting."

Drivers revved their engines as they entered the arena, and the audience applauded.

"And driving a 1983 Chevy Camaro, Number 006, is Willow Patterson, in memory of her fiancé, who loved cars. Willow is driving for Eugene Forsythe, who entered himself in this derby, sponsored by Patterson Hardware." Scott and Ivy turned to each other, mouths open in shock. The crowd went wild with applause as Willow roared into the arena.

The revving of engines and the crowd's cheers made conversation impossible. Cars locked bumpers, spun each other around, bashed each other into logs, and got entangled in a big mass of metal. Smoke puffed from engines, sparks flew, and tires spun.

Partway through the show, Ivy said she was going to the washroom. Scott, engrossed in the derby, simply nodded.

When one of the vehicles burst into flames, Scott thought she was missing out on all the action, then he spotted her. There was a sense of both concern and excitement in the crowd as the fire shot into the air, the car barreling toward a woman in front of the grandstand.

It was Ivy. She stood frozen.

"Whoa!" cried the spectators. As a crew rushed to extinguish the fire, the vehicle rolled backwards over the logs and came to a halt. Smoke and chemicals mingled in the air as the car was sprayed down, and the driver walked away, arms triumphantly up in the air as the crowd cheered even though he was out of the running.

Ivy climbed the stairs and sat beside Scott, her face white. "Did you see that?"

"Everyone saw that. Do you always have to be the center of all the action? Trying to steal the attention away from the poor driver?" He hoped his joke would calm her nerves. "Next trip to the bathroom, I'm going with you." He shook his head in bewilderment, wondering how she managed to always be involved in disasters.

"I'm accident-prone. Cursed. Don't worry. I always seem to land on my feet. It's the people around me that get hurt." One by one, the vehicles dropped out. Willow seemed to be the crowd's favorite, with everyone rooting for her. When it was over, she emerged victorious to the crowd's roars and a standing ovation. Riley joined her in the center of the ring, pumping her hand up in the air as she accepted her trophy with the other.

"Wow, I wasn't expecting that," Scott said. "I had no idea Willow knew her way around cars. Did you?"

"She's a lot tougher than she looks."

They were on their way out of the stadium when Scott noticed Ivy wasn't wearing her purple hoodie.

"I took it off and set it underneath my seat. I was getting too hot with the sun shining down." She turned around, climbing while everyone else descended the wooden steps.

"It's not there," Ivy groaned as she came back down.

Scott assured her they would check the Lost and Found later. "Surely no one would steal it. It's too recognizable with that Western logo on the back."

"A lot of people from the area went to Western. It wouldn't stand out. But you're right, it'll probably end up in the Lost and Found.

They walked through the fairgrounds, taking in the excitement. When Scott suggested the Ferris wheel, Ivy said, "You can't be serious?"

"I know perfectly well you don't like heights. But it's not that high. And it's completely closed in." He pointed out there were no feet dangling, and no one was screaming. Ivy shook her head, shielding her eyes from the sun as she gazed upwards. "I think it'd be fun, but, if you're too *chicken*... Come on, Ivy, let me take you higher."

Ivy gave his arm an affectionate punch. "Take me higher? Does that line work with other women? Because it won't work on me. And I'm not chicken. I just don't feel like going up and down and spinning around in the air."

"What *will* work with you?" Scott's arms encircled Ivy's waist, his eyes locking on hers. "Because I have lots of other lines I'm dying to try out on you."

"Maybe you shouldn't waste them on me. I don't want you to be disappointed."

"I won't be. Not as long as we're together." Scott bent to kiss her, but she turned away, saying a public display wouldn't win him any points.

"Come on, we're at a fair. We *have* to go on rides. How about the kiddie rides? Or is that too scary for you?"

"Maybe the Ferris wheel wouldn't be so bad," she acquiesced.

Once they were securely fastened into their seats, Scott wrapped his arm around Ivy. She gazed into his eyes. "I can do this. I'm not *chicken*."

"Look at this view," Scott urged Ivy as her hand gripped his other arm.

She seemed to be calm as the enclosed gondola rotated and even pointed out what she saw—bumper cars, the arena, tented booths, kiddie rides, the Zipper, the petting zoo.

And then she froze as they came to a stop at the very top of the wheel.

"It's over? Good." She let out a huge sigh. After waiting for all of thirty seconds, she asked why people weren't getting off. Scott told her to be patient, but the wheel remained motionless.

"I want to get off!" Ivy shrieked in a voice he hardly recognized. "Why aren't we moving? Get me down," she whimpered, burying her face in his shoulder. "Please, please, please. I need one of my pills—in my purse, the inside pocket."

As Scott found a vial of anti-anxiety pills and assured Ivy they'd be on the ground in no time, a small crowd gathered below, and other riders hollered, wanting to be let down.

To get Ivy's mind off the fact that she was dangling in the sky, he touched her cheek, and his lips brushed hers. He spoke softly, telling her about his children, providing her with little anecdotes. She relaxed, and her breathing slowed, her face and hand against his chest as he tried to steady his own heartbeat.

After a while, the wheel moved, and people cheered.

"A bit of a power glitch. All fixed now." A man with a 'Ride Supervisor' tag apologized and handed out strings of tickets as people dismounted. "Free rides for everyone."

CHAPTER THIRTY-FOUR

Scott showed the supervisor his ID. "Any idea what caused the power glitch?"

"In my thirty years with the midway, I've never seen a freak accident like this. Someone set a drink on top of one of the electric motors, and the vibration toppled it over. But the circuit breaker did what it was supposed to do. It's all good now."

"An accident?" Ivy's voice trembled.

Scott thanked the man and accepted his free tickets. "Maybe we could try out those kiddie rides," he quipped, leading Ivy away from the wheel.

"How about bumper cars? Just try not to ram me too hard."

"Don't worry, I'll be gentle with you."

They slid into their separate vehicles, and Ivy moved forward to find herself stuck along the wall. Scott came directly at her, hitting Ivy from the side and dislodging her. She lurched forward, then straightened around to counterattack. Scott dodged her as she aimed for him head-on. In doing so, he was sideswiped by another bumper car and shoved against the wall himself. Ivy laughed as she headed for him again.

A sudden realization hit him. They had spent the last couple of hours being entertained by car crashes. Although Ivy was the one who suggested both the demolition derby and the bumper cars, it occurred to him that those activities might bring back bad memories for her—memories of her husband's fatal car crash and that of her parents. Yet she appeared to be having a good time. And then there was Willow. It must have taken a lot of courage for her to take Eugene's place in the derby, right on the heels of his car accident.

Chapter Thirty-Five

As they strolled through the kiddie section, Ivy enjoyed watching the little kids on the rides. They stopped next to the train, Ivy saying she wouldn't mind going on it. "It reminds me of happy times with the kids. And Jim."

"I think you have to have kids *with* you to be allowed on," Scott said. "Do you want me to see if I can round some up?" With a serious expression planted on his face, he surveyed the area to see if there were any unattended kids. "What about those two?" he joked. "Will they do?"

Ivy laughed and shook her head. "I don't think it will look good on your police record if you abduct a couple of toddlers so we can get on the kiddie rides."

"Yeah." He stroked his stubble. "Probably not a good idea."

"Hi, Paige," Ivy waved to her friend, who was with her husband, Matt, and their children. Paige smiled and waved, then lowered her head and kept moving, with one child sitting in the stroller and the other standing on the bench seat behind.

As Scott and Ivy strolled through the midway, eerie music and a neon sign flashing 'Enter if you Dare', surrounded by ghosts and skeletons attracted Scott. "How about it? Do you dare?"

When Ivy responded she hated haunted houses, Scott teased her. "Chicken?" She shook her head. "Come on, don't tell me you're afraid of ghosts? First rides, and now ghosts? What aren't you afraid of? Look, there are kids going in. How scary can it be?" Scott flashed her one of his irresistible smiles and took her by the hand. "No way are we going to miss out on the haunted house. Look, Valerie's running it."

Valerie gestured to them. "It's a lot of fun. I'm here volunteering, along with a friend of mine."

"Sorry," Ivy voiced her aversion to haunted houses. "I had a bad experience with a haunted house a long time ago. Of course, that was a real haunted house. I guess you could say I've dealt with my share of ghosts and skeletons in the closet."

Valerie said she understood. "What about you, Detective Evans? Care for a scare?"

Scott mulled it over. "Thanks, but it won't be any fun if I can't scare Ivy silly," he joked, giving Ivy a look to let her know she was the reason he was missing out on a good time in the haunted house. "She's chicken." His comment brought out the response he wanted. Ivy rolled her eyes and said if it was that important to him, she'd go through the stupid house. Valerie laughed and said she'd let them have a private tour.

Passing through the arched wooden doorway, hand in hand, they entered the nearly pitch-dark house. Streamers hanging from the ceiling brushed against their heads as they stumbled through the corridors. Creepy music from the Halloween movie playing in the background and screams and laughter of the ghouls and monsters that popped out, added to the fun, as far as Scott was concerned, but Ivy stiffened next to him. "It's not real." His lips brushed her ear.

She responded that she was okay as long as he was with her.

That was until they entered a smoke-filled room. Tombstones, with ghosts floating above and skeletons rising from graves, stood behind wrought-iron fencing with skulls adorning the gate posts. A mausoleum in the background, the shadow of bare trees cast over it, with a full moon above and bats overhead, completed the cemetery. The wailing of the dead permeated the room along with the fog.

"I have to get out of here," Ivy cried, rushing ahead to the next doorway.

"It's stuck." Scott pushed, but it didn't budge. They were trapped, with the fog thickening.

Ivy coughed. "I can't...breathe."

Scott led her back the way they came. The door wouldn't open when Ivy frantically pulled the handle. "We're trapped!" Ivy wailed, coughing into her sleeve. Scott pushed against the door, and it unbolted.

They stumbled into the fresh air. Seeing Ivy's face drained of color gave Scott a fright. Holding her tight and rubbing her back, he said, "It's okay. You're safe. I'm sorry I made you go through that. I didn't realize…"

"No. I'm okay," Ivy whispered. "And I am *not* chicken." After a few deep breaths, she added, "I would have made it through if the stupid door wasn't stuck."

They informed Valerie about the door malfunction. "Oh no, are you okay?" she asked, touching Ivy's arm.

As Scott led Ivy away from the midway, he remarked, "I guess any further rides or attractions are out of the question. You're white as a ghost. How about we get some food into you?"

"Is that supposed to be funny?" Then she noticed the candy floss booth. "I guess some sugar wouldn't hurt."

Scott purchased a bag of pink and blue cotton candy. "I'm going to need some grease, though. Sugar doesn't quite do it for me." He indicated the pizza vendor again, several booths down, then something else caught his eye. "Is that a beer tent?"

They were sharing a large pizza when Alice and Will joined them in the tent. "Thank goodness you didn't get killed at school! But your poor substitute. And did you hear about Carter?" Alice asked. When Ivy confirmed they did, Alice continued. "It's the strangest thing. One of the judges from last night contacted the rest of us and said he'd read an unpublished manuscript that described a murder by carbon monoxide poisoning in a closed garage. Someone tampered with the car, causing the victim to be trapped in the running vehicle. It was written by Clark Helmsley, who fell off a cliff last month."

Ivy's cup slipped from her hand, spilling beer down Scott's left thigh. She grabbed some napkins. "Oh, no! I'm sorry," she gasped, patting him down until most of the wetness was absorbed.

"The police will likely be looking into Carter's death as another possible homicide," Will suggested. Scott simply nodded, not wanting to give away any information in front of Alice. To Ivy, he said, "I'll get you another beer. You'll be parched, since you spilled most of it on me."

"Well, I am a bit dry, unlike you." A smile formed on her lips.

"Will, want to join me at the bar?"

When he had Will on his own, Scott asked what he knew about the deaths in other parts of the county.

"Clark Helmsley's body showed signs of a struggle—some bruising on his arms and chest—that could have been inflicted just prior to his fall. He was found lying on his back. It's been ruled inconclusive, but there's definitely doubt, especially in light of the other accidents." Will added, "But I'm sure you're already aware of that. And, of course, you know about Phillip Reece's gunshot wounds?"

There were two wounds, one from a distance and one at close range, but that hadn't been made public yet. "Obviously not a hunter. Whoever pulled the trigger knew who they were pointing the gun at. Off the record, what are your thoughts about all of this?" Scott asked.

"I think since we've never had this sort of situation before, we should be looking at *all* accidents as potential homicides or attempted murder."

"One killer?" Scott wanted the coroner's opinion. He himself suspected it was too much for one person to carry out. "Two? Or a group?"

"Hard to believe only one person could be involved, but it's possible. The deaths are spread out enough; the county's not that big. Conceivably, the killer could be traveling around choosing a victim every few days. If you want my opinion, I'd be looking for a male, young to middle-aged," Will said, as they carried their refreshments back to their table. "Someone strong with a lot of mechanical knowledge. And by the way, I'm sorry about Alice. I let it slip about the murder at the school, and then she got hysterical and asked if it was Ivy or Olivia, so I had to tell her the truth to calm her down."

Ivy and Alice were engaged in their own conversation when the men set down the drinks. "It's just hitting too close to home," Ivy warned her friend. "The killer is targeting writers and people we know. I hope you're being careful."

"Surely you don't think he'd be after us just because we're writers?" Alice asked.

"Or she."

Alice sipped her beer. "You really…think…a woman…could be…capable of this?" she managed in spite of her coughing fit.

"Most serial killers are men." Will offered his opinion. "I don't see a woman carrying out all these accidents."

Scott didn't voice his thoughts.

Not all, but maybe some of the accidents.

Once they finished their drinks, Alice said, "We're going to see the exhibits in the hall. I entered the Arts Council short story contest. Of course, I didn't place, but I want to read the winning entries."

Once Will and Alice left, Scott raised his eyebrows. "You didn't happen to enter the short story contest, did you? I get the feeling Alice wouldn't be happy to lose to you."

The sun was setting, but the crowds weren't thinning. As they jostled their way past the colorful booths, Scott pointed out the various games. He stopped in front of the shooting gallery, laid down tickets, took the gun out of its holder, and aimed, hitting each target, sending off sounds and movement with each shot.

"I'm impressed," Ivy praised Scott as she cuddled the prize she'd been eyeing. "Tom's going to love you," she said to the stuffed Maine Coon.

"Okay, your turn."

"It's hardly fair. You've had a lot of training. I'm not very good with guns."

Scott coaxed her till she grabbed the gun. She shot wildly, working her way around the gallery, missing the first half dozen targets. "Not as easy as it looks," Scott teased. "Maybe we should check out the kiddie games."

Ivy gave him an 'I'll show you' look and tried again, this time methodically. One by one, with her hand steady and her eyes focused, she hit the targets dead on. "And that, Detective, is how it's done," she boasted, lowering the gun.

He stared at the woman beside him with fresh eyes. The Cheryl he once knew—young, bold, sassy—was gone. Still there under the surface, but there was so much more to her now. To look at her, you'd never suspect she'd lived through tragedies and horrors most people couldn't even imagine. Ivy Rose was a sweet, kind, gentle woman, with two kids she had birthed and raised and a school full of kids she thought of as her own. She was vulnerable. A child at heart herself. He'd seen that side of her several times in the last week. But there was another side to her. She was also strong. Resilient. Tough. Unexpectedly so. Not to be underestimated.

Chapter Thirty-Six

A crowd gathered around the haunted house as Scott and Ivy wandered through the midway. Valerie coughed and sputtered while a uniformed police officer stood by.

Scott showed his ID to the officer. "What's going on?"

"The fog machine malfunctioned when some kids were inside," the young cop answered, indicating the smoke billowing out the doors. "Came out coughing and complaining. Valerie put up a closed sign and went in to investigate the problem. She got trapped inside."

"Who called the police?"

"I did. It's a good thing I came back when I did," Valerie's friend had his arm around her. "I couldn't find Valerie, and then I heard screaming and banging on the emergency door. She could have been killed. Especially with her asthma. If someone's tampered with the equipment…"

"When the smoke clears, do a thorough search. See if there's any sign this was caused intentionally," Scott advised the officers. Turning to Valerie, he said, "Maybe you should get checked out by a doctor."

When Valerie left with her friend, Scott asked Ivy if she remembered him.

She answered, "Yes, he was with her at the banquet last night. And he talked to me at the book festival. Why?"

"I'm just wondering if either of them is a writer. If someone intentionally rigged this accident, was it intended to kill one of them?"

"Carbon monoxide? Again? If that's the case, someone must have a good knowledge of mechanics and science to cause the recent accidents."

Scott agreed and said he wanted to take a quick tour through the house.

He didn't need to convince Ivy to wait outside. "Why don't you go on to the agricultural hall, and I'll meet you there in an hour?"

"Are you sure you can let me out of your sight, *Dad*?"

Chapter Thirty-Seven

Blue Water Writes:

Stop by the writing exhibit at the fair today. My story took 1st place! Ahhh! Check it out. I still can't believe I won.

Hey, if you're at the fairgrounds today, my poem's on display. I placed third. Not too shabby.

The Writer

Is it just me, or does everything in Blue Water revolve around writing? More awards. None for me. Why I bother to submit anything is beyond me. It's all anonymous, they say. So the judging is fair. But I know better. It's who you know and what you're willing to do.

The Blue Water Arts Council can go take a flying leap. Handing out grants and prize money to local creatives who contribute to the community. *I* contribute. What the hell did I ever get from them? Not good enough for the snooty artsy crowd.

I've been told enough times that the way to improve my writing is to read more and to examine successful writers' work. As if I don't read enough. Ha! Between reading the best sellers, the local authors, literary magazines, critiquing, beta reading, reviewing, and all the online writing groups, it's a wonder I find time to write at all.

The agricultural hall is empty compared to the midway. I wander over to the photography, art, and literature section. Not much of a crowd in this area. Hmm. There's more interest in the flower and crop displays.

Okay, let's see what's so great about these. I take the time to read the top three entries in the short story category. And I don't get it. Complete and utter hogwash. The winning story makes no sense whatsoever. Some sort of literary masterpiece, according to the judges. Or someone drunk out of their mind scribbling whatever pops into their head, if you ask me. The other two aren't much better.

"So, what do you think of the winning stories?" A voice from behind startles me.

Turning, I smile. "Brilliant! Wish I could write like that."

Chapter Thirty-Eight

When Scott caught up with Ivy, she was at the poetry entries, absorbed in reading. "I figured I'd find you at the writing exhibits."

She turned to face him and gasped. "You found it!"

"Inside the Haunted House."

Ivy took the purple hoodie from his hands, looked it over, and checked out the tags. "It's not mine."

"What makes you say that?" If Ivy's hoodie was missing and he found the exact same hoodie in the Haunted House, where she had been earlier…

"It's a size Medium. I'm a Large. And I wrote my name on the tag in marker after the last time I lost it." she stated. "And besides, Detective, you saw me wearing my hoodie when we got to the stadium, but not when we left. So that's where I lost it."

That made perfect sense. Except, someone could have taken it from the stadium and left it at the Haunted House. He decided it was best to take it into evidence.

"It's almost 9:15. We'd better get going if we want to get seats for the fireworks," Ivy said. As they headed back to the stands, Celia and Dylan waved to them.

"I didn't realize Celia and Dylan were dating," Ivy whispered as her friends walked arm in arm toward the fireworks. "I wasn't even aware they knew each other outside of Murder Club."

"And are either of them married?" When Ivy said they were both divorced, Scott whispered back, "Then I guess they're free to date whoever they want.

Like you and I."

The stands were nearly full even though it was thirty minutes to start time. They sat near the bottom, next to Celia and Dylan. "My hoodie!" Ivy exclaimed. "We forgot to check the Lost and Found. And I'm getting cold."

To Scott's surprise, Celia, on the pretext of going to the washroom, joined him when he said he'd go check the Lost and Found before the fireworks began.

"There's something that's been bothering me," Celia said as they hurried to the booth. "I didn't say anything before, and maybe I should have, but since there's been another death, I think you should know."

"What is that?"

"You have to believe me when I say I'm not involved in any way," she prefaced her confession. "But I have been withholding information."

Scott stopped walking. "Whatever it is, you need to tell me now. Withholding evidence is a crime."

The lights from the fairground illuminated the fear in her eyes. "But I didn't do anything. I just thought it was odd. Like I said, I probably should have mentioned something before, but I didn't know what it meant, if anything." She proceeded to tell him she critiqued a manuscript Wendall wrote.

"I see. And?"

"It was pretty good, actually. But he didn't want his wife to know. She belittled his writing, so he hid it from her. He was going to tell her he had completed a book when she accused him of having an affair, but he wasn't sure which was worse—having her think he was wasting his time writing or seeing someone else."

Scott was flabbergasted to think Claire might prefer a cheating husband to a writer husband. He encouraged Celia to continue as they neared the Lost and Found.

"The strange thing is Wendall grew up on a farm, and one of the murders in his book was made to look like accidental poisoning inside a manure tank. When I heard about Floyd Weber's accident, I thought it was a weird coincidence. But then I heard about Lindsay Hollinger and her electrocution in the bathtub. It was a scene right out of the book *I* wrote." She stopped to check Scott's reaction.

"Did anyone else read your book or Wendall's?" Scott's brow furrowed, as he tried to connect writers to manuscripts.

"Riley Patterson beta read mine. I don't know if he read Wendall's. But Wendall did tell me something else that I've been trying to understand."

"What is that?" Maybe Celia would make the connections for him.

"Well, he said Alice asked him to read over her manuscript. According to Wendall, Alice wasn't happy with the critique she got from her partner, that's Ivy, so she asked him if he would read it. He said he tried to be as sensitive as possible, but he wasn't drawn into her story."

"So, Alice was getting negative feedback?"

"Yes, I guess so. But the thing that really bothers me is she wrote about a hunting accident. Then when I heard about Phillip Reece, I didn't know what to think. And that teacher, Connie Schultz? Her death was right out of Ivy's *Murder Collections*. How is it possible that four accidental deaths in the county are connected to books written by people in my book club?"

Scott told her to hold on for a minute as he approached the attendant at the Lost and Found. "Did anyone happen to turn in a hoodie like this one?"

The attendant looked through a shelf. "Yes, here it is." It was a size Large, identical in every other way to the one he held in his hands.

Carrying both hoodies, he accompanied Celia to the stadium. "So why were you hesitant to tell me about the possible connections between writers and victims?"

"I guess I felt you might think I was somehow involved. Which I'm *not*," she reiterated. "I thought it might incriminate me, since I wrote about the electrocution before it happened. And then there's Eugene." Her voice changed when she said his name, sadness creeping in mixed with a darker emotion. "Eugene and I were, you know, seeing each other. Until I found out he was cheating on me. I could have killed him myself. But I *didn't*."

Scott considered how Eugene could be cheating on Celia when he was engaged to Willow. "I thought Eugene and Willow were…"

"They were. But Eugene and I were in a relationship, too. Or I thought we were. I understood he was engaged to Willow, but I kept thinking he'd leave her for me. I even told Willow that Eugene wasn't being faithful, although I didn't give her any particulars. When I found out he was having sex with other women, I was hurt. And mad. Especially when I found out about him and Alice. The final straw was when Alice told me what happened between Eugene and Paige."

When Alice had talked to Scott about Eugene's flirtations, she was upset by his behavior, but insisted there was nothing going on between herself and Eugene. Why did she lie?

There's more drama in this small town than on June's TV programs.

Just in time to see the first of the fireworks set off, Scott and Celia returned to their seats. Olivia and Cliff had joined their group. Placing Ivy's hoodie over her shoulders, Scott greeted Ivy's best friend and her husband.

So, the whole gang's here.

He'd been right—everyone was out wandering around Port Ripley in plain view. Potential victims and the killer.

"Oh, thank goodness. You found it." Ivy wiggled her arms into her hoodie. "It's getting chilly." He responded by pressing his body as close to hers as possible, his arm around her, her head resting on his shoulder. At this point, he had no concern about what anyone thought of their relationship. The air resounded with big bangs, and the sky lit up in a wondrous color. He was exactly where he wanted to be.

Chapter Thirty-Nine

"It's been an eventful day at the fair. Always exciting to be with you, Ms. *Ivy Rose*," Scott stated as he walked me to my door.

"I told you. Bad things happen to me all the time. I'm cursed."

Scott was right behind me, arms around my waist, his body pressed against mine, lips on my neck as I fumbled with the key. How was I going to manage to confine him to the couch?

"So, I guess you're staying over again?" I finally inserted the key right way up, and we spilled into the hall. Scott closed the door with his foot and unzipped my hoodie from behind, sliding the sleeves down, while continuing to work his mouth down my neck. He spun me around, his mouth claiming mine. We were locked in a kiss when the ringing of my home phone made me jump.

"Leave it," Scott murmured. He kissed me again, his fingers undoing the buttons of my gray cardigan. The phone kept ringing. Scott's lips moved down to my neck, but the shrill sound continued. "You might as well get it. Must be pretty damn important if they won't give up."

I tried to catch my breath as I answered. "Hello? Yes, he's right here." I listened, then said, "You're kidding! "Oh! Oh, my! Yes, of course, I'll tell him. Thank goodness it all worked out the way it did. I can't imagine how you must feel. Keep a good eye on her."

Scott heaved a huge sigh. "What happened now?"

"It's Alice. She got home from the fireworks and Valerie told her what happened at the Haunted House. Valerie's fine, but Alice is really upset. She's sure someone tried to kill her daughter."

When Scott asked why she was so certain it was an attempt on Valerie's life, Ivy explained. "Carter Loewen's manuscript that won the prize last night? Alice read it, being one of the judges. She said there was a scene where teenagers set up a haunted house at a Halloween party. They used a fog machine."

"Don't tell me. Someone got killed."

"Yes, they were overcome by the fumes. All six kids. Victims of a serial killer, killing for fun—someone they knew from school. This town is cursed."

We sat side by side in the living room, discussing Valerie's lucky escape. "I don't know about you, but I'm tired," I said. "Maybe we should get some sleep and talk tomorrow."

With another heavy sigh, Scott agreed. "I'm just going to do a bit of work first. I'll be right back. I need to get my notebook out of the car." He shouted as he stepped out. "Hello, June! How are you?"

I picked my hoodie off the bench and slipped it onto a heavy plastic hanger in the closet. Something was in the pocket. I remembered. It was the note someone left me last Saturday at the Book Festival. The note that asked if I had ever killed anyone in real life.

But wait, that wasn't right. I had disposed of that note.

Sticking my hand inside, I pulled out the paper and unfolded it as a sense of dread swept over me.

Which method do you prefer? A bullet through the heart or a shove off a cliff?

My world collapsed, and so did I, slumping onto the tiled floor, my head hitting the corner of the table on my way down.

"Ivy! Ivy! Wake up!" Someone called my name, but it wasn't really *my* name, was it? Who was Ivy? I faded further into the blackness. "Ivy? Are you okay? Ivy!"

Images from long ago flashed through my brain. From when I used to be Lana.

Lana, taking the gun out of her purse. Darko, locking eyes with her, hands on the barrel, saying, "Careful with that. You might shoot me by accident."

The danger of loving a criminal. The fear. The terror. For her unborn child and for herself.

"No, no, I won't shoot you by accident," Lana, promising as she pulled the trigger. The disbelief in his eyes as he crumpled to the ground. And the horror of it.

Another flash from another life.

Stefan, pointing the gun at her. Brent, distracting him for a moment as he cried for his mom. Cheryl, knocking the gun out of his hand, kicking Stefan again and again and again.

The fear for her life. The anger. The outrage. For her dead husband and her kidnapped child.

Rolling Stefan over the side of the cliff. The scream as he went over the edge. The shock of it.

Something warm ran down my face. The sound of a siren assailed my ears. All the while, someone kept calling for Ivy.

Who is Ivy?

Chapter Forty

I awoke in an unfamiliar place. The sounds, the smells, the feel of the bed—they were wrong. "Where…?" My tongue refused to move, a dead weight, the taste in my mouth sour.

I forced my eyes fully open. Scott held my hand, looking like he'd lost his best friend. Why was he so old-looking? And where was Jim?

"Ivy? Wake up, Ivy," Scott pleaded. "Keep your eyes open."

Ivy? Was it Christmas? Someone entered the room, dressed in white. An angel? Was I dead? No, I wouldn't be in heaven. I blinked to clear my vision, and hopefully, my mind with it.

"She's waking again," Scott said through the fog as the woman in white approached.

"Hello, Ivy. How are you doing?" she asked. "I see you're trying to wake up. That's good. Can you squeeze my finger?"

I just wanted to sleep. *So* tired. It was too much effort to squeeze anything. "No, no, don't close your eyes, Ivy," Scott begged. "It's time to wake up. Come on, Ivy. Wake up, Ivy."

Why did Scott keep calling me Ivy?

I tried to remember what happened before I ended up here. The woman squeezed my hand, prompting me to squeeze back. "Good, that's good," she praised. "Now, let's get you sitting up."

My body folded in two as she cranked me to a sitting position. Through the slits in my eyes, Scott sat in a chair, hands clasped as though in prayer, forehead resting on his fingers. "Scott…" I wanted to see him smile.

He looked up. "Ivy? Are you okay?" He looked like he could use some sleep himself. What was wrong with him? I'd never seen him so…tired. Was that gray in his hair? And his face was…wrinkly? As he leaned closer, the woman in white said she needed to ask me some questions. Scott nodded and moved away.

The woman asked, "Can you tell me your name?"

Why was that such a hard question? "Ivy?" It seemed to be a good guess.

"Yes, Ivy. That's good. And what's your last name?"

"Evans." It was the only last name that came to mind. The woman looked at Scott with a concerned expression.

"Okay. And your children's names?"

"Brent." That was an easy one. Then I remembered. Brent had been taken. "Where's Brent? Is he okay?" The woman gently restrained me as I attempted to jump over the bed rail.

"Everything's fine. I talked to Brent," Scott reassured me. "And Jamie. I let them know you're getting checked out, and I'm looking after you."

"Jamie?" Were the kids with Jim?

"She's worried, but I told her the doctor said it was a mild concussion, and you should be back to normal soon." Scott wasn't making sense. I closed my eyes against the madness.

"Ivy, can you tell me where you live?" The woman persisted with the stupid questions.

"In a house. We bought a new house."

"Where is your house, Ivy? What town is it in?"

"Lake Kipling."

The woman spoke in a quieter voice and brought a glass of water to my mouth. "It's okay. It's not unusual to be confused with a head injury."

"When will she get her memory back?" Scott said in a hushed tone.

"Hard to say, but let's try to keep her awake."

The woman patted my arm. "Why don't we see if we can get you some Jello or pudding, and maybe a few cookies. Would you like that?"

"Cookies?" I perked up. "Chocolate?"

"Yes, I'll be right back. Keep talking to her."

Then there was just Scott. I smiled at him. He smiled back, holding my hand. Everything was going to be okay.

"You had me worried. When I came back inside, you were unconscious on the floor, and your head was bleeding. I called 911."

I touched the gauze on my head. "Why was my head bleeding?"

"You fell and hit your head on the entrance table. Do you remember *anything*? I went to the car to get my notebook so I could record what happened at the Haunted House."

Haunted House? Right. I had visited it the summer my parents died. The house in Croatia where Mom and Dad attended a party years ago. The start of the curse on my family. How did Scott know about that?

Scott kept talking nonsense. "At first, I thought maybe someone was already in the house when we got home, and they hit you on the head. I did a quick search while I waited for the ambulance, and there was no sign of anyone. The back doors were all locked. And I was at the front, and no one came or went that way."

The woman returned with an apple juice, a chocolate pudding, and a couple of large chocolate chip cookies. A reward for answering her questions. "Push the button if you need anything else. The doctor will be back to check on you in the morning."

"Eat. You haven't had any sugar for hours." Scott unwrapped the food.

"What time is it?" Struggling to keep my eyelids open, I assumed it was the middle of the night. "I want to go home."

"Almost midnight. You were out of it for ten minutes, woke up a bit, then slipped away again for five minutes. You had me scared. I'm glad to see you're feeling better." Hands on my face, he bent over and kissed me, his tongue parting my lips.

I pulled away and slapped his face. "Where's Jim? Why isn't he here?"

Chapter Forty-One

ou don't need to keep fussing." The doctor discharged me in the morning, saying someone should stay with me for the next twenty-four hours. I wasn't sure why Scott brought me to a strange house, but I trusted him. As long as he didn't try to kiss me again.

Scott fluffed up pillows and showed me how to use the remote control, pulling a throw over me. He brought peppermint tea and Tylenol. "What kind of cookies do you want? Are you warm enough?" He turned on the fireplace. "I'll get something delivered for lunch. What do you want to eat, Ivy?"

Scott constantly asking what I needed was getting on my nerves. My head hurt, my brain was foggy, and all I wanted was to sleep. But Scott seemed afraid to let me doze. He kept bothering me every time I closed my eyes. I wished he would explain.

Why is he calling me Ivy? Whose house is this? Where are Jim and the kids?

Tylenol took the edge off my headache, and the fire's warmth relaxed me. Then I remembered something. The note. I lifted my head. Scott sat at my feet, reading.

I eased myself off the couch and shuffled to the bathroom, feeling his eyes on my back. The face in the mirror had nearly given me a heart attack when I saw it earlier. Scott tried to explain my memory loss, but I hadn't really believed him until he made me look in the mirror. The strange old lady staring back convinced me this was all a nightmare. Short blond hair, blue eyes, on the chubby side—

That can't be me.

I needed to find that note. Wasn't I in the entrance hall when I read it?

I crept down the hall, eyes on the floor, peering under the entry table and bench. Scott glanced up. I removed my hoodie from the closet, put it on, and felt around in the pockets. "Just a bit chilly still," I lied. No note anywhere. I didn't know why, but the note was important.

"Are you looking for this? It was on the floor beside you last night." Scott held up a piece of paper.

Which method do you prefer? A bullet through the heart or a shove off a cliff?

Feeling a rush of anxiety, I held onto the table. Scott helped me back to the couch. "It's okay. I'm not going to let anyone hurt you," he promised, stroking my head. Don't worry. I'm not letting you out of my sight."

Someone *knew*. "I think it's someone from my past."

"You mean someone who knows about Darko and Stefan?"

My mouth flew open. None of this made sense. I had never told anyone but Jim the truth. Only he knew about Darko's shooting and how Stefan was unjustly serving time in prison for his son's death. Was Stefan after me, threatening to shoot me or shove me off a cliff? Was he out of prison? Was someone else doing his dirty work for him? "Brent! Where's Brent?"

"Brent's fine. He's in Oakridge." Scott patted my back. "It's probably a coincidence. Clark died from a fall off a cliff. Phillip was shot."

Whatever blood had still been reaching my brain drained right out. I had no idea what that was about. Was something wrong with Scott? He was talking crazy. I put my arms around myself, shielding myself from the thought of Stefan out there somewhere.

"I do think it's a clear threat, though." Scott sat closer and rubbed my shoulders. "We're going to have to be careful. But I think I'm closing in on the killer. It won't be long now."

I stiffened. Scott was good at his job. It was only a matter of time until he discovered the *whole* truth. Best to get some rest while Scott was there keeping watch over me. I lay down and closed my eyes, knowing I would need all my strength to get through this. Whatever *this* was.

Chapter Forty-Two

The smell of pizza brought me fully awake.

"You should eat." Scott placed a plate in front of me, and I picked it up obediently. "How are you feeling? You've got some color in your cheeks."

"Better. I wouldn't mind getting some fresh air after lunch, though." My eyes focused on the sun shining through the bay window. "Can we go for a short walk?"

"Sure. There's something else I want to do. I've been going over my notes and thinking about Wendall. The book you found on the beach last week—Eugene's *Beach Bodies*. I had assumed it was left there intentionally by the killer, as a joke to taunt the police, after Eugene was killed. But what if there's more to it? Was someone trying to point the finger at Eugene for Wendall's death? I read Eugene's book, *You're Killing Me*. I don't know if you've read it. It's about a serial killer who leaves calling cards at the scene of each murder."

I *did* remember. I read that. Or maybe I *wrote* it? "The killer leaves a book at each crime scene. A mystery novel describing the killing. He carries out a murder from the book. It turns out the killer is a stand-up comedian who suffers from antisocial personality disorder. He gets a kick out of committing the fictional murders in real life. But his main motivation is to see whether the writer's got it right—is the fictional murder possible, and can the killer get away with it?"

"Exactly." Scott explained the parallels to the situation in Blue Water. "What if Eugene was behind the killings himself? I know…I know…he's dead." Scott raised his palms as I tried to interrupt him to tell him I had no idea what he was talking about. "*But...he was alive for some of the murders. What if someone else was inspired by Eugene and You're Killing Me? And they're continuing his work. A fan. Or what if he had a partner who turned on him? Is it possible? And if so, could there be a clue in his latest book, Beach Bodies?* I know it's a stretch, but I'm going to talk to Alice. She's the one who recommended Eugene's books to me in the first place."

"I have a copy in my—" I stopped abruptly, remembering Darko's gun buried in the bottom of my night table drawer, underneath the book.

"Are you okay? You look confused."

"Yes, I'm fine. Just having some memory issues. Good kitty." I petted the cat dozing by the fireplace. "Are you cozy, Tom? We used to have a cat, but Jim developed an allergy. Then we got a dog for the kids."

"Cookie."

"No, thanks. Maybe later."

"Your dog's name. It was Cookie."

"Oh. Oh, right. Cookie." An image of a cute Yorkie Poo pup popped into my head. The kids loved Cookie.

What was our cat's name?

It was just on the tip of my tongue.

Scott polished off the last piece of pizza and opened the front door. "How about that walk? I could use some exercise, if you're up for it. It's a bit cool. You might want a coat."

I removed a navy windbreaker from the closet and put it over my hoodie. "That's strange. My black scarf's missing." I flipped through hangers and looked on the shelf, grabbing a white cotton scarf.

"You're starting to remember small details, Ivy. Tom, Cookie, your scarf, books you've read. That's good." Scott led the way, stopping to grab a heavier coat from his car. The sun's brightness was deceptive. "I told June I'd see her on the weekend. After our walk, we should check on her. Are you up for it? And to see Alice? Maybe stop at the station? I don't want to leave you alone."

"I'm fine either way. Stop worrying about me. I've looked after myself for most of my life." I stood with my hands on my hips. "I don't need your constant supervision, Detective." Although I did wonder who June and Alice were.

"You're definitely getting back to normal."

Ivy. That's what it was. Jim and I named our cat Ivy. So why is Scott calling me that?

Hand in hand, we descended to the lake, Scott insisting I hold the railing.

"I'll be careful. I don't want to fall," I agreed. My head was already messed up enough without an accident. "I won't be able to help you with the case if I get hurt."

The few people along the boardwalk greeted us, as did the crash of the waves on the shore. We approached the pier. "It's beautiful here. Maybe Jim and the kids and I can move here someday." Scott drew his eyebrows together, telling me I must have said something wrong again.

At the end of the pier stood a lone figure. The channel to the right was wide open, no freighters in sight. Across the deep turquoise water, a few boats were docked at the harbor. To the left, waves crashed against the cement wall. Scott pulled me closer as I shivered. "Brrr...I want hot chocolate when we get back."

The person on the end of the pier hadn't moved, seemingly mesmerized by the water smashing into the breakwater, as we approached from behind. At the sound of our laughter, she turned around, then jumped off the edge of the pier into the cold lake.

Scott shouted, "Claire!"

Throwing off his coat, Scott swore profusely, looked down at the frigid waves, and took the plunge.

Chapter Forty-Three

I stood frozen. I couldn't even scream. Panic paralyzed me, leaving me ineffectual. In the recesses of my mind, I knew I should do something but couldn't think what that something was. Scott was gone. Under the water. Gone, like Darko. Gone, like Jim. And I hadn't even told him how I felt about him.

I stared into the frothy blue water.

Call for help.

No sound came out of my open mouth. It didn't matter. There was no one nearby.

Phone.

I fumbled around in my pockets. It wasn't there. I had left it at home. Because I didn't need it. I was safe with Scott. But now *Scott* wasn't safe.

Removing my jacket and scarf, I eased myself into the waves, the ice-like needles stinging. Scott couldn't be gone. I loved him too much to live without him.

One hand gripping the ladder, I searched the water, calling out his name. I was ready to slip my head under when he surfaced, dragging the woman. I climbed onto the pier and pulled her up while Scott pushed. The weight of the woman's body knocked me onto the concrete.

And with a sudden jolt, I remembered it all. I was Ivy Rose—schoolteacher, widowed mother, and hopeful mystery author. And Scott Evans was back in my life. Because of the murders.

"Ivy? Are you okay?" Scott sputtered, coughing as he proceeded to administer CPR. "Call 911!" he shouted during the compressions. "Phone's in my coat pocket."

Wendall's wife, Claire, was breathing when the emergency crew arrived, Scott's coat tucked around her. I placed my jacket around Scott's shoulders, my body pressed against his, as we stood dripping and shivering.

Once Claire was transported to the hospital and Scott and I were dropped off at home, I turned on the fireplace, led him to the downstairs bathroom, and pulled a fluffy white bath towel from the shelf. "Just throw your wet clothes in the washing machine," I said, unbuttoning his shirt.

His eyes met mine. "Finally. I've been waiting a long time for you to undress me." His teeth chattered as he tried to smile, pulling me toward him.

"I'd suggest a cold shower, but considering the circumstances...a hot shower for you, Detective Evans, and then some hot chocolate."

I myself stayed in the upstairs shower for a long time, trying to warm up, trying to come to terms with my current reality. Warm water flowed over my face until calm settled in.

I entered the kitchen where Scott was preparing hot chocolate, feeling overdressed in my fluffy pink robe as my eyes fell to the towel wrapped around his waist. "So that's what a superhero looks like. I was picturing a cape."

To my total shock, Scott unknotted the towel and pulled it around his shoulders. "How's that?" He wore nothing but a cape and a big smile.

"Oh my..." I diverted my eyes, feeling my face flush. Nervous laughter overtook me, snorts leading to hiccoughs.

"That's not the reaction I was going for."

"I can't believe you just...hic...did that." I rushed to the living room to grab the throw from the couch and tried to cover him. "Go sit down. I'll finish the hot chocolate."

He pulled me to him, wrapped me inside the throw with him, and put his mouth to my ear. "How about *you* warm me up, Ivy?"

"Um...I...Well, I..." But when his lips claimed mine, I didn't protest. "Mmm..." He moved his hands to the sash on my robe, undoing it, letting the throw and his towel slip to the floor, his body pressing mine against the kitchen counter.

"Maybe you *should* have a cold shower." I pushed him away and reached down for the throw. As I rose and fumbled with it, we burst into a fit of laughter and stumbled onto the floor, Scott on top of me.

"No…no…don't…stop." Breathless, my words conflicted with my feelings.

Scott rolled off and gazed into my eyes. "Was that 'no, don't stop' or 'No. Don't. Stop'?"

"The latter. I'm sorry." I picked myself off the floor, tying up my sash. "I'm not interested in being another one of your conquests, another name on a long list of women you've slept with. And I don't want to sully my memories of Jim by having sex with you."

Scott gaped at me, rising from the kitchen tiles. I escaped to the couch.

Moments later, Scott followed, fully wrapped in the towel and the throw, setting two mugs of hot chocolate on the coffee table. Sitting on the opposite end of the couch, he turned to face me. "That's not what this is about. You and me. You know how I feel about you. I—"

"I'm still in love with Jim. I know that sounds silly, but this feels like I'm betraying him."

Scott slid over and grasped my hands in his. "It's not silly. Of course, you still love Jim. He was an amazing guy. A great husband and father. And I'm not trying to take his place…"

"No one could ever take his place."

"No, that's not what I meant. But I think you have room in your heart to love again. And Jim would want you to be happy. Not waste the rest of your life mourning him."

Tears threatened. I pulled away. "You don't understand. It's my fault Jim died. *I* was supposed to die. He was driving my car. Stefan had no idea we were switching vehicles that day. *I* killed Jim."

"No. No, no, no." Scott gathered me in his arms. "That was totally Stefan's doing, not yours. Don't you dare take the blame for what he did. Don't let him take your life away, too. Jim wouldn't want that."

I sat up straight. "Your friendship means everything to me. Let's not spoil that."

Scott spoke softly, "You know I'm here for you, whatever you need, right?"

I nodded, biting my lip, struggling to hold back the tears, and picked up my cup of hot chocolate. The liquid burned my tongue, the sting welcome, distracting me from my guilt and grief. "So, is Claire Collins behind the murders?"

"She wasn't my prime suspect. But now, I don't know…"

"So, who *was* your prime suspect?" I wiped my eyes with a tissue.

"You mean besides you?"

I yelped as hot chocolate spilled onto my robe. "Me? Are you serious?"

Scott dabbed at the liquid with his napkin. His broad grin settled my nerves and stopped me from feeling sorry for myself. "Yes. Ivy Rose, mild-mannered schoolteacher turned serial killer. You're definitely my prime suspect. I do have someone in mind, though, but I need more evidence. I have a hunch. I don't want to name anyone just yet. But I'm mulling over the possibility of it being Eugene and an accomplice. A jealous accomplice. I wasn't thinking of Claire, but she's obviously carrying a lot of guilt about something."

I realized this was his way of steering me away from the pain of losing Jim. Scott always had a way of drawing a line between his personal and professional life. We were in work mode, the case back on the table.

"A jealous woman accomplice?"

"Like I said, it's just a hunch."

He wasn't going to give away any more information. "Cookie?" I held up the plate. "Are you warm enough? I can get another blanket." I brought the comforter from my bed. "This should keep you toasty. You must be frozen after diving into the lake. I was in for just a minute and froze. And what about supper? What do you want to eat?"

"Stop fussing. I'm supposed to be taking care of you," Scott complained about having our roles switched. "It was no big deal. Just a little dip in the lake on a cool September afternoon."

"Well, if you're sure you're okay, I'll just slip over to see June."

"No. I want to keep an eye on you. If someone's threatening you…"

"Nothing is going to happen to me at June's house. Unless you think *she's* your serial killer?" I raised my eyebrows, daring him to give me a reason not to check on my neighbor. "Wouldn't *that* be a twist? A nice little eighty-year-old woman doing away with the townspeople. I'll have to use that in my next book."

"I guess you're right. And you seem to have completely recovered your memory, by the way. But I'll come with you," he insisted, rising from the couch.

"Your clothes are in the washing machine. You're not thinking of going over there in a towel, are you? What will June think?" The image of him walking into June's house with nothing on got me started again, my tears welling from laughter. "Can you imagine… Poor June…I'll bet that would be a first…a naked man coming to call on her…for tea…and biscuits." I brought my hand to my mouth, trying to stifle the snorts as he glared at me. "Even if it is your second date…I really don't think…and what if you dropped your towel…oh my gosh!" I heaved, drops moistening my lower lashes.

"Well, I'm pleased to see I can be such a source of amusement for you," Scott said, straight-faced.

"Oh, you are, you definitely are." I took a deep breath and swiped the tears off my cheeks with the back of my hand. Then I gave my nose a good blow and got dressed before leaving the house.

Minutes later, I stormed back in. "Help! June's house is on fire! I need you to get her out!"

Scott jumped up, exposing himself as the towel fell. I ran back outside. He followed not long after, having donned the pink robe on my bed.

"I managed to wake her up," I said, with June by my side. "But the house is full of smoke."

"It's probably just from the fireplace downstairs. Sometimes it gets a bit smoky…" June paused at the sight of Scott in a pink robe. "I'm sorry if I interrupted your…date…or whatever you young people call it these days."

Scott rushed into June's house as I ran home to call 911, but my door was locked.

"I'm going next door to call the fire department," I yelled to June who stood staring at Scott as he came through her door, coughing, carrying a scorched couch cushion, embers still glowing on one end.

By the time the fire trucks pulled up, all the cushions were on the lawn. "I need help getting the couch out," Scott yelled to the firefighters. "It's still smoldering, but everything's under control."

When they brought the couch out and set it on the grass, June remarked, "I never did like that couch anyway."

Riley Patterson was one of the crew. "We've opened the windows. Just let the smoke air out," he advised. "We've also put batteries in the smoke detectors." He gave a sermon about how important it was to check them frequently.

When Scott asked what caused the fire, Riley answered, "Looks like a spark flew out of the fireplace onto the sofa. Fortunately, the cushions are fire-retardant. Let the fireplace cool down before using it again. And be careful when you're putting wood in; don't leave the door open."

Riley noticed Scott's attire. The sash had fallen off the robe, letting it hang open. Riley patted Scott on the back. "Hey, I'm not one to judge." Giving June and me the once over, he shook his head and chuckled. "Your secret's safe with me."

"I'm not involved in any of their shenanigans." June threw her hands in the air. "But they're good people, whatever their proclivities. They've saved me more than once."

"Can you help me get into my house?" I asked Riley. "We seem to be locked out."

Riley removed some tools from the firetruck. "All set," he said a few minutes later. "And it's good to keep your door locked, with a serial killer on the loose. But next time you're role-playing, take the key with you. It might save you some embarrassment."

Chapter Forty-Four

"That was another interesting day." Scott shook his head after the fire department drove off. "I'd almost forgotten how much fun it is hanging out with you. Not much has changed over the last few years. Now that half the town has seen me like this…" Scott moved his hand down the length of Ivy's robe, "I'm going to get dressed before the police show up and arrest me for indecent exposure."

"It wasn't half the town. Maybe half the street. A few people over at the park. Most of the fire department. And probably a lot of women on their first date with you." Ivy's mouth twitched upwards.

"Very funny. And for the record, it's not that long a list. A lot longer than yours, but not as long as you seem to think."

"What list?" Ivy asked.

"What's long?" June's eyes shot downwards, taking in Scott's physique. "Oh, my."

"The women I slept with." Scott tied the sash on his robe, eyes glued to Ivy's. "And none of them hold a candle to you. Including my ex-wife."

"Why don't you come join us? Let your house air out for a couple of hours?" Ivy invited June, turning away from Scott.

"Thanks. I hope I'm not intruding on your…" June glanced at the pink robe again. "er, privacy."

"Not at all. Detective Evans was just waiting for his clothes to dry after his plunge into the lake. That's why he's wearing my robe."

June nodded. "I wasn't born yesterday, dearie."

The late afternoon sun coming through the window added to the warmth of the fireplace. Scott settled Ivy on the couch, with June next to her, and put the kettle on for tea. "Get some rest," he told Ivy, setting down two mugs of chamomile tea on the coffee table. He explained Ivy's head injury to June and added, "Keep an eye on her."

Scott exchanged the robe for his own clothes once they were dry. He could still smell the lake on his jeans and shirt, and he detected the odor of smoky, scorched foam on his skin. At least now, he was dry and decent. He washed his face, rinsed out his mouth, and ran a hand through his hair. His fatigue was reflected in the bathroom mirror.

What I should do is get some sleep. What I need to do is get to the bottom of this.

Scott didn't believe the fire was caused by June's negligence. This was the second close call she'd had in a week.

"I need to check into a few things," Scott announced as he came out of the bathroom. "Do you want to come with…" He stopped suddenly, as June shushed him. Ivy was asleep, the comforter drawn up to her chin, quietly snoring, with Tom curled on top of her. June was watching an old black and white film on TV, Clarence lounging in her lap. He wasn't sure if June was shushing him because Ivy was sleeping, or because he was interrupting her viewing.

Placing Ivy's cell phone in June's hand, Scott gave her instructions. "I'll be back in a couple of hours. And I'll bring chicken for supper." He stood in the entranceway, considering whether it was wise to leave them alone. "I'll call every half hour to check on things. My number's in Ivy's phone. Call if there's any problem. And call 911 if it's urgent. Keep the door locked. Don't let anyone in the house till I get back. And don't let Ivy talk you into going out." He grabbed the fireplace poker and propped it next to June. "For protection, if you need it."

"Yes, sir," June saluted him. "You can count on me."

Scott had second thoughts as he grabbed the doorknob, but he brushed them away.

They'll be fine for a couple of hours. What could possibly happen?

His first stop was the hospital. He had a short conversation with Claire in her private room. "I'm glad to see you're doing okay. Do you want to tell me what happened on the pier?"

Claire looked down at the magazine she had been flipping through. "I don't know. I wasn't thinking clearly. When Celia called me this morning..."

"Celia Parkins?"

"Yes, she was in Wendall's book club. I never approved of him joining their group. All those people interested in murder and getting together every week to talk about it, like it's some sort of normal hobby. It's sick." Claire wiped away a tear. "I should never have let him join in the first place."

"Why did Celia call you?"

Claire told him Celia read Wendall's manuscript. "It made me feel bad, knowing he had to hide it from me. I wasn't supportive of Wendall's writing. I had no idea he'd completed a whole book. Celia said she'd been debating whether to call me ever since Wendall's death." Celia told Claire what she told Scott last night. Wendall thought his wife suspected he was having an affair. Celia assured her that wasn't the case, but Wendall thought it was better for her to think that than to know he'd been writing behind her back. "If only I had talked to him. I was driving myself crazy thinking he was going to leave me, afraid to confront him about it. And all that time, all he wanted to do was write. It's my fault he went down to the pier himself. I should have been with him, spending more time with him, going for walks together, supporting him in his writing, even if his hobby *was* a waste of time."

Scott put his hand on hers, saying he was sure Wendall wouldn't want her blaming herself.

"I know...it's just hard...but I want to thank you, Detective, for saving me." Claire told him she was going to seek help for her grief and guilt over Wendall's death. "I have an appointment with Matt Thornton for counseling."

Scott was relieved to hear Claire was going to be a survivor, both physically and emotionally. When he called home, June answered. "Tell Ivy that Claire blamed herself for Wendall's death, but she's agreed to get counseling. I'll be home shortly. Don't let anyone in."

Chapter Forty-Five

The doorbell rang. When it rang again, the sound of pounding on the door accompanied the chime. "What...what's going on?" I sat up on the third ring, June sitting next to me, a poker in her hand. "I think there's someone at the door."

June explained Scott's instructions. I pulled myself off the couch and peeked through the tinted glass in the door. "It's okay. It's a friend of mine." The purple hoodie covered her head, but I recognized her right away. "Come in, Paige."

"I don't know, Ivy. Detective Evans said we shouldn't..." June warned. Clarence yipped around Paige's legs.

"He meant strangers. Sorry, Paige. June's just being cautious. She had a bit of an accident today, and Detective Evans is concerned for her safety."

"Oh no, are you okay?" Paige sat next to the elderly woman. "What happened?"

June waved her hand in the air. "Oh, it was nothing. I'm perfectly fine. Just a bit forgetful lately. Normal at my age. They're making a mountain out of a molehill. But her..." She pointed to me. "I'm not so sure about. She bumped her head last night. Went to the hospital. And then she and the detective jumped off the pier. I'm just glad they were there for me. Even if he was wearing a fluffy pink robe when they rescued me."

"Oh." Paige blinked, then turned to me. "I'm sorry to bother you. I wouldn't have come if I'd known you were having a bad day. I was here earlier, and you weren't home. I was just about to give up now, too, and then you came to the door."

"I'm glad you dropped by. Would you like some coffee or tea?"

Paige sat with her head down, picking at the skin around her fingernails. "Tea would be nice. If it's not too much trouble." Following me into the kitchen, she continued in a quiet voice, "There's something I'd like to talk to you about in private. Something of a personal nature."

June followed us to the kitchen, a firm grip on the poker. "You'll have to speak up. My hearing's not that good." Gently prying the poker out of June's hand, I returned it to the fireplace. "That was for protection," June protested. She shot Paige a warning look. "Not that I need it. I'm a black belt."

I was sure June never had a martial arts lesson in her life. "Yes, it's a good thing you're here."

We each carried a mug of tea into the living room, and I placed a plate of cookies on the coffee table.

"So, what was the personal thing you wanted to talk about?" June blurted out. As Paige sank back into the cushions. I suggested she might like to speak to me alone, perhaps downstairs in the family room.

June insisted she needed to keep her eyes on me. "Besides, I can keep a secret. Nothing you say will leave this room. Just like Detective Evans wearing a pink robe. It's not like I'm going to go around town gossiping. What he does in the privacy of his girlfriend's home, that's his business."

Paige raised her eyebrows. "I know you saw me and Riley at the hotel."

"Riley, the hardware guy? He's not your husband. What were you doing with him at the hotel?" June interrupted.

I looked down at my hands. "Oh, well…I guess you were having breakfast together. So were Detective Evans and I. They have an excellent buffet."

Tears streamed down Paige's face. "Please don't…don't tell my husband. He thinks I spent the night with a friend who wasn't feeling well." She put her head in her hands as I patted her back. "He knows about my…well, my indiscretions…not the details, of course. But this thing with Riley, it's different. It's been going on for a while. And there's more to it than just sex. He's helping me…weaning me off other men. He cares about me. And I really care about him. But I think Riley may expect more from me than I can give."

"He's old enough to be your father." June tsk-tsked Paige, adding, "What *would* your father say?" That sent Paige into an uncontrollable fit of sobbing.

Putting an arm around Paige, who had her knees drawn up on the coffee table with her head buried in her lap, I shot June a look to shush her.

"It's okay. I'm not going to say anything to Matt," I reassured Paige. "But you can't think he won't find out. You're either going to have to tell him or break things off with Riley." I had never cheated on Jim, but I knew what it was like to be tempted. Every time I was alone with Scott during that year of our friendship, the sexual tension between us simmered. I had to remind myself how much I loved my husband. Yes, I understood how Paige could be tempted.

"I need you to understand. I've been trying to get help," Paige said, sitting up. "I really have. But it just isn't working for me. I have a problem…an addiction…to…you know…"

"Men?" June ventured. "Don't worry, dearie. Everyone's addicted to something."

Paige took some comfort in that. "Do you really think so?" She sat up straighter. "What are you addicted to?"

"Daytime television, for one thing. I'm not proud of it, but it's a hard habit to break," June chuckled. "And not nearly as entertaining as your addiction, I'll bet. And Ivy, here, seems to have some sort of kinky thing going on with the detective, so she's not one to judge." June raised her eyebrows and pursed her lips, tilting her head toward me.

I denied there was anything at all going on between myself and Detective Evans. "We knew each other a long time ago. We used to be best friends."

"Mmhmm, friends," was all June had to say, sitting back on the sofa, arms crossed.

"But I do have addictions of my own, of course. Sweets, for one, especially chocolate. And I spend my spare time watching, reading, and writing murder mysteries, so I guess you could call that an addiction of sorts," I confessed.

"It's not really the same, though, is it?" Paige asked, eyes on her lap. "TV, books, chocolate—none of those things really hurt anyone. And what I'm doing…I'm ashamed to even think about it, much less talk about it. I'm ruining my marriage."

"Just like that good-for-nothing great nephew-in-law of mine, Reggie. He's gambling away his money. Brags about how he's doing so well with his sales job, selling pharmaceuticals, but he's not fooling me. Emma told me about his problem. She's the one paying all the bills. I don't know why she puts up with him." June shook her head.

"Reggie Kloppen?" Paige looked up.

"Don't tell me he's one of the men you're…Wait till I get my hands on him. The gambling is bad enough, and leeching off my grandniece, but if he's stepping out on her…"

"Oh no, no, it's not like that. I only know him through my group—All Addicts Welcome. It's just odd that you mentioned him. I saw him today, hanging around the house next door when I was here earlier looking for Ivy." She turned to me. "I didn't know he lived next door to you."

"June lives next door. Reggie was…maybe visiting?" I looked to June for confirmation, but June said she hadn't seen him since yesterday, at Larissa's place. "Maybe he came around when you were out walking Clarence."

June nodded and said that was possible. "But I don't know why he'd come without Emma. He knows I'm not overly fond of him, to put it mildly."

I filed away the information about Reggie Kloppen in my head—gambling, pharmaceuticals, money problems, son-in-law to Rick, who was involved with the Mafia. I was sure Scott would be interested. "Is there anyone else in this AAW group that I might know?"

"I don't want to break anyone's confidence. I've already said too much." Paige rose to leave. "I just wanted to ask you to not say anything to Matt. I need some time to break it off with Riley."

"Of course."

As she went out the door, Paige turned around and said I reminded her of something. There *was* someone in her group I knew well, someone with a very strange and uncommon addiction. "Similar to what you mentioned. But I've said too much. We're sworn to secrecy. AAW is a safe place."

Chapter Forty-Six

lice asked Scott if he would prefer tea or coffee. "Tea, thanks," he replied. "I hope you don't mind me dropping in like this."

She assured him she was always glad to have company. Showing Scott to the sofa, she excused herself to make a pot of tea.

When she returned with a tray holding two cups, he told her he was there on police business.

Her smile faded. "Oh? What exactly is it about?"

"I was hoping to talk to you about Eugene's book, *Beach Bodies*."

"Oh, is that all?" She breathed a sigh of relief.

"Have you read it?"

"Yes, of course. Why do you ask?"

Scott observed Alice as she tucked a lock of blond hair behind her ear. "I wondered whether there was anything in the book that connects to the recent deaths in Blue Water. Some clue or similarity?"

Alice's hand trembled as she laid her cup on the saucer. "Well, obviously, the title relates to what happened to Eugene. His book is about a reality show at a beach resort. People with tanned, buff bodies. They have to solve a fake murder mystery, like in a murder mystery theater. But then someone actually gets murdered. The body washes up on the shore while they're filming. I can give you my copy if you want to read it yourself."

Scott didn't want to let on that a copy had been found on the beach, and that he had already skimmed through it. "That would be great, thanks."

The shelves surrounding the fireplace were filled with books. "I see you really enjoy reading."

"There's nothing like a good book to lose yourself in," Alice confirmed, her face lighting up. "It's almost as good as sec…." Her face flushed, then she added, "writing," explaining the joy of losing oneself in a fictional world of their own creation.

When Scott asked about her writing, she animatedly talked about her work, modestly stating it wasn't very good, but she enjoyed it.

Alice put on a pair of reading glasses as she perused the titles on her shelf. "It doesn't seem to be here. I'll get Valerie to fetch one from the store. It won't take long."

"Do you happen to wear contacts?" He looked into her blue eyes as her eyelids fluttered.

"I…sometimes wear reading glasses. Why are you asking? Is that somehow related to the case you're working on?"

Scott admitted it was, but he couldn't elaborate. Standing to stretch his legs, Scott asked if he could use the washroom.

The blinds on the patio doors overlooking the backyard were open, giving Scott a good view of the pool and hot tub as Alice showed him the way. Scott *thought* he had seen a pool in the back the night he was there for Murder Club.

When he returned to the living room, he asked Alice the name of the company that did her pool maintenance. She wrinkled her forehead, staring at him. "Why do you ask? Are you thinking of moving into town and putting in a pool yourself? You and Ivy?"

The idea of moving in with Ivy appealed to him. But with the lake right across from her house, a pool wasn't necessary. "Just asking for a buddy of mine at the station."

"I've just recently switched, and it's too early for me to recommend them or not." Alice flinched. The name she gave was the same company Olivia and Cliff used. Lakeshore Pools.

"And who did you use before that?"

"Townsend Pool Services. And I can't recommend them."

"Was there a problem with their work?"

Alice stared at her hands. "Let's just say their customer service was less than professional."

Scott shifted the conversation to what happened at the Haunted House and how that was connected to Carter's book. "And then there's Carter's death, described by one of the writers in the contest," Scott pointed out. "I also wanted to ask about your book. I've heard there's a murder made to look like a hunting accident."

"Who told you…? Oh, it was Ivy, of course. She critiqued my book."

"You didn't think Phillip Reece's death was connected?"

Alice admitted she *did* think it was odd. "But my work's unpublished, so no one knows I wrote about a hunting accident. Except Ivy. And Wendall, who was dead before Phillip." Alice wrinkled her forehead again. "So, I couldn't imagine there was a connection. But now, given what happened to Carter and what almost happened to Valerie, I'm not so sure."

Valerie came through the door with a copy of *Beach Bodies*. "Nice to see you again, Detective Evans. Did you have more questions for Mom? I'm sure she told you everything she knows. Here you go, Mom. Sorry you can't find your copy. Maybe you lent it out to someone? You're always doing that."

"Actually, I'm going to lend this one to Detective Evans."

Valerie turned to Scott. "By the way, I was checking out your Camaro. I hope you don't mind. I'm a car enthusiast. I was looking at the interior and noticed a Western hoodie in your back seat. That wouldn't happen to be mine, would it? I lost it at the Haunted House yesterday. People joke that Mom and I look like twins when we wear our school hoodies. Of course, a lot of people in town have one."

Chapter Forty-Seven

"I *told* you to lock the door and not answer it for anyone," Scott admonished June. "For all we know, Paige could be the killer."

"What? That tiny little slip of a girl?" June's face wrinkled up even more than it already was. "She seemed like such a meek thing, afraid of her own shadow. Besides, I had the poker trained on her the whole time. And it's Ivy's fault, not mine. *She* let her in."

When Scott informed us killers were often good at hiding who they really were, I flinched. Was he talking about me? "You can't seriously think Paige is behind all these deaths."

Would Scott understand sometimes you had to commit a horrific deed to save yourself and your family? Life wasn't always black and white. There were gray areas, muddy areas, areas most people never thought they'd find themselves traversing.

"I don't think she's a cold-blooded killer." I was speaking about myself as well as Paige. "But we think we've figured out who *is*. You won't believe it. It's someone right under our noses. Paige saw Reggie hanging around June's house earlier. What if *he* caused the fire?"

"Hmm…" Scott stroked the stubble on his chin, glancing over at June. "Tell me more about Reggie."

"He's not on my list of favorite people, but I wouldn't peg him as a serial killer," June said. "He hasn't got the balls to kill me."

I told Scott about Reggie's gambling debts and how his wife, Emma, along with her siblings, would inherit not only June's share of Larissa's estate, but also June's money. "He works in pharmaceutical sales. So, he'd have access to drugs, and he'd know something about them, wouldn't he? He could have easily drugged Larissa and messed with June's pills."

Scott agreed that was possible. "But why kill all those other people?"

"I don't know. But there's also Reggie's connection to the Mafia through his father-in-law, Rick. Like I said before, maybe the other victims are just to cover up the real motive for the murder."

"Maybe. It just seems far-fetched. But it does make me wonder about what you said. Red herrings. What if all these murders *are* meant to throw the police off track? What if someone has something to hide? What if there was a danger their secret was going to be published by one of the writers? What if one of the writers was blackmailing the killer? Or threatening to expose him or her?"

Goosebumps erupted over my arm as Scott's fingers caressed it. What if? Someone had something to hide. What if that was the motive behind the murders that initially appeared to be accidents? The murders that seemed to be the work of a serial killer. Someone trying to make it look like something it *wasn't*. What if? I gazed into Scott Evans' warm brown eyes and wondered.

Is it all about to blow wide open?

Chapter Forty-Eight

A mini-break for the students and staff of Blue Water High. Things were locked down tight while the police investigated the death of Connie Schultz. The bad news was everyone in town was on edge. No longer did anyone believe the recent accidents *were* accidental.

Doug McLaren had been wrong when he said things would die down by the time the Arts and Crafts Festival took place. The media was having a field day. A dead parent. A dead teacher. A closed school. One suspicious accident after another. A visible police presence on the streets.

Scott refused to leave my side. "I can't trust you to follow instructions and do what you're told. Whether this is about a serial killer of writers or a writer threatening and blackmailing someone with a secret worth killing for or the Mafia exacting vengeance, you're in the center of it."

Although I wouldn't admit it to Scott, I didn't mind spending time with him. He handed me a copy of Eugene's first published book, *You're Killing Me*. "Here, read this again. I think there's a clue in there we're missing."

"What am I looking for?"

"I don't know. But I think this book inspired the killer. And I still think it could be Eugene himself."

"That's impossible. Dead men don't tell tales or commit murder."

Scott tapped his fingers on the steering wheel of his Camaro. "He was alive for the three out-of-town deaths. And for Wendall's and Larissa's."

"But not for Phillip's and Connie's and Carter's. So, it wasn't him."

"Unless…he *isn't* dead. Why are two of his books connected to the murders?"

I furrowed my brow, my mouth flew open, and I brought my hand to my left cheek. "Not dead? But there was a funeral. His car…"

"He went through the windshield, head first. No seat belt. His body smashed on the rocks. I'm wondering how recognizable his body was. Maybe it wasn't him."

"Wow." Scott's theory was so out there that I couldn't begin to understand it. "How would that even be possible?"

A sharp intake of breath left me dizzy as I held it in. Of course, it was possible. I thought about my parents. Unrecognizable bodies. Closed caskets.

When we arrived at the station, Scott pointed to a chair in the lobby. "Sit. Stay. Look for clues in the book. I'll try not to be long."

Rolling my eyes, I opened Eugene's book and read while Scott brainstormed with Mike behind closed doors. When he returned a couple of hours later, his eyes held a question.

"What is it?" I asked.

"Willow. She identified his body. He had no other family. His body was examined by Will Jenkins, who confirmed the crash was the cause of Eugene's death."

"And…" I rolled my hands in the air to encourage him to continue.

"Willow said Eugene had her name tattooed on his left bicep. It checked out. No further tests were done. He was cremated shortly after his death as per his wishes. It just strikes me as odd."

"What does?"

"Willow and Will. Will accepted her identification and didn't question it any further. They were both satisfied it was Eugene."

"Shouldn't they have been?"

"It threw a wrench into my theory about Eugene and an accomplice and it being a publicity stunt to sell more books. I'm off-track. What about you? Did you find anything useful?" He pointed to the book I held.

"No, not so far. But I thought of something that's kind of strange."

Scott sat next to me. "What's that?"

"Wendall was the first in-town death, and Will was the first to question the accidents in the county. Wendall critiqued Larissa's manuscript, which was about a car accident on a bridge. Will questioned Larissa's death. Will was good friends with Wendall and Larissa. But…Steph said he was jealous of his two friends when he saw them together. Then Eugene died in the car crash."

"I'm not following. What does that mean?"

"I have no idea, but it's all connected."

Scott steepled his fingers. "Let's go."

"Where?"

"To the scene of the crime. The first one in Port Ripley."

Scott's Camaro cruised up and down the length of the beach road while I kept my eyes open looking for the source of a possible witness who didn't *realize* they were a witness, according to Scott.

"You're right. Will was the first person to question the accidents. He insisted that someone killed Wendall. Wendall died out in the open, in a very public spot. We need to keep looking for a clue, a witness…something." Scott slammed the brakes and stared out his window toward the beach.

A shrill horn blasted, and a vehicle pulled up next to us from behind, the driver flipping Scott his middle finger and mouthing obscenities before taking off, tires screeching.

"And I thought people here were friendly," Scott said, turning to me.

"Probably a tourist. From the city. Why the sudden stop?"

Scott signaled before turning into an angled parking spot. "That old woman over there. What is she doing?"

"Oh, Janine. She's looking for treasures with her metal detector. Why?"

Scott didn't wait for me. He slammed his door shut and ran toward Janine. Janine ignored him as he greeted her and showed his ID, talking and gesturing, while she continued to skim the sand for coins and jewelry as though he wasn't there.

I jogged up to Scott and nudged him. "Janine doesn't trust strangers. Or cops. So…double whammy."

Janine moved away, ignoring both of us. She must have decided I wasn't to be trusted by way of my association with a strange cop.

"Put your badge away," I whispered to Scott. "Janine's a free spirit. Between the shelter and friends, she finds a safe place for the winter. But she loves to be outdoors in decent weather."

"Will she talk to you?"

"What did you want to ask her?"

As I drifted toward Janine, trying not to spook her, Scott followed at a respectable distance.

"Janine, hi. It's Ivy, you remember me, don't you?"

She glanced at me and nodded, jutting a thumb at Scott. "What's with the undercover cop? I'm not doing anything illegal."

"Oh, no. It's nothing to do with you, Janine. And Scott's not working right now. We're just out on a beach date. He's my boyfriend."

"Humph. Boyfriend. Since when do you have a boyfriend? You're always alone whenever I see you. I thought you didn't like men. Boyfriend, my ass."

Scott cleared his throat.

"I've known him for years. He's a good friend. We've been getting to know each other better this past week as more than friends."

Janine took a full minute to scan Scott from head to toe, then focused on his eyes. "Well, if you're gonna get yourself a man, he's as fine a specimen as you're gonna be able to snag. I'd hold on to him if I were you."

Scott cleared his throat again.

"I was just wondering, Janine, if maybe you had seen anything strange on the beach lately." I waved my hand and did a three hundred and sixty-degree turn to indicate the area I was referring to. "On the pier or in the water? The parking lot? Sand?"

"Lots of strange things happen, especially after the sun goes down."

"What about Wendall Collins? His body was found on the beach a few weeks ago. Did you happen to see anyone or anything connected to his death?"

Janine shuffled her foot through the sand, picked up a necklace and pocketed it. "You never know what you'll find. But I've never found a body on the beach."

"Well, I wouldn't imagine that bodies on the beach are all that common.

Unless they're live beach bodies."

"I bet *he's* got a good beach body. A *real* live one. Are you two…fooling around?" Janine nodded toward Scott.

Scott's heavy sigh behind me indicated I was wasting time talking to Janine.

"We'll let you get back to work," I said. "Have a good afternoon."

As Scott and I walked away, Janine yelled, "By the way, I read a book called *Beach Bodies.* There was some pretty heavy fooling around going on there. And murder to boot."

Scott and I stopped walking and turned around.

"Some fella buried it in the sand one night. Got out of his van, ran over to the beach, and dug a hole with his hands, plopped something in. I pulled it out after he left. It was quite the story. But those books are a dime a dozen. Worthless. So, I put it back where I found it the next day."

Scott and I gawked at her.

"I'm a fast reader."

"What fella? What did he look like?" Scott asked.

"It was dark. He had his hood pulled over his head and part of his face."

"You're sure it was a man?"

"Either that or a real muscular-type woman."

"What sort of vehicle was he driving? Color? Make?"

"It was dark. But it was a large van."

"Why didn't you call the police? You must have heard about the deaths. Eugene was one of the victims."

"Police? Humph." Janine spit on the sand. "And what's with all the questions?"

"Thank you, Janine. You've been very helpful." I smiled my appreciation.

"Some sort of delivery or work van. I couldn't read the words on the side. And he was youngish. More your age than mine."

"I thought you couldn't see his face," Scott said.

"I saw him move. He was in a hurry." Janine spat again. "Humph. Police."

As we headed to the car, Janine shouted, "He may be a looker, but he's still a cop. Don't forget that, Ivy."

Scott turned on the ignition. "She seems nice."

"She gave you what you wanted."

"Speaking of getting what I want." He fixed his eyes on me. "I'm your boyfriend? So, when does the fooling around part start?"

I punched him hard.

"Ouch!" He rubbed his arm. "I don't like it rough. But if it turns you on...feel free to punch away."

I reached over and punched his other arm.

Chapter Forty-Nine

You were right when you said there's always something happening in Port Ripley." Scott accompanied me to the Fall Arts and Crafts Market Wednesday evening, his arm around my waist as we strolled through the exhibits, stopping to chat with people we knew. Scott had become a fixture in town in a very short time.

I smiled and waved at Doreen Morris as she beamed at one of her music students, singing *Live the Magic* on the stage. Doreen needn't have stressed about preparing her students to provide the evening's entertainment—their natural talent shone through regardless of their nervousness or the lack of time they had to practice. Proud parents looked on, recording their kids' performances.

Attendance was up from last year's market. People throughout the county came to sell and to buy. Whether it was because of curiosity or the belief that there was safety in numbers, people wandered around checking out the wares for sale. If it weren't for the current situation, I would have set up a booth with my books. Several other authors from the county hadn't been deterred by the recent events, and readers' interests in local books were piqued. My attention was drawn to the baked goods and jewelry, while Scott admired the art.

"You should have set up a cinnamon bun/book booth," Scott said.

"Books, maybe. I don't remember the last time I baked cinnamon buns. Jim loved my buns." I sighed.

"I loved your buns, too. Maybe you'd consider making some for me. In the meantime, how about some of these butter tarts?" Scott pulled out his wallet and handed a ten-dollar bill to the woman seated behind the table.

As she bagged his treats and they discussed the nice weather, my eyes drifted to the jewelry display a few tables down. Gorgeous stones glittered in the sun. Although I didn't usually wear a lot of jewelry, I was attracted by the art and beauty of the designs.

"I make these all myself," the woman said. "Crystals have natural healing powers as well as being a beautiful accessory."

"They're lovely." I admired the various colors and designs. A chart posted some of the properties of each stone.

"Each one is unique. Hand-crafted one-of-a-kind."

I was drawn to one in particular. A silver and turquoise bracelet called my name. I couldn't resist picking it up.

"What's your astrological sign?"

"Sagittarius. Why?"

"That's your zodiac stone." She handed me a card that spelled out the properties and benefits of turquoise.

I skimmed the information. The green-blue gem, one of the oldest stones, reminiscent of the ocean, is associated with good fortune and warding off negativity. A symbol of friendship and enduring love, it brings balance and calm.

I fingered the stones, immediately feeling the peace of water flowing over me. The small white price tag was face down. Flipping it over, I said, "It's so pretty. I'll give it some thought."

Far from pricey, but I rarely splurged on myself.

Scott touched my shoulder, startling me. "There you are. For a minute, I thought I'd lost you. Did you drop something?" He pointed to the ground behind me.

I turned around and searched the grass, bending over to get a closer look. "I don't see anything."

"Further back. Something shiny."

I moved toward the next table, my eyes glued to the ground. "There's nothing…"

"Never mind. It's just a piece of garbage. How about we get some fries? If they taste as good as they smell…" He tilted his head toward the food truck at the end of the aisle.

"They do. They're the best fries you'll ever have."

"Oh, you've had them before?"

"Phil's Fries are famous on the beach. People line up all summer."

Scott's eyes popped wide. "Really? Why haven't I seen the truck down there?"

"She closes down after Labor Day. She'll still do a few events here and there till the snow comes."

"She?"

"Philomena. She and her husband run the food truck."

Scott rubbed his chin with his free hand. "On the beach? Till Labor Day? Let's go."

Joining the line-up in front of Phil's, I said, "Get the jumbo size."

Scott raised his eyebrows. "Extra hungry?"

"I don't want you eating them all on me. With the jumbo box, I might be able to snag a few before you wolf them down."

When we got to the counter, Scott pulled out his ID and asked to speak with Phil, the young woman dipping baskets into the fryer.

"Seriously?" her husband, Don, asked. "Can't you see she's busy? Come back after nine, when we close."

Scott and I sat on a bench overlooking the lake, fighting over the fries.

"Stop hogging them," I complained.

"It's my first time, so I'm entitled." He swiped a fry from my hand before it made it to my mouth.

We watched the sun set over Blue Water Lake, then strolled through the booths once more as lampposts illuminated the park. Just before nine, we returned to the food booth.

"Wait here," I said, "I just need to slip off to the bathroom."

On my way, I stopped at the booth with the crystals and jewelry. My eyes scanned the display. "That turquoise bracelet I was looking at before…"

"Oh, I'm sorry. It sold," the vendor said. "Is there something else…"

"No, it's okay. I guess it wasn't meant for me, after all. I probably wouldn't have many occasions to wear it anyway. Thanks. Have a good night."

By the time I returned to the food truck, Scott was ready to head home.

"Did you talk to Phil?" I asked as we walked down the street.

"I did. She was very helpful. I asked whether she saw anyone at the beach the night of Wendall's death."

"Oh?" I waited for him to elaborate. "And…?"

"She happened to come back to the truck that evening. Said she forgot her rings, like she sometimes does, when she cleaned up the kitchen at the end of the night."

"And…?"

"Someone was walking back from the end of the pier. She saw them under the lamppost after she locked up and sat on the grassy mound to gaze at the stars."

I gasped. "It could have been the killer. Did she recognize them?"

"No, it was too dark. And the hoodie covered their head."

"Did they see her? Phil could be in danger if she's a witness."

"No. She was on the other side of the mound. The truck isn't visible from the pier because of it. But she saw the back of the person as they passed by her. And she recognized the hoodie. It's one of those purple Western hoodies. Like the one you have."

My jaw dropped.

* * *

Sitting on my front porch, Scott said, "I've got something for you."

The last five minutes, walking home, my mind had been on the hoodie, trying to figure out whether that was the clue that would provide Scott with the killer's identity.

"Oh?"

He opened the bag containing the butter tarts and pulled out another plastic bag. Inside it was a paper bag filled with fries. "These were left over at the end of the night. Phil offered them to me. For free."

"Oh."

We shared the left-over fries, Scott's arm slung over my shoulder, enjoying the quiet of a cool, starry night. When the bag was empty, we continued to sit in silence. I hadn't felt such peace since I was in Jim's arms.

Apart from a bit of teasing, Scott hadn't made a move on me since Sunday, after the fire at June's house. Maybe he had lost interest in me already. A huge part of me regretted not giving in to my feelings when I had the chance. But I knew I'd end up getting hurt in the end.

I tucked my head into Scott's shoulder. "This is really nice."

"Mmmm, it's perfect." He kissed the top of my head.

"I feel so safe with you."

"Safe?"

"From the world. I wish we could stay like this forever. Just me and you and the stars. It's magical."

Scott pulled something out of his pocket and slipped it around my left wrist. "Oh, and I got you a little something else."

As he closed the clasp, I stared at my wrist, knowing it was the turquoise bracelet I had admired earlier, even though the porch lights were off.

"It's one of a kind. Like you. I hope you'll wear it all the time. I understand it's a friendship bracelet, or a symbol of enduring love. If friendship is all you have to give for now, then let me be your best friend. Always. Forever. No matter what happens."

"How on earth did you…?"

He brushed his hand against my cheek. "Don't question the magic, Ivy. Just live it."

Chapter Fifty

When school reopened on Thursday, Scott worried about me returning to the scene of the crime. "Make sure there are always lots of people around you. Come directly home after school and lock the doors," he instructed as we left the house at the same time. "And make sure you text me every chance you get."

As much as I shook inwardly, I had to hold myself together for the sake of the kids. My students stared at me the first day back as though they expected me to have answers. Why was Friday's substitute teacher dead?

After a moment of silence for the victim, I assured the students they were safe with a police officer stationed at the school. They knew I was meant to be the victim. I overheard kids whispering in the hall.

"My dad said the killer was after Ms. Rose," Melanie Thompson said to a circle of friends. Her dad was an officer at one of the nearby police detachments. "And the substitute teacher was in the wrong place at the wrong time."

"Mom said to be extra careful. First Uncle Floyd's farm accident, and now my substitute teacher," Willy Weber whispered to his ninth-grade classmates. "I'm not going to tell her someone's trying to kill Ms. Rose. She'll probably send me off to the private school."

Celia's son, Toby, one of my brighter students, asked if he could speak with me privately. "Ms. Rose, I don't know if it's important. But I noticed something the day Mrs. Schultz died. When I walked home from school, there was a white utility van parked on the road. It looked like the vans the school board uses when they come to fix stuff. But usually, they park in the school lot."

When I asked if he told the police, Toby scratched his head. "Naw. I didn't want to make a big deal out of it. But it's been bugging me."

During lunch, Olivia said, "I still can't get over how you were away the day the killer struck. You're never off. What are the odds of that? What made you stay home that day?"

I told Olivia about Scott. Not just that I knew him from before—I had already explained our past relationship. But about my present feelings for him. "We were up late that night, just talking." I lowered my eyes, feeling the heat creep up my neck when Olivia raised her eyebrows. "And I took the next day off. I don't think I should feel guilty."

Olivia agreed I deserved a day off. "I'm just saying fate stepped in. You were lucky."

I had never considered myself lucky. Except during the twelve and a half years I was married to Jim. Those were *very* lucky years. I didn't deserve them.

"Speaking of Detective Evans, is he any closer to finding who's causing the accidents?" Olivia asked. "I've been thinking. My manuscript, Eugene's *Beach Bodies*, your story "My Life in Shreds," the awards banquet…is the killer a mystery reader? Or a writer? Someone in the online critique group? One of the people in Murder Club? Is it possible it's someone we know?"

I nearly jumped out of my chair, knocking some things from my desk onto the linoleum in the process. "That's exactly what Scott and I were thinking. Mystery writers. Mystery novels. But someone we *know*? Surely not. We should make a list. Of all the victims. The books that are connected. All the writers that described their deaths. And all the people we know who love mystery novels."

As I gathered up the objects that had fallen to the floor, a pen caught my eye. It had a logo: Townsend Pool Services. I assumed it must belong to one of my students. Grabbing a piece of blank paper, I began a list. First, Wendall. His death was connected to Eugene's book. Then Larissa. Olivia's manuscript was about a woman who died from a fall. Then Eugene.

The bell rang. Frustrated, I put the pen and paper in my purse to continue later. For the rest of the afternoon, I tried to put all thoughts of murder aside. The day dragged on. At the final bell, I gathered up my materials, anxious to leave. Judging by the looks on my colleague's faces, no one intended to hang around after school. The locked workroom and police officer posted in the middle of the hall served as a constant reminder of Connie's death.

Going to the library.

I texted Scott to remind him I had some overdue books. He responded he'd meet me there. Before leaving, I stopped at the office. It was a new safety policy Doug McLaren put in place. All staff were to report to the office upon arrival and departure. All student absences were to be investigated with immediate phone calls to parents. This was the new reality at Blue Water High. This was the new way of living in Blue Water County, formerly one of the safest places in Ontario. Now it was one of the deadliest.

Chapter Fifty-One

"You owe twelve dollars," Valerie said when I inquired about my overdue books. I handed her a ten-dollar bill and looked for change.

"Sorry about that. I completely forgot. With school starting and everything else going on, I just didn't have time…I shouldn't have been selfish and taken out three bestsellers when other people were waiting to read them."

I dug around in my change purse, and a dollar slipped out of my hand, fell on the floor, and rolled out of sight under the library counter.

I fished around my purse some more. "I don't seem to have enough."

"I know where you live," Valerie joked. She placed my books on the cart and walked away to help a patron at the computer station. In the center of the library, where comfortable chairs and a couple of sofas were arranged around the large double-sided stone fireplace, Scott sat with his ankle over his knee, reading a *Camaro Performers* magazine.

"I can sign that out for you if you want," I offered. "Even though I'm a delinquent." I explained what happened. Bringing his magazine, along with two others, to the counter, Scott said he'd take care of the amount owed.

"You know, you probably should try to find that dollar you dropped," Scott suggested as we waited. "It could be your lucky coin."

"My lucky coin? You believe in luck and serendipity, but not curses?" I snickered.

"I do. And it's not funny. I got lucky with a lost coin once. Took me ten minutes to find it in the tall grass next to the parking meter," he said with a serious expression.

"You must have been really desperate for those few cents."

"I bought a lottery ticket with that coin. Won twenty thousand dollars."

"You did not," I scoffed. "Well, I don't usually buy tickets. With my luck, there's no chance of a win."

Scott set down his magazines on the wooden counter and knelt to look for the coin. "There it is—almost on the other side of the counter."

I slid in behind and knelt beside the librarian's chair. "Got it." As I rose, something familiar caught my eye on the top shelf of the counter, next to a library repair kit and a stack of damaged books. The thick brown envelope had a label on the front, addressed to Justin Newark.

So, Valerie is sending him a manuscript, too.

Underneath it were two other similar envelopes.

I barely returned to the front of the counter before the library assistant spotted me. "Is there something I can help you with?" she asked, taking the magazines from Scott and raising her eyebrows at me.

"Just these, and on my account, please. I owe a couple bucks. Here's one. I'll pay the rest next time."

Taking a five-dollar bill out of his pocket, Scott advised me to keep the lucky coin. I gave him an eye roll. Opening a hidden zippered side compartment in my purse, I slipped the coin inside for safekeeping. Scott noticed the folded sheet of paper with a pen clipped to it. "Can I have a look at that?" he asked.

I explained I was making a list of victims and books, looking for a connection we might have missed.

"I meant the pen. Where'd you get it?"

I handed it over, the paper attached. "One of the students must have dropped it and the custodian probably picked it up and set it on my desk."

As we walked to Scott's Camaro, I asked, "Did you seriously win the lottery?"

"How do you think I could afford this car with alimony and child support?"

Scott winked as he started up his Camaro. "I'd hold onto that coin. You never know. Maybe it'll change your luck. Time to put that curse behind you."

I ran my fingers over my turquoise bracelet. Maybe it *was* time.

231

Chapter Fifty-Two

"What are you thinking?" Scott asked as we sat in front of the TV. "You've been lost in your thoughts since you found that dollar."

"There were three thick envelopes behind the library counter, all addressed to Justin Newark, this literary agent in Oakridge. It's strange."

"What's strange?"

"People I know are submitting mystery novels to him. Olivia told me about Justin when she submitted her manuscript to him. It was the day we heard about Wendall's death. There's something odd about this agent."

"I don't know a lot about the publishing industry and how it all works. Enlighten me."

I explained the usual process for submitting a manuscript to an agent. "But with Justin, there was no email address or online form to complete, only a postal box. And he requested *full* manuscripts be sent to him without reading a sample."

We locked eyes. "So, you think he's connected to the murders?" Scott asked at the same time I blurted out, "What if he's involved...?"

Scott decided to go to Oakridge in the morning to check out Justin's post office box.

"Why don't you pop in to see Brent while you're there? His office is nearby. I'm sure he'll be glad to see you." I had fond memories of how Scott always found time to play with the kids when he dropped in for a visit. He was like one of the family.

Scott inquired about what Brent did for a living. "I heard he's a lawyer. I always thought he'd do something with cars."

I laughed, thinking of how impressed Brent was with Scott's Camaro. "Actually, he's a defense attorney. He grew up believing there are two sides to every story."

"Good for him," Scott said. "I'd love to see him. In my mind, he's still a twelve-year-old kid. Those were good times."

I remembered them well. The laughter and friendship. How Scott always made the kids' eyes light up when he came for a visit. The mutual attraction we couldn't act on because I was happily married. The way Scott respected Jim. What was holding me back now? Scott was right—Jim would want me to be happy.

I pried the remote from Scott's hand and set it on the coffee table. Scooting closer to him, I laid my hand over his heart and snuggled my head into his right shoulder, tilting my head up to meet his eyes. "I was thinking maybe we could entertain ourselves instead of watching TV."

"What did you have in mind?" His lips brushed mine. Then, the corners of his mouth turned up. "Do you still have that Clue game?"

We used to play the mystery board game years ago, the five of us—me, Jim, Brent, Jamie, and Scott. I took my hand from his heart, cradled his face, and kissed him. Scott's laughter was replaced by a moan.

I stood and took him by the hand. "I was thinking a little more along the lines of a bedtime activity."

"You're going to read me one of your stories?" He grinned up at me. "You have *no* idea how long I've waited for that."

I sat again, my lips trailing down his chest while unbuttoning his shirt and undoing his belt buckle. When I looked into his face, his eyes were closed. "Let's go to bed then," I whispered in his ear. "I've been waiting a long time, too."

Scott's eyes opened, full of pent-up desire, as I untucked his shirt from his jeans. "How many more clues do you need, Detective?"

My heart pounded as Scott's breathing quickened. He pulled away, his eyes still on mine, his voice soft. "Ivy, no. We should wait." He buttoned up his shirt. "I don't want to jeopardize our relationship."

"I thought this was what you wanted." Hurt and embarrassed, I stood and walked toward the door. "Maybe you should go back to the hotel tonight."

Scott joined me in the entry. "I do. Want this. More than anything. But not if you're not ready. Good night, Ivy."

As he turned the doorknob, I blurted out, "I want what you want, Scott. Please stay."

He turned to face me. "I don't want to rush you."

"I want what you want," I repeated.

"Are you sure?"

"Yes. I'm definitely sure," I whispered, taking his hand and leading him to the bedroom.

"I told you that coin could turn out to be lucky." Scott pressed me against the hallway wall, his mouth claiming mine as he unbuttoned my blouse.

*　*　*

We woke to the music alarm, spooning in the center of the bed. I groaned, then realized I wasn't alone. For the first time in years, there was a man in my bed, a naked one.

As I tugged the covers over our bodies, Scott kissed my forehead, my eyes, my lips. "Good morning." He worked his way down.

"It's c…c…cold," I shivered, more from desire than from the temperature.

"I'll warm you up," he said, his mouth trailing across my stomach.

"Did I mention that you have a lot of skills, Detective?"

"Several times last night," he chuckled. "How about I show you a few more?"

The heat coursed through me. It had been so natural with him last night; we were a perfect fit, we had a perfect rhythm, as though we'd always been together. Comfortable. Safe. And yet not too comfortable…no, definitely not too…Just perfect. Perfectly natural.

And he made my toes tingle.

"I've been waiting fourteen years for this," he confessed, lifting his face to gaze into my eyes and caress my face. "Since the first moment I saw you, I wanted you."

"I know. I've been waiting, too."

"I didn't act on my feelings, out of respect for you and Jim."

"I know…I couldn't…I loved Jim."

"But now you can."

"Yes, now I can."

I lay in his arms afterwards, Scott stroking my head as he asked, "What do you think about coming up north with me after this is all over?"

I stiffened. "I don't want to go back north. It would be too painful. The memories."

He lay silent, only his breathing and the beating of his heart speaking to me. We had no future. Only memories. Only the moment.

The 7:30 news came on the radio, reminding me I couldn't stay with Scott. "Oh, no! I'm late."

He pulled me back as I struggled to get out of bed. "I could spend all day in bed with you."

"I think we spent most of the night… Anyway, I need to get going. I can't just roll into work any time of the day, like you."

"Why don't you call in sick?"

"I can't do that. What will people think? The last time I was off, my substitute got murdered. No one's going to want to cover for me ever again." I disentangled myself from him and pulled on my robe. "I'm going to shower."

Scott followed me into the bathroom, without even a modicum of modesty. After we brushed our teeth and showered, I wrapped a towel around myself, pushing him away when he tried to kiss me. "I need to go."

"Remember to stay in a group and come directly home after school. Keep your doors locked and…"

"Yes, Dad." I moved my hands to my hips, and the towel unknotted.

Scott pulled me close and whispered in my ear. "Tell me you'll think about moving back up north."

I pulled away. "My life is here. My kids. My job. Which I need to get to right now."

Scott blocked the door as I reached for the bathroom door handle. "And my life is up north. Where does that leave *us?*"

"I don't know. But don't tell Brent about *us* just yet."

I wasn't sure what exactly I would tell my son. Scott was no longer just my detective buddy. We were friends with benefits. But to me, it was so much more. I was sure I was very much in love with him. And he hadn't mentioned a word about love last night. Not that it would matter. I had no plans to move up north with him and live the 'happily ever after' I should be living with Jim.

Chapter Fifty-Three

It took an hour and ten minutes to get to Oakridge with rush hour traffic. As Scott approached the city, he pulled over to call Brent. "Hi, Brent. It's Scott Evans. I'm wondering if I could drop by, for old time's sake, if you've got a few minutes."

"Sure, sounds good." They agreed to meet for lunch at a restaurant just down the block from Brent's office.

As Scott drove to the city center, most of the rush hour traffic had thinned out. He parked on the street, close to the post office. From the sidewalk, the postal boxes were visible inside the glass and concrete structure. PO Box 275 was one of the larger lock boxes. Scott strode to the long service counter, showing his ID, and asked to speak to the manager.

"How can I help you?" An efficient-looking middle-aged brunette introduced herself as branch manager. When he explained the purpose of his visit, she said they couldn't divulge customers' private details.

"Excuse me," the young blond clerk said when the manager left the counter. "I *know* Justin. He's a literary agent."

"Would you be able to describe him?" Scott asked.

"Sure, just a sec." She stepped out from behind the counter. "Older guy, good-looking. Dark brown hair, about six feet tall, muscular. Friendly," she said.

"And how do you know him?"

"I'm the one who rented him the box. Under his business name—Newark Literary. Said he was expecting a lot of thick manuscripts in the mail, and I signed him up for an extra-large box. I'm a writer, so I was super excited to make a connection with an agent, but he doesn't rep literary fiction. We talk about books and writing when he comes in. Are you a writer, too?"

"No, just a detective. But a good friend of mine is. A mystery writer. Maybe you've heard of her? Ivy Rose?" She hadn't, of course. And Scott hated to lie, but perhaps she had information that could be useful to his case. "She sent her manuscript to Justin, then her computer crashed and that was her only copy. She hasn't heard back from him and was hoping to get his phone number."

"Oh, no! That's brutal! I don't know what I'd do if I lost my work. I'm sorry I can't give out his number or address, but I *can* tell you what he drives, if that helps. I was coming in to work one day when I saw him pull up in his white utility van. It's a Chevy. I know that because my boyfriend drives one like it for the plumbing company where he works."

"Any signage on it?"

"No, sorry. I didn't notice."

Scott thanked the young woman for her help and headed out to meet with Brent. As he maneuvered the busy main street, he spotted a white delivery van behind him. He slowed down, expecting the driver to pass so he could get a good look at the license plate. The van slowed as well, allowing a vehicle to pass and then another. Waiting for the traffic to thin, Scott signaled and pulled into the first available parking spot, watching for the van to drive past.

Seeing no sign of the white vehicle, he made a U-turn and backtracked. A few blocks back, he spotted it, parked with no driver in sight. Scott took down the license plate number and radioed it to the station.

"An Oakridge-based courier delivery company," came the reply.

Scott sighed. Of course, it wouldn't be Justin's vehicle. How many white Chevy vans were there in the city? He couldn't chase them all. Still, there was no reason why a literary agent couldn't work a day job as a courier.

Minutes later, a fit-looking young woman in her courier's uniform bounced down the sidewalk and hopped into the van. Not Justin.

Scott turned right at the next corner and circled the block, heading back in the direction of his lunch date with Brent. In the parking lot of the chain restaurant, someone called his name.

"Brent?" He had a hard time reconciling the tall, handsome man with wavy black hair with the kid he once knew. As he approached, Scott recognized some of Ivy's facial features in his. "How are you? So good to see you."

They shook hands, and Brent chuckled, "I see you still drive a silver Camaro."

"I've always been a Camaro man. I still have the one I drove when you were a kid. It holds a lot of good memories for me. I keep it in storage and take it out for a spin now and then."

"Wow, that's something. I've got one of my own." Brent told him about his classic 1998 silver Camaro. "I'm restoring it. That Camaro of yours was one of the happy memories from my childhood in Lake Kipling. I told all my friends at school my best friend was a detective and drove a cool Camaro."

"Just the Camaro was cool, I wasn't?" Scott laughed. "To tell the truth, I wasn't sure you'd even remember me. I was a good friend of your mom's." He thought it prudent to add, "And your dad's."

"Yes, yes, of course, I remember."

They were seated, and the waitress took their orders. Brent chose the burger and fries. "I see you've still got a taste for junk food," he commented when Scott followed his lead. The two men discussed the past, mainly focusing on cars, food, and the games they played as a family—Brent, Jamie, Mom and Dad, and Mom's detective friend, Scott.

"So, I hear you're a lawyer now." Scott changed the conversation to the present. They talked shop for a while, the defense lawyer and the detective. "Glad to hear things are going well for you."

"How is the investigation into the mystery writer murders going? That's what Mom calls it." Brent stopped eating and stared at Scott. "And what *exactly* is going on between you and Mom?"

Scott nearly choked on his burger. Coughing into his napkin, he thought of how to answer that question. Last night was amazing, especially after longing for her for when they knew each other in Lake Kipling and knowing he could never have her. But he didn't know what the future would bring with over four hundred miles between them. "We're just getting to know each other again. I'm glad she's back in my life. It was a real stroke of luck, my coming to Port Ripley. I couldn't believe it when I ran into her."

They discussed the case, and Scott told Brent they were closing in on the killer. "Just take care of Mom," Brent said. "She's had a rough life. I don't know how much she told you…"

"She told me you were abducted by a deluded old man who thought you were his grandson. I'm just glad she found you safe and unharmed."

"Yeah, didn't end so well for the old man." Brent gazed off into the distance. "And with Dad gone, she had a lot to handle."

Scott nodded. "I wish I could have been there for your mom, and for you and Jamie."

"So do I. But Mom said we couldn't go backwards. We needed a fresh start." Brent placed his hand on Scott's arm. "I'm glad you're back in her life. She's been lonely."

The meal ended with the two men saying they hoped to see more of each other. As Scott drove back to Port Ripley, he considered how fortunate he was to have been given this second chance with Ivy. If he could just solve the case and make sure she was out of danger…but then he would have no excuse for staying in Port Ripley.

There was one other lead to follow up on before returning to the station. Scott stopped at a small industrial strip mall on the main highway at the south end of Port Ripley. A storefront with a sign, Townsend Pool Services, held shelves filled with pool and hot tub equipment at the front. Scott was greeted by an older woman who approached from her desk in the partly glass-enclosed office adjoining the warehouse.

"Hello. What can I do for you?"

Scott showed his badge. "I'm wondering if one of your staff was at Blue Water High recently." When she said the high school didn't have a pool, Scott showed her the pen with their logo. "This was found at the school."

"We give out hundreds to customers, potential clients. The staff, students, parents—a lot of them would have one of our pens."

Scott asked what type of litmus paper they used. The sample piece he showed her was a match to the strip found in Carter's garage. Scott was sure he was about to break open the case. He asked the woman if she knew Carter Loewen.

"Yes, he used to work here, doing pool maintenance. Quit a couple of weeks ago. I heard about his death. Such a shock. He didn't seem like the suicidal type."

Chapter Fifty-Four

I was having a tough time staying awake through my morning classes, much less concentrating on my students. By the time lunch break came around, I had consumed four cups of sugar-laden coffee and was running high on adrenaline. I asked Olivia to join me in my classroom.

"Are you feeling okay?" Olivia asked, behind closed doors. "You look a little on edge."

"I'm fine, just didn't get enough sleep last night." It wasn't the appropriate time to tell Olivia about Scott. And besides, I wasn't sure what to say. Just because we spent one night together, it didn't necessarily mean anything. "Just tossing and turning. I guess it's the stress of knowing there's a killer amongst us and not knowing who it is."

Olivia shuddered and rubbed her hands over her arms. "It's downright creepy. Everyone's suspicious of everyone else. It's hard to know who to trust. Does Scott have any more leads on the case?"

"He's in Oakridge today, looking into something. It's Justin Newark. He's wondering whether there's a connection between him and the victims."

Olivia's mouth flew open, and she leaned in closer. "Why would he think that?"

I explained the theory that Scott and I discussed last night. "Don't you think it's really odd that he placed ads looking for mystery writers about the same time mystery writers began mysteriously dying?"

Olivia's eyes grew wider. "Oh, my goodness! So, you think we've made ourselves potential victims by submitting our manuscripts?"

"Yes. And I think he's using the methods from our manuscripts to kill people."

Olivia thought that over for a minute. "But that's just absolutely…" Olivia searched for the right word.

"Crazy," I finished for her.

"I wish I'd never written that book. I feel responsible for Larissa's death. I can't believe I may have inspired someone to actually carry out my stupid plot."

"It's not stupid, and it's not your fault any more than my writing a story about an accident with a shredder is mine. We can't control what other people do with our fiction."

Olivia sighed. "I don't even know why I wrote it. I've dabbled in personal writing, just letters and diary entries, some poetry, my memoir—but all those books we read for Murder Club got me thinking I could write my own murder mystery. I'm too old to be thinking of starting a writing career. I should be looking ahead to retirement."

I reminded Olivia that I started with personal writing, went on to become a reporter, and then to publish short stories in literary magazines. "It's only this past year that I became a published author of a book. It's never too late to do what you want to do. Not until you're…" I was about to say 'dead'. "Really old. And, I don't know about you, but I'm not old yet."

Olivia nodded. "I know what you're saying. And you're right. Better late than never. And you're the one who has inspired me. I see you working hard to achieve your childhood dream, and I want something of my own, too. Something special that I can create and enjoy. I'm not sure it's writing murder mysteries, though."

"Maybe we could co-author a book?" I had recently read a thriller that worked well with two points of view, each written by a different author.

"Partners in crime fiction?"

"Once this whole true crime is behind us."

Olivia sprang from her chair as the bell pealed, signaling a return to class. The rest of the afternoon moved along at a snail's pace. I couldn't wait to hear what Scott discovered in Oakridge. During my spare period, I sat at my desk, eyes closed, hands supporting my head. The memory of last night was bittersweet. Finally, after fourteen years, we were together. But soon, it would all be over. Once Scott solved the case, he'd go back home to Lake Kipling, leaving me behind.

I forced my eyes open and looked at the student work on my desk, waiting to be marked. Sweeping it aside, I pulled out an empty sheet of paper. Something had been bothering me since last night. Being in Scott's arms made me temporarily forget it, but it was still niggling at the back of my brain.

I picked up my pen and began to write a new list. On the left-hand side of the paper, I wrote down the names of the known accident/murder victims in the county during the last couple of months. On the right-hand side, I recorded the names of the writers whose manuscripts were connected to the deaths. Who had read each of the manuscripts? I needed to add that piece of information. Was there an obvious clue there? Writers, books, readers, accidents.

When the buzzer rang for the next class, I stared at the piece of paper.

I wonder if...is it possible? Should I warn them?

I wasn't sure if I'd found a pattern or if I was trying too hard to see one. Regardless, the students were filing in, sitting down, and looking to me for direction. Time to pack away my sleuthing persona and put on my teacher's hat.

When the final bell of the day rang, following the lead of the students and most teachers, I left the building promptly and set off for the weekend. There was something I needed to do.

Chapter Fifty-Five

Blue Water Writes:

Did anyone else notice that some of the accident victims seem to be mystery writers? Hope everyone is being extra careful. Meet in groups. It's bound to be safer that way.

The Writer

The walls are closing in. What if...? It's not possible. But the evidence is there. And it points directly to...

It won't be long until Detective Evans pieces it all together. He needs to be stopped.

That's the problem with living in a small town. Everyone knows your business. It's no secret I have a problem. The rumors go around. But everyone pretends they're just rumors because everyone has something to lose. They all battle their own private demons. The alcohol. The drugs. The sex addiction. The gambler. The philandering fiancé. The affairs. The writers. The secrets. The murders.

What about the detective? He must have an Achilles heel.

Chapter Fifty-Six

lice was setting up a new window display of escapist books—romance, fantasy, adventure, science fiction. I peered in, startling Alice, causing books to fall like dominoes.

"Oh, I'm so sorry. Here, let me help you." I stepped into the alcove and picked books off the floor. "I shouldn't have gawked in at you like that."

"It's fine, it's not your fault. I'm just on edge with what's been going on lately."

"We all are." I helped her set books back onto the tables. "I see you're putting up quite a range of genres. I don't see any mysteries, though."

"I think everyone's had about enough murder for now," Alice responded, with a shiver. "It's hitting too close to home, and sales are down the last couple of weeks. Hardly anyone is shopping late because they're too afraid to be out at night. I was hoping to get people's minds off the murders by suggesting other types of fiction."

"Sounds like a good idea. I'm sorry to interrupt, but I wanted to warn you in person." I put the last book in its spot and turned to face Alice. "I think you might be in danger. I've noticed a pattern in the murders."

Alice made an abrupt movement and toppled over the display again. "Pattern? What pattern?"

"I'm pretty sure the killer is getting ideas for the murders from mystery books. And the writers of those books are also his victims. They're intertwined somehow."

"What? That's insane!"

"I think the hunting accident in your manuscript inspired Phillip Reese's killing. And since there's been no attempt made on your life yet, I'm worried you may be one of the next victims. So, I just wanted to warn you to be extra careful."

"But my book isn't published, and no one's read my manuscript," Alice stammered. "Except...Wendall, who's dead, and...you. And you're beyond suspicion. *You* would never kill anyone."

Chapter Fifty-Seven

"You just missed Ivy," Alice said, as he entered the store.

Scott approached the window alcove where Alice arranged and rearranged books. "Ivy? What was she doing here?"

He had told her to go directly home after school. Why couldn't that woman do as she was told? Her life was in danger.

"She wanted to warn me to be careful."

Scott took a deep breath. If only Ivy would heed her own advice. He exhaled loudly.

"Is everything okay, Detective?"

When Scott indicated he wanted to ask her a few more questions about the case, Alice turned around the Open sign and locked the door. "Let's go back where we can speak in private. There *is* something I wanted to discuss with you."

She led him to the back corner and motioned for him to have a seat on one of the chairs by the fireplace as she lowered herself into the other. "Ivy confided something to me about the case, and maybe she shouldn't have, but she said she's worried about me. Am I in danger?"

"Oh? What did she say?" Scott fought to contain his displeasure at Ivy sharing information about the case, especially when he was so close to nailing his main suspect.

"The killer is targeting mystery writers and using ideas from their books."

"That is one theory I'm working on." Scott didn't think there was any point in denying what Alice already knew to be true. "But we're still gathering information and evidence. Which is why I stopped by to see you. I wondered whether Carter Loewen had ever been to your house to service your pool."

Alice's eyes shifted, and she hesitated before answering. "Yes, yes, he has."

"You didn't mention he worked for Townsend Pools."

"Was that important? Was he involved in the deaths? Do you think he killed himself out of guilt?"

Scott waited for her eyes to meet his. "Everything is important in a murder investigation."

Alice kept her eyes locked on Scott's. "Well, then maybe I should share a few things I've been mulling over. Ivy's thoughts about the killer mimic Eugene's book *You're Killing Me*. You've probably already figured that out. And everyone has access to his book. Then, there's *Beach Bodies*. Eugene wrote about a body washing ashore, just like what happened to Wendall."

Scott nodded.

"But what you might *not* know is, and I shouldn't be breaking a confidence, Eugene was far from faithful to Willow. He got his kicks out of using women. Paige, Celia, for starters. What he did to Paige was…criminal. He had Celia believing he was leaving Willow for her. And who knows what else he was capable of? Murder?"

"Eugene was a victim," Scott reminded her. He wondered why she was so reluctant to bring up her own relationship with Eugene.

"Humph. Was he?" Alice looked away. "It's a shame he's dead, but…maybe he brought it upon himself."

"How so?"

"It's a small town, Detective. Everybody knows everybody's business. And the writing community is even tighter."

"Meaning?"

"Wendall critiqued my manuscript about a hunting accident. He told me he also critiqued a manuscript about a car accident. And he said he was giving his manuscript, about a manure tank accident, to Celia to critique. I'm wondering whether Celia read anyone else's books. What is she privy to?"

"Celia?"

"Celia and Eugene. A man who wrote a book about the serial killing of mystery authors and a woman who has her nose in everybody's business involved in an illicit affair. Think about it, Detective. Love can make you do crazy things." Alice rose and took a step forward.

He certainly had thought about it. Taking that as a sign the discussion was over, Scott eased himself out of his chair. Alice slid toward him. She placed her hand on his chest and ran it downwards, lowering herself, tugging at his belt buckle. "If Ivy is right, perhaps I need personal police protection. I'm willing to discuss this further in private, if you're interested."

Scott tripped over the chair leg as he jolted away from Alice, who was kneeling on the floor at this point. "The door's locked. No one needs to know," she said.

What the hell?

"Thank you for speaking to me about the case," Scott tried to salvage the uncomfortable situation, moving further away. "And I'm sorry, but I'm already taken."

"You mean Ivy?" Alice shouted as he bolted for the front door. "Maybe you should know something else. Wendall read my manuscript about the hunting accident. He's dead, as per Eugene's book. The only other person who read my manuscript was Ivy. Maybe you should be looking for the killer closer to home."

Chapter Fifty-Eight

After the bookstore, I dropped by Paige Thornton's house, in one of the newer subdivisions on the edge of town. Paige looked harried when she answered the doorbell of her gray brick loft bungalow, brushing hair out of her eyes.

"Come in," she said. "I'm getting supper ready." Her two little boys were in the family room off the kitchen, playing, or rather fighting, with their toy vehicles. It made me nostalgic for the days when Brent and Jamie played with their vehicles. The difference was, Brent didn't have a sibling to fight with for the first five years. I was so excited when I learned I was pregnant with Jim's baby. Although I regretted that Jim and I had waited till we were financially stable to grow our family, I had the advantage of having a responsible built-in babysitter when Brent turned twelve. It upset me that Jim didn't live to see our children grow up. After my parents were gone, we discussed having a third, and we were trying for a baby when Stefan took Jim from us. Whenever I see a happy family, it reminds me not only of Jim's loss, but that of the child that could have been.

"Sorry for the mess," Paige said, seeing me take in the homey kitchen and family room.

"Oh, no. Don't worry about that. I was just thinking back to when my kids were little. Those were the happiest days of my life. You have a lovely home."

Paige stopped chopping vegetables. "Yes, I'm very lucky."

"I had a thought about the killer today. The methods he's using come from manuscripts of mystery writers in the local area."

Paige gasped. "What? That's nuts!"

"I've also noticed that the writers of the manuscripts end up victims themselves. I thought I should warn you. If I'm right, you could be one of the next victims."

"Me? Why would anyone want to...." She looked over at her two boys who were still fighting. Leading me to the formal dining room, Paige half-closed the door. "Why kill me?"

"I don't think it's about you personally. The killer is simply killing off mystery writers."

"But I'm not a mystery writer. I write children's stories, for Pete's sake."

I told her about Olivia's hot tub accident. "I know you wrote about a hot tub murder, and I know Larissa was your beta reader. Who else read your book? Who else knows about the hot tub murder? The killer must have read it."

"Well, I guess *you* know."

"Apart from me, who else? What about Matt?" Alice once confided in me that she was seeing Matt for counseling, but didn't want anyone to know. Maybe she had shared her idea for her manuscript with him.

"Matt? He doesn't know I'm writing mysteries. I didn't think he'd approve. He doesn't know about my mystery book, and he doesn't know...." Her voice had been quiet, but now she slipped into a whisper. "I've been seeing Riley, you know for—"

"You don't need to explain to me. That's between you and Matt, but you really need to deal with it."

"I can't help myself. Sometimes I think I do these things to see how far I can go. It's like I want to get caught doing something terrible enough for him to leave me. Matt is always so calm and understanding about everything. Maybe it's just a cry for attention. I'd like to get a reaction out of him, maybe have him lay down the law. But he keeps putting up with it."

"He must love you a lot." I tried to understand Paige's self-destructive behavior and her husband's blind acceptance of it. Jim was aware of the attraction between Scott and me, and we discussed it openly. Jim knew Scott was important to me and accepted our friendship, knowing I would never put our marriage or our family at risk. I had almost destroyed my relationship with Jim years ago when I dated Darko and got pregnant. But Jim loved me enough to put that behind us. I put my hand on Paige's, hoping to stop her from making a mistake she would always regret. "You should talk to Matt and be honest about what you're feeling. Don't put your family in jeopardy because of your addictions. Let Matt help you." As an afterthought, I added, "And you really should break it off with Riley. It's one thing having sex with strangers. But Matt sees Riley every time he goes to the hardware store, and they're bound to cross paths in town. It's going to be a very uncomfortable situation when he finds out. And he will find out. If he hasn't already. You know how rumors spread."

"I know. I will. Break it off. Soon."

"Sorry, I didn't come here to stick my nose in your business and preach about being faithful to your husband. I just wanted to warn you. And by the way, if Larissa read your manuscript, did you read hers?"

"No, but I did read Riley's, and he read mine. He started his book with a shove off a cliff."

"Thanks, that really helps."

Paige said she needed to get back to the kitchen. "I can't be late with supper tonight. I've got a meeting at the bookstore at seven to talk about another book signing. Riley's going to be there. Well, you'll probably be there, too."

"No, I didn't know anything about it. I guess I'm not invited."

My next stop was the hardware store. Riley was behind the counter, serving his last customer. The store was closing in five minutes, the evening hours shortened the last few weeks as people weren't venturing out at night as much. I waited till the store was empty.

"How are you, Ivy? What can I do for you?"

When I explained I was there on personal business, Riley raised his eyebrows. "Oh?"

I explained my theory that mystery writers in the area were being killed with methods used by local writers in their manuscripts.

Confusion crossed Riley's face. "That's what you wanted to see me about?"

He narrowed his eyes. "So, what does that have to do with me? My book's non-fiction, and no one's tried to kill me."

"I'm talking about your mystery novel, the one where the killer shoves the victim off a cliff." Riley's mouth flew open as I continued, "One of the accidents in the county was the result of a fall off a cliff, just like in your book. I think you may be one of the next victims."

"How could you possibly know about my book? It's not published. No one's even read it." He backed away. "And why would someone want to kill *me*?"

"It was Paige."

"Paige? She would never hurt me! We're friends. Well, more than just friends, actually." He looked like he wanted to take back that last bit.

"No, no, I didn't mean Paige would hurt you."

"Her husband, though...*he* might kill me. You're not going to tell him about us, are you?"

"That's not my business. What I meant was Paige told me about your book. I know she beta-read your manuscript."

"So, you and Paige know about the cliff murder scene in my book. And the killer used it to actually kill someone? And now you're telling me I could be next?"

"Yes."

"But how could the killer know I wrote that scene?"

"I was hoping you could tell me."

Riley stared at me, as though assessing my intentions. "If it's not Paige, then it must be—you. But it *couldn't* be, could it?"

Chapter Fifty-Nine

Blue Water Writes:
Public Group - A community of writers in the Blue Water area - 1K members and shrinking

Mystery writer here. Anyone out there looking for a critique partner? I'm in the market for a new one. If you love a good murder, let's swap manuscripts.

As she described the next murder scene, her face lit up, and her eyes sparkled. With a smile, she announced, "The next accident is a double homicide."

"Perfect," he crooned, next to her on the couch. "You're so smart. That's what I like best about you." As he pushed his partner onto her back and kissed her, she shoved him away. He pinned her arms above her head with one hand and began to undo the zipper on her hoodie with his other. She usually liked it when he took charge, even if things got a bit rough.

This time, she bit his lip and spat, "Well, it's a good thing one of us is smart. Now get off me, you moron. I'm not in the mood."

Slowly, he rose from the couch and stood at the window, looking out, composing himself. The red-hot anger rose within him. But he wouldn't let it win. Turning back to face her, he calmly said, "Okay. Whatever you want, babe. However you want it. You know that." He smiled, his face showing none of the rage and humiliation he felt at being belittled and rejected. It certainly wasn't the first time she had treated him like this.

The domineering bitch was used to getting her own way. He found it a turn-on at first. But lately, it was wearing thin. She was a poor substitute. A clone, a replica, an imitation of the woman he really wanted but who had tossed him aside. He formulated a plan of his own. He'd show her who the moron was. The double homicide she so carefully planned was going to play out a bit differently. Murder by the books. With a twist she wouldn't see coming.

Chapter Sixty

The Writer

I could be in danger? The killer is after *me*? It would be almost funny if this whole thing wasn't so sad. Tragic. Absolutely unbelievably irrefutably catastrophic.

And now I've made a fool of myself in front of the detective. Will he take anything I said seriously now? Or anything else I say from this point forward?

What am I supposed to do? Wait and see? Pretend nothing's wrong?

Confront him? Talk to her?

Confess?

Point the finger yet elsewhere?

The nerve of some people. Cheating on me. And involving her in *this*? *This*...I can't even say the words. It's too horrific.

Eugene was a real piece of work.

Cheating on his fiancée? On Celia? On me? With who knows how many people?

Taking advantage of women. Drugging victims and luring them to a hotel room with his buddies. Filming them for his own pleasure.

They say confession is good for the soul. A confession at AAW helps, but it doesn't change things. *Everybody* knows. And it's always the woman who lives with the shame. Men get away with everything.

But there are worse things than sex scandals.

Writing that book. Putting ideas in people's heads. *He* started all *this*.

People are dead. And dying.

You think you know people. But…

You can't trust *anyone*.

Chapter Sixty-One

It was nearly six p.m. when I got home. Scott had texted earlier in the day, saying he'd be late and would pick up pizza for supper. Tom meowed to be fed as soon as I stepped through the door. He wasn't having any of this late dinner nonsense. "Okay, okay," I agreed, dodging him as he tried to trip me on the way to the kitchen.

At 6:45, I finished sketching out lesson plans for Monday and was about to call it 'good enough' when a thought entered my head. The meeting about book signings that Paige mentioned. Riley, Paige, Alice—they were going to be at the bookstore tonight. All three were mystery writers, their manuscripts used in the recent accidents. But none of them had suffered an accident themselves. Could that change tonight?

I pulled a wide binder off my bookshelf. It contained a copy of the manuscript of the first book in my series. Setting it on the coffee table and turning the floor lamp to maximum light, I flipped through the chapters till I came upon the scene I was looking for. The victim was in the bookstore, perusing shelves containing hardcover books, looking for a mystery novel. As luck would have it, he wouldn't get the opportunity to enjoy it. The entire bookcase came crashing down on him, catching him completely unaware. He was pinned down by the weight of hundreds of mystery books, his last breath crushed out of him by the genre he loved best.

Tonight's meeting could be just the opportunity the killer was waiting for.

Chapter Sixty-Two

Maybe she'd parked her car in the garage. Scott reached into his passenger seat to remove the pizza box. The house was unlocked.

"Ivy? Ivy? I'm home." He liked the sound of that. Home with Ivy.

Hearing no answer, he placed the pizza box on the stove. Tom rubbed against his legs, meowing for attention and food. "Here you go." Scott peeled off some ham from the pizza and tossed it down. "Sorry supper's late. Where's your mom? I've got some bad news to tell her about her friend, Alice."

His latest meeting with Alice confirmed his suspicions. He just needed more proof.

The office door was open. In the bedroom, Ivy's phone sat on the dresser, her purse on a chair. Finding the house empty, he ran outside. He was about to knock on June's door when she opened it.

"Are you looking for Ivy? You just missed her. She drove out of here like a bat out of hell. Acted like I was invisible. Didn't even answer when I said hello."

"Where was she going?" His stomach was in knots.

"I have no idea. Didn't she leave any clues?"

Scott ran back to check Ivy's phone. The last message was from him saying he'd be late. On his way through the hall, he noticed a binder on the coffee table. He read the page Ivy had left open. Five minutes later, he was downtown, in front of Worth a Read. A loud crash resounded through the store.

Chapter Sixty-Three

The closed sign was up, the lights were dim, and the door to the bookstore was locked. I peered through the display window. The place was so crammed full of shelving and books, it was difficult to see if anyone was inside.

I hurried to the back entrance where Paige's maroon Honda CR-V and Riley's white delivery van were parked next to Valerie's bright blue Ford Fusion. Concrete steps led to the lower-level exit, which was usually locked, unless there was a meeting. As I slipped through the door and rushed to the stairs, Valerie's voice drifted down from the main level.

"…in the display windows. Then we'll set up a table with your books and author merchandise. Oh wait, I forgot to bring the product catalog. Anyway, here are some of the samples: pens, notepads, bookmarks… Why don't you take a look while I get the catalog?" Footsteps went off in the direction of the sales counter, opposite the stairwell.

I crept up the stairs, tiptoed around shelves, and froze. With their backs to me, Paige and Riley stood next to the fireplace. Riley leaned over to kiss her.

"I really shouldn't…This needs to end," Paige whispered, pulling away. "Matt—"

"Matt doesn't understand your needs the way I do. You and I are good together. Maybe you should tell Matt about us and ask for a divorce. I can give you what you want. He obviously doesn't."

I stepped back and hid behind the end of a bookcase as Valerie returned. "Here we are." As they flipped through the catalog, Valerie made suggestions.

"Mugs with your photos of the lake would work well. Or calendars featuring your photography of historical buildings. Nice souvenirs for the tourists and a great way for you to keep your name out there. And for the kids, Paige, what about a coloring book or stickers featuring some of your cute characters?"

As they discussed options, from out of the corner of my eye, a bookshelf moved. I blinked and looked again. Sure enough, it was teetering. All the shelving was screw nailed into the hardwood, wasn't it? Someone else must be in the store. Behind the bookshelf, loosening it from the flooring, trying to push it over. Just like in my manuscript.

Chapter Sixty-Four

Paige, Riley, and Valerie stood in the path of the wobbling bookshelf. Move!" I screamed. "The bookcase is falling!" Seeing me running toward them, gesturing, they jumped back out of the way, just before the wooden bookshelf, laden with hardcovers, crashed down onto the table, crushing it.

"What the hell?" Valerie shouted.

Trapped in the corner, they crouched as a shadow flew past an unlit section of the store, dodging the shelving and displays. At the same time, a gunshot rang out, and glass shattered. Without thinking, I chased the shadow down the stairs.

I ran on adrenaline, through the center of the game aisles, on the heels of the suspect, who was wearing a hoodie. Picking up a game of Clue, I threw it like a Frisbee, clipping the assailant on the back of the head. Stunned for a moment, the shape swayed back and forth.

"Stop! Police! Put your hands up in the air!" I shouted. For a minute, the hooded figure looked ready to comply, but then turned to face me.

"*You?*" I pulled down the hood and was knocked to the floor. The bright security lights allowed me to identify the person who aimed a battery-operated screwdriver at my forehead.

Chapter Sixty-Five

The crash came from somewhere near the back. Scott fired a shot through the glass and darted through the store, stopping abruptly upon seeing the three people trapped beside the stairwell. "Downstairs," Paige yelled. "Help Ivy!"

Jolted back into action, he took the stairs two at a time. When he saw the screwdriver at Ivy's forehead, he didn't hesitate. "Police!" A bullet to the man's shoulder kicked the tool out of his hand. "Don't move!" Scott held his gun steady. "On your knees, hands where I can see them."

Scott cuffed him to a shelf and called for assistance. "If you've hurt her, you're a dead man." He knelt next to Ivy and cradled her.

"Scott?" she said, her voice weak. "I love you."

* * *

"Do you have any idea why he did it?" Olivia sat next to me, in the emergency room. Scott had called her to be with me while he went to the station to explain what happened at the bookstore and to fill out a report. "Is it just a random serial killing?"

"I don't know. We'll have to wait for Scott to tell us. I can't believe it. Valerie's boyfriend. Poor Valerie. This will be such a shock to her. She was nearly one of his victims."

"It's a good thing he's not that good at murder. He got caught. And you escaped, Valerie, June, and so did I," said Olivia. "Maybe others."

I considered all those who didn't survive.

After the doctor examined me, I was free to go home. "You need to rest," the doctor ordered. "No more murders, real or fictional, for the next couple of days. Stay away from books, TV. No writing, no school. And no more detective work. I don't want to see you back here with another head injury."

I agreed to stay out of trouble. I'd had enough murder to last a lifetime. Maybe I would switch to reading and writing romance.

We were on the couch, making our way through a box of a dozen doughnuts and a pot of tea when Scott came home. "I brought a fresh pizza. But I see you've already got supper covered. Did you save any for me, for dessert?"

"There might be a couple yet, if you hurry," I joked.

Scott placed a couple pieces of pizza on a plate for each of us and grabbed a beer out of the fridge and four slices for himself. Tom rubbed up against his legs.

"So?" I picked up a slice. "Why did he do it?"

"So." Scott put his feet up on the coffee table, chewed his pizza, and tossed some pieces of meat to Tom. "Unbelievable story. He was happy to tell it. Bragged, actually. Brock Townsend, owner of Townsend Pool Services, is a mystery writer. He wrote a novel about some crazed lunatic who kills mystery writers to decrease the competition and to get back at those who find the success she hasn't. Personally, I think it's more of an autobiography. Anyway, long crazy story short, his main character, the killer, gets her ideas for the murders from other mystery novels. The murders are made to look like accidents. She gets away with it, and writes a novel about it, which becomes a bestseller. It's a rip-off of Eugene's book, *You're Killing Me.* But not nearly as good. A copycat writer, not a copycat killer like we considered when we thought there might be an accomplice. Unfortunately for Brock, his own story didn't end as well as his main character's did." Scott leaned back on the couch, Tom on his lap, and polished off his slice.

Olivia stared at him, her eyes and mouth open wide. "That's insane," she finally said.

"Yep." He started into his second slice.

"What about Justin Newark? We thought the literary agent was involved,"

I reminded him. "Was that a coincidence?"

"No." He chewed and swallowed. "Brock *is* Justin. That's how he got fresh new ideas for his own writing and for the murders. Desperate writers looking for an agent. Potential competition. Victims. Justin was never a real agent. I'm sorry about your books. You'll have to submit elsewhere."

"It doesn't matter. The important thing is you caught the killer."

"Actually, I think *you* did that. I just showed up to arrest him."

After Olivia left, I wrapped my arms around Scott. "Thank you for saving my life. If you hadn't been there…" I convulsed at the memory of the screwdriver. The shock, the relief, realizing how much I needed Scott. And knowing now that the case was solved, he was going to leave.

"Shh…it's okay. Everything's going to be all right. I owed you. You saved my life once, remember?" He scooted closer on the couch and pulled me down on top of him. "You said you love me. Show me how much."

"I hit my head on the floor when I got knocked down. I may not have been thinking clearly when I said that," I said through my tears. "The doctor said a concussion can cause confusion. I've had two concussions, so I'm probably really confused."

Scott grinned. "Well, let me unconfuse things for you. I've been crazy about you since the first moment I saw you, all those years ago when I couldn't have you. I love you, Ivy, Cheryl, Lana, whatever you want to call yourself. I'll always love you. And I have every intention of having you to myself, all of you." He leaned over to kiss me when Tom jumped up and stuck his nose between us. "Maybe we should continue this behind closed doors."

Chapter Sixty-Six

Blue Water Writes:
Public Group - A community of writers in the Blue Water area - 1.1K members and growing again

Did you hear what went down at Worth A Read last night? Crazier than fiction! Thank goodness it's over. Blue Water is safe again.

"We were meant to be together. It was fate that brought you into my life," she had said.

"I know. We make a good team, you and I."

They were lounging in bed one Saturday afternoon when she asked, "Do you think she'd get away with it?"

"Who? Get away with what?" he asked as she raked her fingernails up and down his bare back. Much of their time together was spent in bed, at his place. They did go out occasionally, but she preferred to stay in. Take out food, Netflix, a couple bottles of wine, maybe a game of Scrabble, and she was happy. They talked about work and their families, but mainly, they concentrated on discussing their writing. They were, after all, critique partners.

"Your main character—the writer. Do you really believe she'd get away with killing off fellow mystery writers?"

"Sure. Why not? The cops think the killings are the work of a random serial killer. There's no real connection between all the victims, other than they love to read and write murder mysteries. And the killer doesn't even know all of her victims. It would be hard for the police to come up with a motive. Who would want to kill a bunch of writers? Especially ones they don't know?"

"A dissatisfied reader who hates their books and doesn't want to see any more published?"

He laughed. "That's a bit extreme."

"But a fellow *writer* killing them off isn't?"

"You know what I think? I think you're overthinking the whole premise. It's fiction. So, the chick's a bit delusional." He tried to get her mind off his book by pulling her on top of him.

"I suppose with all the different methods used in the killings, it would make it hard for the police to connect all the murders to one person," she acquiesced. "But…"

"But what?"

"What if it wasn't just one person?" She sprang up to a sitting position. "It would be really hard to prove opportunity."

"What do you mean?" He sat up alongside her and listened. "You think I should change my main character to two main characters?"

"Exactly! With no clear motive, all different murder methods…and…proof that she wasn't at the scene, or at least all of the scenes…well, then she'd probably get away with it." He watched her face as the wheels turned in her head, revising his manuscript.

"So…a partner in crime?" he asked, considering it. "But why would someone want to help her? You're already questioning the credibility of my character wanting to kill off other writers because she's jealous and wants to get rid of a few of them, then steal their work. One psycho writer, maybe. But who's going to believe two crazed writers going on a killing binge?"

"I've got a story of my own to tell," she had said. "Hear me out, and then you can decide whether it's believable or not. I think we just might make a best seller out of your book, after all."

Chapter Sixty-Seven

I t wasn't over yet.

When Scott showed up at Alice's door the next morning, she wouldn't allow him in. "Why are you here? You caught the killer. And I think I've been humiliated enough, throwing myself at you."

"I have some more questions. Unless you have something to hide?" Scott asked. He wanted to catch her off guard.

"Of course not." Alice huffed, standing aside.

Once inside, Scott produced his warrant and radioed for the two officers down the road to join him. As they pressed forward into the house. Alice brought her hand to her mouth. "No, no, no," she wailed.

Will Jenkins was drinking his morning coffee in the kitchen. "I thought it was all over. Suspect in custody, caught red-handed. What's this about?"

Valerie descended the stairs, still dressed in pajamas. "Detective Evans. What's going on? Why are the police here?"

"We need to make sure we have enough evidence to put Brock Townsend away for a long time," Scott explained. "I'm hoping you can help me with that. Perhaps you have some information that the police don't. I understand he's your boyfriend."

"Yeah, well, not anymore. I'm willing to do whatever I can to help. I want to make sure he goes to prison, especially after what he did to me. And all those other people, of course. It's just hard to believe...I thought I knew him."

"Is this really necessary?" Alice interjected. "My daughter was almost killed by someone she cared about. I don't understand why you need to go through our home. You won't find anything to incriminate Brock. He's never been inside the house."

Scott apologized for the inconvenience and addressed Valerie once again. "We need to be sure we haven't overlooked something. Can we speak in private?"

"I had no idea it was him," Valerie said as they moved to the basement family room. "We were seeing each other for the past couple of months."

Scott informed her Brock claimed he had an accomplice who masterminded the killings, but he hadn't named them yet. "Perhaps you might know whom he could have been involved with."

There was a look of disbelief on Valerie's face. Then she calmly spoke. "I have no idea. I can't believe this. He's an absolute psychopath. I never imagined. I guess you can't spot a psychopath. They look like regular people, don't they? Act perfectly normal most of the time. You'd never know you were talking to one."

Scott searched Valerie's cool blue eyes. "Yes, I suppose so. You'd never know. But there's some evidence to suggest he's telling the truth."

"Evidence? What kind of evidence?" She looked cool and collected, except for the slight fluttering of her eyelids.

"Eugene's book found on the beach, for one thing. We were able to get fingerprints from it that aren't his. And then there's the blond hair found in Eugene's Corvette." Scott stopped to gauge Valerie's reaction.

"Oh?" She remained composed. "What does that mean?"

Scott explained the blond hair was a match to a hair he pulled from a brush in the bathroom of her mother's house. "We know Alice was in Eugene's car. And a fingerprint from the book she lent me is also a match to the copy of *Beach Bodies* found on the beach. That ties her to the scene of Wendall and Eugene's deaths. Your mother knew the two men. We also know Townsend Pool Services worked on your mother's pool. Brock's neighbors have seen Alice coming and going from his house at all hours. I'm sorry to break this to you, but it looks like your mother was his accomplice."

Valerie's mouth flew open. "Mom? No, that's not possible. Just because she was in Eugene's car doesn't mean anything. She was helping him promote his books. And Mom's fingerprints are on a lot of books in this town. Brock never mentioned knowing Mom personally. The neighbors must have seen someone who looks like her. It can't be Mom. That all sounds circumstantial. Mom?" She shouted up the stairs.

One of the officers conducting the house search called Scott aside.

When Scott resumed his conversation with Valerie, he said, "There's evidence from other murder scenes. Then there are the manuscripts we found."

"I don't understand." Valerie stared at Scott wide-eyed. "What does all this have to do with Mom? What reason would she have for killing all those people?"

Footsteps pounded down the stairs, a high-pitched screech coming from Alice, with Will on her heels.

"Stop!" Alice cried. "It was me. I did it. I killed them. Brock made me."

Will stared at Alice, his mouth gaping wide.

Valerie screamed, "Mom, no!"

"We were having an affair. I'm so sorry, sweetheart." Alice wrapped her arms around her daughter, only to have her pull away, eyes wide in horror.

"I can't help myself. I have a problem," Alice sobbed. "An addiction. To sex. With younger men. And to murder mysteries. Brock took advantage of my weaknesses. That bastard! He used me to make his fiction reality. And now, the whole town is going to know."

Well, there's *a plot twist.*

Chapter Sixty-Eight

"No problem. I appreciate the opportunity. I've been offered a position as Chief of Police up north, and I want to give them my decision today."

I overheard Scott on the phone Sunday morning. "Sounds good. I think a change will be good for me. There's something else I want to check into, but I'll drop by this morning."

It was just as I knew it would be. He was leaving me, going back up north, back to his own life. And I would be alone again. Just as I deserved to be. I came out of the bedroom, trying to hide how upset I was, but it was tough. My bottom lip quivered as I poured the coffee. I avoided his eyes. "What do you want for breakfast?"

"I'll just skip it. I'll see you later." A quick peck on the cheek, and he walked out.

I called Olivia, unable to hold back my tears. "He's leaving. I heard him… on the phone…he has a new job…up north." I held the phone in one hand while I grabbed a tissue and wiped my drippy nose with the other.

"Are you sure?" Olivia asked. "This all sounds suspiciously like one of those romance movies we love, where there's a misunderstanding overheard on the phone. Did he specifically *say* he was leaving?"

"No, but he's…" I didn't know how to explain it. "He's been distracted since Brock's arrest Friday night. Like he's preparing to leave me now that the case has been solved."

Olivia told me to tell him how I felt. "Lots of people have long-distance relationships. Just because he's leaving doesn't mean he's gone for good."

When I got off the phone, I sat next to Tom on the couch with my coffee. "It's just the two of us again." I stroked his silky fur. "At least I can depend on you." I picked up the remote and watched the morning talk show, although my mind was elsewhere.

Scott saved my life. I shouldn't have been so foolish as to go after the killer on my own. What was I thinking? A schoolteacher isn't a trained police officer. I was lucky to be alive, sitting in my living room with Tom, drinking coffee, watching TV. Plenty of other people weren't so lucky. Scott was right. I wasn't cursed. I needed to look on the bright side of things. Be more optimistic. Maybe we could maintain our relationship across the miles.

I broke down into a complete mess, sobbing like it was Scott's funeral. Of course, we couldn't have a long-distance relationship. How would that work?

It's for the best anyway.

Scott was really good at his job. If he had stayed with me any longer, he would have found out the truth about my past. He certainly uncovered Brock's sick relationship with a fellow murder enthusiast. Two psycho writers turned crazed killers, turning fiction into reality. Brock, caught in the act, claimed an accomplice instigated the murders.

Alice's confession had thrown Scott until Valerie broke down, confirming what the evidence showed. Traces of Wendall's blood on Valerie's Western hoodie, her contact lens matching the one found in Larissa's house, the muddy footprint on Lindsay's walkway, some of the manuscripts describing the murders hidden in her room and at the town library. Scott's implication that her mother was going to prison was enough to make Valerie finally lose her cool and break down with a full confession, including the threatening notes she wrote to me.

"Why did she do it?" I asked.

"Who knows why anyone kills someone else? I don't know if there's ever a reasonable answer. Valerie's admission was off the wall. She said she didn't want to hurt anyone. She just wanted to provide more opportunities for her mother, whose life goal was to be a writer, by cutting down the local competition. She wanted Alice to be proud of her for wanting to write, too, and maybe they would co-write a series together, using some of the ideas she had gathered from other authors. It's crazy how people can justify murder and carry it out so easily," Scott tried to explain Valerie's motive. "Even in my line of work, I've never had to end someone's life. I don't really understand the workings of a killer's mind."

What did that say about his understanding of *me*?

"Maybe there are cases where it's justified. Sometimes people have to defend themselves or their loved ones."

Scott shook his head. "Sadly, yes. But I like to think there could be other ways to deal with threats."

I nodded, wishing I had dealt with the threats against me in a different way. It was too late now. There are some things you just can't take back. I wondered whether Valerie wished the same thing.

As the town librarian and the local pool guy, Valerie and Brock knew a lot of people and were readily invited into people's homes. No one would have suspected what evil lay beneath the surface. The Haunted House incident was meant to throw the police off her trail. But the bookstore? That was all his doing, and he meant for her to die. According to him, he was sick and tired of taking orders from the psycho bitch.

"Valerie was just messing with you. The similarity to what happened to Darko and Stefan was pure coincidence. Nothing to do with you," Scott had explained. "She saw how jealous Alice was of your writing, and how your critique of her work upset her. Valerie really had it in for you because you were good friends, and she knew her mother's writing wasn't near the caliber of yours. To be honest, I was convinced that Alice and Eugene were working together, and she killed him because of his cheating. But Alice was just protecting her daughter." Alice had confessed under the strain of suspecting her own daughter of murder and having the police show up at her door. She had discovered some incriminating manuscripts in Valerie's room and overheard her on the phone after Connie's murder. The police accessed a record of her call. "You idiot! How stupid can you be? First, you screwed up and let some of them survive. Now you've killed the wrong person. You're completely useless! Do I have to do everything myself?

You're such an imbecile! Can't get anything right. I don't know what I ever saw in you."

Alice tried to take the blame for her daughter, but Scott got the truth out of them in the end. Alice's only crime was an obsession with fictional murder. I knew Alice was really into mysteries. But then, so was I. Nothing wrong with a little murder in your life. It was a hobby, not an addiction. Did it really warrant going to AAW? To think Alice was so obsessed with murder mysteries that she needed professional help…But what really shocked me was Alice's sexual addiction to younger men. She had been involved with Eugene, who was engaged to be married. Of course, she wasn't the only one. Celia had been involved with him, too. Who knew how many others? Eugene had a problem sticking to just one woman. And then there was Alice's affair with Brock Townsend, of all people. No wonder she didn't approve of her daughter dating him. I knew Alice was seeing Matt, Paige's husband, professionally. Now I knew *why*. Matt was counseling her, helping her to deal with her obsessions. She was going to need a lot more counseling now that her daughter was charged with murder.

Poor Alice. At least she would have Will to help her through it. He truly cared for Alice, and he promised he would accompany her to visit Valerie in prison. Will had been going to break it off with Larissa just before she died. He'd fallen for Alice when he walked into her bookstore one day looking for a mystery book, and she started up a conversation about murder. It was something they had in common. The obsessive mystery buff and the town coroner. A perfect match.

The ringing interrupted my thoughts. I picked up the phone.

"I just wanted to thank you again. If you hadn't been there…" Paige sobbed. "My kids would be without a mom."

"I was just at the right place at the right time. Anyone else would have done the same thing."

"No, they wouldn't. Not everyone is as selfless as you, Ivy. You're a good person."

I knew that wasn't true. I wanted to be, tried to be, a good person, but didn't always succeed. As much as I wanted to redeem myself, I knew I couldn't take back the terrible things I had done. "Thank you. I'm just relieved that you and Riley are okay. I never suspected Valerie could be involved in something so…I don't even know the word for it. I can't imagine what Alice is going through, discovering her daughter is a cold-blooded killer."

"The secret lives people lead," Paige stated. "And even those closest to them don't know. Matt's going to have his hands full helping Alice through this. He's never dealt with murder before."

"What about you? How are you doing?"

"I broke it off with Riley. Matt knows everything. He's referring me to another psychologist, a woman, to get help. I'm still going to attend AAW. Matt says it takes time to overcome an addiction."

An email came through on my phone. When I finished my conversation with Paige, I opened it. It was a literary agent—a request for the full manuscript of *Secret Lives, Secret Lies.* I wasn't sure I would ever trust an agent again. I decided to research the agent thoroughly before sending off my work.

I was making a gooey grilled cheese sandwich for comfort when Scott texted.

Be home soon. We need to talk.

No 'love you' or 'miss you'. I wallowed in tomato soup and grilled cheese, perched in front of the local noon news. There was plenty to report. Two arrests had been made in the recent murders in the county. The reign of terror in Blue Water County was over. That should give Riley enough material for a sequel to *Blue Water Discoveries*, one that integrated his new-found interest in murder mysteries.

Tom was curled up next to me when Scott woke me from my nap, carrying flowers and a box of chocolates. "What's that for?" I asked, half-asleep.

"To cheer you up." He put the flowers in a vase. "And to celebrate the solving of the case. We work well together, just like in the old days. Let's go for a walk."

* * *

We strolled to the end of the pier in silence, holding hands. I couldn't stand avoiding our breakup any longer. "It's over, isn't it?"

"It is now. The police just made another arrest."

"What? There's a third person involved?" I didn't see that coming.

"Not in the way you think. One of the victims wasn't connected to mystery writing. The other murders were a good cover for it."

I couldn't stand waiting for him to spit it out. "What? Which victim?"

Scott sat me down on a bench and explained how he spoke with Steph LaMante that morning. There had been something bothering him about June's accidents. The fact that she wasn't a writer and wasn't into mysteries didn't fit the victim profiles. "Steph was concerned about her great-aunt. She thought it was odd she made two mistakes in one week—mixing up her pills and taking batteries out of the smoke detectors. She said she wasn't sure it meant anything, but she noticed Reggie had something in his pocket the day of the fire. He pulled it out accidentally and stuffed it back in. But not before Steph saw it."

He had me on the edge of my seat. "*What?* What did she see?"

"Matches. Which she thought was odd since Reggie doesn't smoke, and the more she thought about it, the more she wondered if he had anything to do with the fire."

"Oh! You don't think…"

When Scott confronted Reggie about the matches and his gambling debts, Reggie broke down and confessed. He owed Rick a ton of money for his gambling addiction. Rick extended his debt repayment since Reggie was his son-in-law, but he was getting impatient. According to Reggie, Rick said, 'Family is everything. But business is business.'" Scott added, "With all the accidents happening in town, Reggie thought he'd capitalize on that by getting rid of his old aunt. With June gone, her money would go to the family. Figured the windfall would pay off his wife's father and give them a fresh start. Reggie was so apologetic about what he did to June, saying he was sorry, he'd made a mistake. You'd think he just bumped into someone rather than tried to bump someone off."

"So, the Mafia *was* involved?" I gasped, remembering what June had said about Rick, and trembled at the thought.

"Just loan sharking. And it had absolutely nothing to do with your past," Scott assured me with a hug.

"I guess Reggie will be having a fresh start in prison, then?"

"Looks that way. Attempted murder, maybe manslaughter, with mitigating circumstances because of the strain Rick put him under, and the fact that June wouldn't necessarily have died as a result of his actions. Speaking of fresh starts…." He searched my eyes.

"I know what you're going to say." Tears welled up, threatening to stream down my cheeks.

"You do? So, what do you think?"

Not wanting him to see me cry, I rose and stepped to the edge of the pier. The water was a beautiful blue with gentle waves, deceptively calm and caressing, but deep and deadly beneath the surface.

"I think it's great," I lied.

Scott joined me at the water's edge, his finger touching a tear. "Why do I get the feeling those aren't tears of joy? I thought you'd be happy—"

"I am. I'm happy for you. You deserve to be police chief. It's just…." I tried to stop the tears, but they flowed freely.

"Ivy." He cupped my face in his hands. "I turned down that job. I just came from the station. I talked to Mike's superior and accepted an offer to stay on in Port Ripley."

"You're not leaving?"

"No. I kind of like it here. There's the lake, the town, the people, Tom, my friend June, Clarence…" He kissed my nose. "And then there's you. I was afraid to say anything because I wasn't sure how you would feel. Especially when you were so adamant about not joining me up north. And if it's not what you want, if it's too soon…that's okay. I can wait till you're ready."

"Ready?"

"What do you think about me moving in with you? We're both free to be together. I've always loved you, Ivy. For the past fourteen years. There's nothing keeping us apart anymore, is there?"

"But…"

CHAPTER SIXTY-EIGHT

"I know. You're still in love with Jim. Maybe in time…"

"Scott." I stroked his cheek. "I'll always love Jim. But I'm in love with *you*. I just can't go back there—to Lake Kipling—not to live, anyway. And I can't expect you to switch jobs, give up your home, and leave your family behind. It's a long drive to see your kids."

"The flight's shorter. We can fly up a couple times a month and stay in Julia's spare room in the basement. And we'll visit my parents in Kap. I've been giving it a lot of thought. We can make this work." Scott's voice quivered as he added, "If it's what you want. Please tell me it is."

I looked deep into the warmth of Scott's brown eyes and found what I'd been missing since I lost Jim. Love. Belonging. Home. Maybe I *did* deserve another chance for happiness. Maybe I *could* forgive myself for the sins of my past. And maybe, just maybe, I wasn't doomed to be cursed forever. If I believed in curses, there was no reason I couldn't believe in good luck and serendipity.

"I want what you want. You're right. There's nothing to keep us apart. Nothing at all. Welcome home to Blue Water." My arms around Scott's neck, standing on my tiptoes, I brought my lips to meet his.

We stood wrapped in each other, lost in the kiss, the sound of waves lapping against the pier's edge. I finally broke away, hearing voices. An elderly couple approached, hand in hand, soft laughter accompanying their conversation.

"Let's continue this at home, Ivy," Scott's lips tickled my ear. "I've got some *under cover* work to catch up on."

I giggled like a schoolgirl. "Yes, let's go home, Detective. Maybe I can work with you under the covers. We make a good team."

Scott's smile widened as he chuckled. "In more ways than one."

We gazed over the lake, into the distance where diamonds danced on shades of blue under the bright sun. Hands clasped together, we turned and headed for home.

Epilogue

What a fucking bitch she turned out to be.

She should get the Pulitzer Prize for Fiction.

He wasn't going down for this without her. Sitting in his prison cell, he had all the time in the world to play it over and over in his mind. It was all her idea. He just wrote the book. It wasn't even his own original premise. But if Eugene could make it big with his debut, *You're Killing Me*, surely there was room for another great novel along the same lines. Who could have known his main character would pop out of his novel and lead him around by his nose? He'd heard of authors creating a character and allowing them to take over the plot. But he'd never imagined meeting a character face-to-face until she answered his call for a critique partner.

At first, he had thought she was joking. "Wouldn't it be great if we could get rid of mystery writers?" she had said, with a twinkle in her eye when they discussed his new psycho-thriller.

"Do you have any idea how many mystery writers there are?" His laughter subsided as he noted her expression turning solemn.

"Well, we could get rid of *some* of them."

"But we'd be caught." He attempted a smile, thinking she must be kidding.

"Not if it's done carefully," she insisted. "Think about it. It would put you and your book in the spotlight."

"When they read my book, *if* they do, they'll know I did it. I'm not going to spend the rest of my life behind bars just to get attention for my book." He chuckled again, but she didn't join him.

"No one would figure it out. You'd be using the premise of your book, not following it to the letter. And besides, people would think you got the idea from the actual murders, not the other way around. No one would know you wrote the book before the killings. You could just say you read about the murders in the news, then got the idea for writing your book, *based on actual events*. It happens all the time. Writers take real situations and twist them into fiction. And that's what sells. Your book will make a killing."

The sparkle came back into her eyes as he said, "So you really think we could do it? Actually play out the book in real life?"

"Yes, that's right. Like a movie."

"So, which character would we kill off first?"

"Maybe we should plot it out. I don't think pantsing is going to work for this," she suggested. "We're going to need a plan."

"You keep saying 'we'. What exactly do you get out of this?"

"Satisfaction. All my life, I've had to live with a writer. An unsuccessful one. It's been torture for her and the family. It's like she was born that way. All she ever does is write and think about writing. She's consumed by it. Obsessed. Murder mysteries, in particular. She's getting help to deal with her writing addiction, but I'm not sure it's working. And if she ever found out…if she ever found out that I'm following in her footsteps, it'd kill her. Like mother, like daughter. Two obsessed, unsuccessful mystery writers in the family—it's too much for her to deal with." Tears welled in her eyes, and he wiped them away. "I don't know. Maybe…if there was less competition out there, at least on a local level, she'd have better luck getting recognition. She just needs a break, you know?"

He nodded sympathetically. He knew exactly what she was talking about, and he wanted to do what he could to help. He was well aware her mother was obsessed with writing. And he understood what obsession could do to a person. He himself was obsessed. Or had been obsessed. With her mother. His relationship with her mother had been a mere fling to Alice, but it was everything to him. For months after she broke it off, he hadn't been able to work, write, eat, sleep. But that all changed when he met her daughter. A younger version of the woman he craved made a good substitute.

"Maybe…" she continued, tears trickling down her cheeks. "If there were fewer writers, she'd have a better chance of success herself. I know that sounds crazy."

"No, not crazy at all," he assured her. Her eyes quickly dried up when he added, "It's too bad we couldn't weed out some of that competition."

"Maybe we can. At least locally. That would give her a chance to shine, wouldn't it?"

"I'm listening. Where do we start?" He pulled her into his arms.

When she told him her idea, the excitement on her face worked like an aphrodisiac.

She tossed her hair back and laughed. "Wouldn't it be ironic? What if your fiction becomes reality?"

Acknowledgements

Thank you to my husband, Brian, for his role in the creation of the fictional setting of this book, inspired by a beautiful coastal town overlooking Lake Huron. He first introduced me to the spot decades ago when we were dating, and we are blessed with memories of picnics on the bluff, huge ice cream cones, walks along the boardwalk, and exploring the town and the trails. Part of me will always belong to the lake—the place of our engagement, where our children swam and played, and the spot we still visit several times a year. Thanks to my son, Bryant, for the laughter of his childhood as he splashed in the waves, and to my daughter, Brittany, for spending the summers of her teenage years soaking up the sun and water on the beach with her mom. Don't question the magic. Just live it.

Special thanks to Brian for being the first reader of my work and the last reader before it is sent off to my publisher, and for providing feedback and suggestions. Thanks for accompanying me to every book event, setting up and taking down the display, and talking up my books to potential readers. Thank you to our family for their support and encouragement of my writing and book events. Bryant, Brittany, son-in-law Eric, grandson Rowan and your new baby sister, Violet—you are my world. Thanks to my brother, Joseph, and my sister-in-law, Audrey, my nephews and niece, and my in-laws, for being part of my life. And to T. C. and Scruffy for their unconditional love, snuggles, and purrs as I create my fiction.

I appreciate the support of my friend, Loretta Dunn, and her presence at my library events. To my friend, Deb Robinson, thank you for your continued enthusiasm for my books. As always, thank you to my critique partner, Norah Blakedon, for her expert advice. Also, my appreciation to the beta readers who read early versions of this book. Family, friends, neighbors, people in our community—thank you for asking about my writing and for reading my books.

Thanks to my local libraries, bookstores, markets, book fairs and festivals, and writing group, who have been supportive by inviting me to do book signings and readings.

To Cindy Bullard of Birch Literary, I owe my eternal gratitude for taking me on as a client. Thanks to her, this book and the Blue Water series came together and is now in the hands of readers.

Thank you to Level Best Books for publishing this series. As always, I am so grateful to Shawn Reilly Simmons, for her editing expertise, amazing book covers, and for believing in my work. Thanks as well to Verena Rose and Deb Well and the rest of the team at Level Best.

To my readers, thanks so much for choosing this book. I hope you love reading it as much as I loved writing it!

About the Author

Ivanka Fear is a Slovenian-born Canadian author. She lives in Ontario with her family and feline companions. Ivanka earned her B.A. and B.Ed. in English and French at Western University. After retiring from teaching, she wrote poetry and short stories for various literary journals. Ivanka is the author of the Blue Water Mystery series and the Jake and Mallory Thriller series. She is a member of International Thriller Writers, Sisters in Crime, Crime Writers of Canada, and Vocamus Writers Community. When not reading and writing, Ivanka enjoys watching mystery series and romance movies, gardening, going for walks, and watching the waves roll in at the lake.

AUTHOR WEBSITE:
  https://www.ivankafear.com

SOCIAL MEDIA HANDLES:
  Facebook: https://www.facebook.com/ivankafearauthor
  Instagram: https://www.instagram.com/ivankawrites
  Twitter: https://twitter.com/FearIvanka

Also by Ivanka Fear

The Dead Lie, A Blue Water Mystery

Where is My Husband?, A Jake and Mallory Thriller

Lost Like Me, A Blue Water Mystery

What Lies in the Cornfield?, A Jake and Mallory Thriller